The Limits *of* Enchantment

Also by Graham Joyce

The Limits
of Enchantment

A NOVEL

Graham Joyce

ATRIA BOOKS

New York   London   Toronto   Sydney

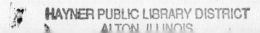

ATRIA BOOKS

Library of Congress Cataloging-in-Publication Data
Joyce, Graham.
The limits of enchantment : a novel / Graham Joyce—1st Atria Books hardcover ed.
p. cm.
ISBN 0-7434-6344-7 (alk. paper)—ISBN 0-7434-6345-5 (TP : alk. paper)
1. Witches—Fiction. 2. Young women—Fiction. 3. Beat generation—Fiction. 4. Midlands
(England)—Fiction. 5. Marginality, Social—Fiction. I. Title.
PR6060.O93L56 2005
823'.914—dc22
2004056683

First Atria Books hardcover edition February 2005

1   3   5   7   9   10   8   6   4   2

ATRIA BOOKS is a trademark of Simon & Schuster, Inc.

For information regarding special discounts for bulk purchases,
please contact Simon & Schuster Special Sales at 1-800-456-6798
or business@simonandschuster.com

Manufactured in the United States of America

To my daughter Ella and to my son Joe

prologue

If I could tell you this in a single sitting, then you might believe all of it, even the strangest part. Even the part about what I found in the hedgerow. If I could unwind this story in a single spool, or peel it like an apple the way Mammy would with her penknife in one unbroken coil, juice a-glistening on the blade, then you might bite in without objection.

But Mammy always said we have lost the art of Listening. She said we live in an age when everyone chatters and no one takes heed, and that, she said, is not a good time in which to live.

And while I offer you my story unbroken, like the apple peel, it hangs by a fiber at every turn of the knife. When you come to know the nature of the teller of this tale you may have good reason to doubt both. You may suspect the balance of my mind, and you may condemn my position. You may start to disbelieve.

Perhaps I once was mad. Briefly. Perhaps that much is true. And this, in an age where we no longer have the patience to listen, may cause you to break off, to give up on me, to turn away. A young woman has so little of interest to offer, after all. A young woman of unsteady temper, even less.

What they did to Mammy they tried to do to me. They released the dogs. And when it comes to telling how it was done, I only ask this: when doubt wrinkles your brow, when incomprehension clouds your eyes, when distaste rests like a rank fog on your lips, then think how we few have held our tongues for so long. How we have choked back the truth. How we have burned in our hearts rather than risk the telling. And when you feel most far from me, then at that moment listen hard. Not to your thoughts, which will mislead you, nor to your heart, which will lie, but to the voice behind the voice, and trust the tale and not the teller.

one

*M*ammy *pressed her ear to* Gwen's distended pink pot, and everyone in the room had to hush up. That was Gwen of course, ready to split like a fruit, and Mammy also of course, and Gwen's friend Clarrie, who stood with her arms folded and a ciggie between her lips and a stick of ash hanging over the bed, and me. And we all listened.

"Make it easier if you told me, Mammy," Gwen said, but Mammy flapped an arm through the air, hush up, and pressed her ear closer to the spot she'd shown me just north-northwest of Gwen's navel.

Mammy straightened her back and turned away from Gwen. "Can't tell."

"I know you can!" Gwen protested, running her chafed hands over her own massive belly. "You'd a looked me in the eye. So now I know."

"She knows, right enough," Clarrie croaked, without removing the ciggie from her mouth, then a tiny cough made the stick of ash just miss the bed. "Old Mammy Cullen knows."

Mammy did know, but wouldn't let on. "Let's see what nature give us and be glad," Mammy always said.

But Gwen wasn't having that. "Oh Mammy, if I just knew, I could relax and this one would be out and it's not as if it will be any less loved either way."

Gwen had four brawling and bawling red-cheeked boys and desperately wanted a little girl to put a bit o' balance in the house. Mammy would listen and was usually right but she was not infallible so she never liked to say.

At last Clarrie took the cigarette out of her mouth. She expertly nipped the lighted end between a finger and a thumb callused from the canning factory and dropped the stub in her apron pocket. "Let the girl have a listen," she said.

My hand flew up, as it always did in these moments, to the three iron hair grips pinning my hair at the temple. Gwen mouthed at me like a fish, go on. Mammy wrinkled her nose and motioned me toward Gwen's swollen mound. I put my ear to the spot and listened hard. Then I got up and because the other two were hard at watching my lips, I touched my left earlobe.

"She thinks it's a girl, and I do, too," Mammy said, and Gwen started blubbering.

"But she ain't said a word!" Clarrie protested.

Mammy was more interested in scolding Gwen. "Now look at you, filling up! And where you going to be if I'm wrong?"

"You ain't never wrong, Mammy, they all say! Thank you, Mammy! Thank you so much! Oh I could die happy!"

"Die? You ain't going to die! And I'm *offen* wrong about it. *Offen.*"

"She never said a bloody word!" Clarrie complained again, lighting up another Craven A and looking at me.

No, but we had our own way of speaking, and just as I'd touched my left earlobe I'd looked at Mammy for a response because I knew we'd both heard trouble. Mammy wiped her forefingers together, just the once, to confirm the difficulty I'd picked up in the heartbeat. There all right, but too flat. Trouble. Oh dear for everyone, and I'm going: stay calm now, Fern, stay calm.

Gwen was right in that she relaxed immediately and within half an hour after Mammy's pronouncement that little baby girl was inching her way out. But where we all wanted to see her boxing the air with her tiny pink fists, something was wrong. The baby had the cord around her neck, like a noose, and you could tell she was starved of oxygen. Mammy got her fingers between neck and cord and quickly freed her, but there was so little.

"Flat," I said to Mammy in an underbreath, not wanting Gwen to hear.

But Clarrie sensed something and stepped round to look. Taking her ciggie from between her lips she blurted, "But she's so blue!"

"Blue?" said Gwen.

"Stand aside and shut it," Mammy said sharply to Clarrie. The baby was all out now, but limp. Mammy flicked its feet hard. Then she slapped it. "Sucker," she said to me, but softly. I rummaged in Mammy's bag and I found the fine-bore length of rubber tube and handed it to her.

"Is it all right? Tell me it's all right, Mammy," Gwen was saying, so I attended to her bleeding with swabs, more to distract her so that Mammy could do whatever she could. Mammy laid the baby down and stuck the tube down its throat and sucked hard. She spat into a bowl. Mammy slapped again, but the blue thing was still flat. Almost lifeless now. Almost nothing.

There was no hiding it. Clarrie had gone silent, and Gwen was paralyzed and I felt the flush of fear travel between us, and we all looked to Mammy. But Mammy seemed to be listening hard, and not at the baby but at the window. Her head was cocked slightly.

"Bucket of cold water, Fern, quick as you can. Use the rainwater barrel. Cold."

I didn't need telling twice. I raced downstairs, grabbed the nearest bowl to hand, and filled it with icy water from the rainwater tub outside and brought it back to the room. I knew what Mammy wanted, but Clarrie said, "They don't do that anymore. It'll ketch pneumonia."

Mammy ignored Clarrie and plunged the baby into the cold water. She held it under and brought it up again. Then she plunged it under again. "Linseed meal, Clarrie, go and get me some, sharpish. And you, Fern, gold dust."

Clarrie was gone for the linseed, but before I left the room I heard a tiny cough, like the spluttering of the water pump when you primed it. The baby coughed. It made a tiny gasp. "Don't dawdle now, Fern."

I had to go down to Gwen's pantry and rummage about for mustard seed, which Mammy called "gold dust." I ground up the seed in a mortar and pestle I found in the kitchen. Before I'd finished, Clarrie—who lived in the next house—was back with her linseed meal. I took it from her and made the wet poultice then took it back up to the room.

Gwen had the baby with her now, wrapped tight in a towel.

Mammy inspected my poultice, took the baby back from Gwen and unwrapped the towel. She smeared the yellow poultice all over the baby's back, then wrapped her in the towel again before handing her back to her mother. "She'll not get pneumonia," Mammy said pointedly, looking hard at Clarrie.

"Oh Mammy!" Gwen said. "It's the little girl I wanted. Will she be all right?"

Well even though the danger had passed, Mammy would never say anything would be all right because she told me nature was imperfect; but she was wise enough to know she had to behave now as if it would be. "Write her down," Mammy said to me. "Write down her time and her weight. Write down as Gwen has had a healthy little girl."

Mammy's precision in these things was her one concession to the bureaucrats who exiled her from her true calling. Though she herself couldn't read or write, and claimed to see no point in the practice, she was proud that I could. It was her way of showing to the other women that we, too, could keep records if records there must be. So I took out my notebook and I wrote: *to Gwen Harding, daughter, eight pounds nine ounces, sixteen minutes past four pm, 4th February, 1966.* And as an extra flourish of my own I wrote *Full moon baby.*

Gwen was lost in the moment of new motherhood. Her friend Clarrie was happy again, too. She puffed away at the fresh ciggie wedged between her teeth, manufacturing a new stick of ash. "They say as you're always right, Mammy. And you was right about that lickle gal, too."

I had tipped off Mammy, when I touched my left ear, that I heard it was a girl. That had confirmed it for Mammy enough to take a chance and tell Gwen, and I was pleased because after dozens and dozens of these I was getting nearly as good as Mammy, who'd taught me not to go by how they were carrying but by the heartbeat, because a girl will beat slower than a boy and after a while you can tell them apart long before you get to look what's between their legs. Though we hadn't known what you can never know, that in this case the slow heartbeat was caused by another thing altogether. But they—that is,

Gwen and Clarrie and all the rest of them—never knew how we did it because it was just one of the many things we few kept to ourselves.

And we mostly did keep to ourselves. Which was why I was so surprised the next day.

Blowing up for a gale it was, rough February weather, though fine enough for washing, and the corner of a hung-out sheet flapped at me, like having a bite at my leg, so I snapped back at it and put it in its place. You don't let them talk at you, those flapping sheets. My tiny Hitachi transistor radio softly broadcast the pirate station Radio Caroline from the doorstep. Though the batteries were a price just to keep it going, I liked it on while I worked and sang along where I could. Not that Mammy liked the pop tunes. Not at all. Rubbish she called it. Rubbish and rot.

But I was singing away when there was a rustle behind a cotton sheet, and a dark shape, and I stopped singing and took a step back. I suddenly wished that Mammy were there. Then the sheet was snatched away to reveal a face, deadpan yet humorous under a head of soft copper-colored curls. It was Arthur McCann, so tall he slouched in his black leather motorcycle jacket. His drainpipe jeans were so blue I wondered how he got them so.

I turned my back on him and carried on hanging out. "You frit me. I was going to grab that garden fork."

"Take a joke, Fern. No harm meant." I remembered Arthur from school. His eyes were as blue as his jeans, and he blinked at me with delicate eyelashes. I checked the three iron grips holding my hair back, and from there my hand went to the hole in the elbow of my cardigan. "You'll catch it if Mammy finds you here. She'll be back from the village anytime now."

Arthur stepped from behind the sheet, and it flapped in the stiff breeze. "Can't keep hiding behind Mammy Cullen, Fern." He inched closer. I could smell beer on the wind. "Got to give some bloke a chance."

Arthur was a tough from the neighboring village of Hallaton. That's a mad place. There are things I could tell you about that village. I had a wooden clothes pin clenched between my teeth. "Chance? What chance?"

I reached up for the clothesline knowing my waist, hips and buttocks were all displayed for him. Though my back was turned, I could feel his ghost arms wanting to settle on my hips. Hussy, Mammy would call me, but I bent over my washing basket, flapped another sheet, stretched again as Arthur breathed over my shoulder. I sensed the moment when he was going to step nearer, so I blocked it by turning. "I don't want a Hallaton barmy. Anyway you're almost the same age as me, Arthur. I want an older man."

"What do you want an older man for? I'm in me prime, I am."

"You're twenty-one. That's not your prime. That's a boy. I want a man who can teach me things." I knew what he would say back to that, and Mammy would call that teasing, no mistake.

"I could teach you a thing or two." Arthur scratched his chin and blinked his white lashes.

I spun my back on him again, hanging out. Do I want him to touch me? I remember thinking. Do I?

"Youch!" went Arthur.

I turned quickly to see Arthur grasping the ham of his leg, up near the buttock. Behind him stood Mammy Cullen with her ash stick raised, threatening him with another blow. "Who said you could come in my garden?" Mammy roared, squinting at the boy with her slate gray eyes. "Who said as you could?"

"We was just talking!"

"Courting! You was courting!" I could see Mammy's huge bosom heaving up and down inside her coat. Her fat jowls manufactured a comical twitch, but her tobacco-leaf brown eyes were a-boil. "And you don't court a gal by sneaking up when her back is turned! We can do without that sort of courting. And you don't court without my say-so!"

"We was just talking, Mammy! No need to take a stick to me!"

"I'll fetch you another blow, my lad. And you wasn't talking, you Hallaton barmy! You was reaching out your hand, and I saw you from the gate there."

He rubbed the ham of his leg, but he was laughing. It hadn't stung him at all, and we all understood it. Though I knew from when I was a girl that Mammy didn't usually let fly with her stick with half measures. This was a game, lucky for Arthur, but she could turn. "Give a young bloke a break, Mammy."

"What?" Mammy roared. "You come in my house and garden, and I'll break my stick over you!"

"Mammy!" I shouted, laughing, too. She was too handy with that ash stick, and I didn't want this to go any further.

Arthur was nimble and strong, and he grabbed the stick off her and vaulted the garden gate. Mammy was old but she could shift, and she was after him. "Bye Fern!" he shouted, taunting, leaving the stick by the gate. He leaped on his motorbike and kicked it into life. Mammy picked up a clod of earth and let fly at him, but he was long gone, the drone of his bike already diminishing. "Get out of my garden you Hallaton ginger-arse, and don't come back!"

After she'd retrieved her stick, Mammy sat down on her garden bench, getting her breath back. I said nothing and finished the job of hanging out the washing. When I was done I sat beside Mammy on the garden bench. We stared ahead in silence. After a while Mammy's shoulders began to tremble. I stayed tight-lipped. Then Mammy snorted. "Ginger-arse," she guffawed, and I shrieked. "Hallaton barmy!" I said, and Mammy's broad shoulders quaked. "Ginger Hallaton barmy hare-chaser!" she said, then she hooted and slapped down her own knee as if it was rising of its own volition, and I howled with her and I was glad we lived far enough from the village so that no one would hear us.

You couldn't help it. Not really. Not when you thought about it.

Old Mammy Cullen was not my natural mother, but had taken me on as her own. So Mammy had told me, I had arrived as a mistake to a woman whose other children were already mature; and they in turn had no interest in taking on a child whose father was, in any event, not the same as their own. I never met my half brother and two half sisters. Mammy Cullen had lost a child of her own long, long before, and that left a hole in her life that yawned and howled until Mammy, already a long way into her fifties, saw a need to fill it again. That was in 1946. With the war just over Mammy had slipped the event past all registration. As I understand it, there was no authority at hand that considered it of enough significance to record the deed. It was a time when finding a warm hearth for a barely walking child was more pressing than writing names in some leather-bound ledger.

"I brung you in from the hospital," she told me, and I never questioned it.

Mammy had a hole to fill, and Mammy took me in. That's all it was. She loved me and treated me no better and no worse than if I had been her own. Which was to fight to make a warm house, with enough food on the table and clean clothes; and just one or two remembered thrashings with the ash stick; and love that came in the form of as much time as could ever be lavished on a child.

Mammy listened, Mammy answered, Mammy interpreted the universe for me. She had a habit of briefly rolling her eyes before offering her report on the world, always carefully explaining where that version might touch her neighbors' and where it might not. And since the day of my first period she had been plain with me what it was all for, and had fought to save me from the boys who appeared at the garden gate. Arthur McCann wasn't the first to be chased away by Mammy Cullen. Though again I thought Mammy had been too interfering, and said so.

"I can look after myself, Mammy."

"I know that. But one of them will come along, and you'll fall on your back for him. I can't hold them off forever. It's against nature. You'll just fall over."

"No I shan't."

"You shall. Don't matter how tough you think you are. He'll stand there and he'll find a cotton loose in your apron and he'll pull it and pull it and you'll let him and the next thing you know you'll be shivering and on your back in the grass and you'll love it and think your-self clever for what's done. That's how it works. Just don't get your-self knocked up. And I've shown you how."

She had shown me, too. But then Mammy had the skill of reckon-ing in a way that left me for dead. *Take away the upper of the eleven-to-eighteen rule from the number of days in the shortest o' your last six bleeds and take away the lower from the number of days of the longest of your prior six bleeds. If your last bleeds were twenty-six to thirty-one days in length, keep your man away with a stick between the eighth day (which is twenty-six take away eighteen, ain't it?) until day twenty (which be thirty-one take away eleven, ain't it?) on month seven. There. And you should be safe enough. Though you might also use your bit of sponge and vinegar.*

"Arthur's got no bad in him."

"I know that, too. But what will you do when I'm gone?"

"You've got plenty of juice left."

"You say that, but I was in the village paying the damned electric-ity bill this morning, and I had a jolt all up my spine and through my chest. Turned me over it did."

"Electricity?"

"No you soft lump. Old age. I'm seventy-seven years old, and I know when I'm being called."

I stood up and turned away. I didn't want her to see the tears squeezing. But you could hide nothing from Mammy. Nothing. Never ever ever.

"You'll be all right, my little chaffinch," she said.

For a while there wasn't a breath of wind in the air. Then a breeze got exercised from nowhere, whipping the sheets high on the wash-ing line, snapping them at us viciously. We both listened to it for a moment.

"You shall have to be," Mammy said.

two

I heard the rain before I felt it as together Mammy and I turned off the road and took a path across the fields. It was a mid-February morning, and it was cold to be up at the crack of dawn like that. Mammy pulled her old-fashioned shawl around her head and I had a transparent plastic foldaway head scarf to wear until it gave over. The fine spray of rain had the leaves winking on the evergreens. We walked in silence, and my shoes were polished by the wet grass. We'd been out gathering. Riding the rolls, Mammy called it, because the land undulated like a great green ocean, and we could get swallowed up and forgotten in the troughs of its waves.

Although my eyes were trained on the country path before me, my mind was elsewhere. Even Mammy, walking three steps behind me, must have heard my brain clacking like an abacus.

"Out with it," said Mammy.

"Oh." I sighed. "Only what I've told you before. Only that I don't believe half of it."

"That's between you and your head. Anyway, you're too much in the head. It makes no difference what you think."

That was Mammy's way. It made no difference what anyone thought. She had an idea that they did what they must, and behaved as they must, and that everything in the world of words had no true bearing on the world as it actually was. She believed that people often spoke against their true nature, said one thing and did another, claimed to be *this* when really they were *that*, and tricked themselves to the point where they didn't know whether they were the hare or the hound.

She was against talking, Mammy was. "What little you know, keep to yourself."

We'd done gathering, so we returned through the woods and

round the outcrop of rock, where the woad grew thick and tall, beyond Keywell. The way up was very steep, and Mammy had to lean on my arm, puffing and blowing and cursing her arthritis. But as we made the bend in our quiet lane Mammy tapped my leg with her ash stick, and whispered, "Hey up! Strangers!"

There were not usually many people up and about at that time of the morning, other than those on their way to work somewhere. So it was a surprise to see a battered old transit van parked not a hundred yards from our cottage, its bonnet yawning open. An odd couple squatted on the grass verge, smoking cigarettes and looking on vacantly while another man hid his face in the guts of the engine, grunting and fiddling with wires.

No fashion plate myself, it did seem to me they were oddly dressed. A rum crew. The woman wore a long skirt, mud-stained at the hem, and a cheesecloth blouse under an army coat with brass buttons. She played with her long, unkempt hair and smiled at their predicament. Her partner, rolling himself a cigarette, wore a battered leather coat and a white shirt with no collar, which you never saw anymore. His skin was unusually tanned for that time of the year, and I could see his nose had been broken and reset. His hair was long, well over his collar, like a woman's, but he wore a felt hat with a broad brim. Of course no one wore hats anymore, either. Around his neck was a bell on a chain, just as you might have expected to see on a favored cow.

I let go a little gasp. I didn't know whether they were a traveling circus or early-morning visitors from the fairy folk.

"Beatniks," Mammy whispered.

Perhaps the man had extraordinary hearing, because he looked up from constructing his cigarette. "Greetings," he said, twinkling his eyes first at Mammy, then at me.

"Grrn," said Mammy. She had this noise she made, halfway between a greeting and a growl, leaving you at liberty to take it either way.

I said nothing. I haven't been far, but I can't be doing with mockery, and I didn't like the look of him. *Greetings* indeed. Unshaved, disheveled, the leather of his coat scuffed and distressed in patches. Just as I was thinking you can keep your greetings, the man jumped up theatrically to let us pass by on the grass verge. He smiled at me and ran his tongue lasciviously along the gummed edge of his cigarette paper.

The man with his head in the car engine looked up at us. "Ain't got a spare distributor cap, have you?" he shouted.

I didn't really know what a distributor cap was. I didn't know what a beatnik was, either. A gypsy with an electric guitar was how I saw it at the time. I put my nose in the air, and we passed by.

Listening behind me, I heard one of them say, "I think that was a no."

The gate to our cottage whined on its hinge. I always said why don't we put a drop of oil on that gate, but Mammy said it let her know when someone was coming, so that's how it stayed. But that morning Mammy mentioned that she'd seen a jenny wren busy in the hedge. "Mark it?" she said. "We shall have visitors."

And we did. A gentle rap on the open door heralded the first of two male visitors before the week was out, both uninvited. I was busy cleaning the hearth, and I looked up to see a dark-haired gentleman in hiking boots. He had knee-length socks secured outside his trousers, but I didn't giggle. He held his sporting trilby aloft in an attitude of exaggerated politeness, and a silver-topped cane in his other hand. An emerald green feather was tucked into the hatband of the trilby. "Good morning!" he cried cheerily. "Forgive me for disturbing you on such a day as this."

The man smiled excessively: something that always unnerves me. And neither was I accustomed to the extreme formality. His accent was BBC radio, and his politeness signaled not warmth but social superiority masked by extreme cordiality. I got to my feet and stood wiping my dusty hands on my apron.

"Might I come in?" he asked.

"Not until you've told me what you're after." For all his airs, it's still bad manners to leave someone guessing about your business. I stooped to pick up the ash pan from the grate and stepped toward him, to make him jump. He did too: leaped back as I swept past him before emptying the ash onto the garden soil. Some of the ash swirled in a naughty breeze, and a fleck went in his eye.

After rubbing his eye he placed his hat and stick across his heart and held up the palm of his free hand in a placating gesture. "I do apologize. I was looking for a Mrs. Megan Cullen. I thought perhaps you might be her daughter. Though I never expected to find one so charming."

I had to stop a smile at that. I went back indoors and fitted the ash pan back in the grate with a rattle. Does this soft soap really work on people in the city? "But I haven't been charming," I said.

He smiled again. "I see I'm no match for you."

"Are you going to say what you want?"

He blinked at me. Perhaps the speck of ash in his eye was still troubling him. "My name is Bennett. I've driven quite a way. From the university, in fact. Cambridge. That's my car over there. I've come in the hope of interviewing Mrs. Cullen."

"Interviewing? You want to interview Mammy?"

"Formal term. More of a chat really. Make a few notes, that sort of thing."

"Mammy's out at market."

Bennett scratched his head. "Really? Do you know when she might be back? Of course I could simply sit in my car until she returns."

I softened a little, thinking I should invite him to wait inside. He seemed harmless enough. But before I'd decided a shadow moved behind him.

"Mammy's already back," she announced. "And who be you?" Mammy brushed past the man, affecting disinterest, but keeping her good ear cocked as he repeated what he'd told me.

"Get that kettle boiling," she said to me, "and don't you know it's bad manners to keep a visitor standing on the threshold?"

"You've always said—"

"Never mind that." She turned to our visitor. "Well, are you coming in or not? Find a seat, no not that one, that's my place. Over there, that's it." She hung up her coat behind the door and settled into her chair beside the fire. "I like to keep my eye on the door."

"Indeed, Mrs. Cullen," the man said, at once amused and chastened. "Indeed you would."

"Who told you to come and speak with me?"

Bennett fumbled in his pocket for a business card. "This gentleman," he said, handing it over.

"That's no good, as I can't read. Give it to the girl."

I took the card. " 'Dr. Montague Butts,' " I read aloud. " 'Trinity College, University of Cambridge.' "

"Means nothing to me," Mammy said. But I saw her cross her legs at the ankle and knew she was lying.

Bennett blushed. "Indeed? But he assured me he'd met you on at least one occasion, you see. That he'd been here to this very cottage. How irregular!" I made to return the card, but he pushed it into my hand, so when his back was turned I threw it on the fire, where it flared in an instant.

I poured tea and handed a cup to the visitor. Though I gave him a chipped cup.

"I'd better explain myself then," Bennett said.

"You'd better," Mammy said.

Bennett held his cane and his hat in one hand as he leaned forward and described how Butts and he were folklorists. More of a hobby than their true academic discipline, he explained, but one about which they were assiduous. That was his word: "assiduous." He and Butts went about the country collecting what he called oral tradition and writing it down. He was looking, he said, for folk songs, folktales, superstitions, hedgerow medicine . . . anything that might be of interest.

Mammy stroked her chin. "Well," she said, "I'm not much of a singer myself. Let me think."

Sometimes I marveled at Mammy. I had to bite my lip.

"No," Mammy said at last. "No, I've never been a great one for singing. Fern here might be better. She can hold a tune. Not that I have much time for these pop tunes and long-haired beatniks."

"Pop tunes are precisely what we don't want," Bennett said, "and since I'm a former army chap, you'll see I prefer a short-back-and-sides."

"Away you go," Mammy said to me.

So I got to my feet and gave him "The Coventry Ploughboy," and treated him to a version that had thirty-two verses and a two-line refrain. Throughout the rendition Bennett tapped his foot mildly, pretended to look enchanted beyond all understanding by my singing, and almost prevented his smile from locking, but didn't quite. When I was done he put his hat and cane on the floor and offered genteel applause.

"She's got plenty like that," Mammy said. "And she's bookish. That girl has read a hundred books. More than a hundred."

"Splendid," Bennett said. He took a notebook from his pocket and withdrew a tiny pencil from inside its spine. "And would you have anything in the way of hedgerow medicines?"

"Give Mr. Bennett a bottle o' that elderberry wine, Fern. Go on, fetch it out of the pantry."

"That's too generous, Mrs. Cullen, I couldn't possibly accept it."

"No, you shall have it. And you shall call me Mammy as everyone else does round here. Go on, you call me Mammy. Go on now!"

I passed him a bottle of cloudy elderberry wine. It was good, but we had too much of the stuff.

"Why if you insist, Mammy. There's a great modern interest, you see, in hedgerow medicine."

"That's more like it. Hedgerow medicine? Let me see. I do know this elderberry wine is very good for keeping you regular. Do you have any problems not being regular?"

"No, I don't say I—"

"Or that Mr. Butts at Cambridge? Is he regular?"

"Well, I can't speak for—"

"Now I've never rubbed *my* back agin a college wall like you have done, but you take a tot o' my elderberry each evening, and you shall be regular. And that friend of yours, Mr. Butts, he shall be regular, too."

"I'm sure he'll be very pleased."

"Write it down in your little book, then."

"Mrs. Cullen?"

I had to turn away and stuff a corner of my apron in my mouth while he wasn't looking.

"Make a note. Hedgerow medicine. Write down elderberry wine. One tot per evening keeps your bowels regular."

Bennett made a note. Then he closed his book and leaned forward confidentially. "Mrs. Cullen . . . Mammy . . . can we speak more generally, about hedgerow medicine?"

But Mammy was already hauling herself out of her chair. She screwed up her face and pushed the heels of her hands into the small of her back. "I've to lie down now. It's the arthritis, it gives me such pains if I sit a while. Fern, you look after our visitor." Mammy parted the curtain across the staircase at the back of the room and hauled her bulk up the creaking wooden steps.

Bennett looked sadly in my direction. "I don't suppose you have anything to tell me about hedgerow medicine?"

"No," I said, "but I know another tune you may enjoy." And I got to my feet again and parted my lips in song.

three

I heard voices on the radio—
American voices—talking about the first docking in orbit by a space-
ship called Gemini 8. The astronauts would come back safely, they
said, and the Russians were actually going to land a ship on the lunar
surface. The speaker claimed that a man would walk on the moon before the end of the decade. Three years to go. It fascinated me that
they could do these things. Mammy observed me listening hard and
opened her mouth to comment. She said all these things they were
firing off into space were changing the weather, and for the worse.

But before she could say it again she turned her good ear toward
the window. "Hark! Was that the gate? Go and look, Fern."

Mammy thought she'd heard the gate hinge squeaking, but when I
went to the window to look out there was nobody there. I thought
perhaps she was expecting the postman, though you would just as
likely see an astronaut coming up our path unless it was to deliver a
bill. Mammy was anxious because money was short. She spoke of big
trouble unless we had a good summer.

Mammy garnered from various sources; too many she said, always
bemoaning the fact that unlike other folk we didn't have one steady
source of income. The midwifery was irregular, and Mammy was de-
pendent on payment at the discretion of the women we attended.
There was no fixed fee, nor could there be: Mammy didn't have a certificate.

There was a shadow at the back of her practice that had passed up
all chance of proper qualification. Anyway the National Health Service offered a free and localized service to all pregnant mothers. The
days of the freelance midwife were long over, and Mammy knew that
only her strong local reputation kept her in any of that work at all. It
was a tragedy because she loved it, and in that field she had no peer.

She had the touch. She had the know. She just wasn't allowed to use it enough.

We kept scrawny chickens in the backyard, selling eggs and the occasional fowl for little more than it cost to feed. We bottled jams from the fruit of our tiny orchard and the berries of the heath. We stunk out the house making florescences, and we sold those; and our fingers were swollen and numbed on needles when we took in sewing. We baked, for weddings and parties and the like, though for some reason we were being asked less and less. Sometimes we took in washing, though Mammy hated that more than anything. And even though our outgoings were parsimonious in the extreme, it was all never enough.

The reason Mammy had been struck off the register was because sometimes she would do work for girls who were at the end of their tether. That was Mammy. Though she never let anyone go without a lecture, she never said no to a desperate girl.

Meanwhile, there was some gossip Mammy had gleaned concerning the hippies, or beatniks as Mammy persisted in calling them, who had moved into the tumbledown Croker's Farm. Some of these hippies we'd already encountered fixing their van by the side of the road.

No one in the village was much impressed by them. They didn't work and by all accounts they were a bunch of soap-dodgers. But they couldn't be moved because the property had been inherited by one amongst their number. The Stokes estate (which also owned our cottage, and Mammy felt that Lord Stokes—or his estate manager— was always looking for small excuses to turn us out) had tried to acquire the land. But the new owner had held out, and invited his fellow soap-dodgers to stay at the farm with him.

When Mammy had finished treating me to her views on beatniks and other scourges on the countryside, our conversation turned to whether we might help one Jane Louth. Before we had decided what to do, I left the table and nipped across the yard to the outhouse. I opened the toilet door and what I saw there made me scream. I slammed the door shut.

Mammy came running out with her stick to see what the commotion was.

"You know those hippies you was just talking about?" I said.

"What of it?"

"One of 'em is in our shithouse."

Mammy faltered, her huge bosom heaving again. Then she stepped forward and nudged open the outhouse door with her stick, as if there were a fat rat or snake inside. Sure enough, the young man we'd seen with the broken-down van was perched on the toilet seat. His trousers were round his ankles and he wore dark glasses that made him look like an insect, though I recognized him from his broken nose.

So this was our second male visitor, though of course he wasn't as formal as that chap from Cambridge University. "What you doing in there?" Mammy said, still holding the door ajar with her stick.

He smacked his lips, once. "I'll give you three guesses," said the hippie, "and if you can't come up with the answer between you, then you're both thick."

"I'll call the police on you, I will."

"What you gonna tell 'em? I stole a bucket of shit?"

He did look a sight in his sunglasses, debagged, pale as a ghost and his hair stuck to his face. He was sweating heavily.

"You've no right," Mammy said. "Going in places as don't belong to you."

Now he took his dark glasses off and looked Mammy in the eye. "I'd love to debate this. Any chance I can finish my business first?"

Mammy let the door swing shut. We stood off a bit and waited. After a few minutes the man came out. "How do you flush it?"

"You fill the bucket from the pump," Mammy said. "Don't you know anything at all?"

"You're living in the Dark Ages."

"Well," I said, "if you're coming all superior, you can shit in the street."

He cast me a look as old as time. Sweat trickling from his brow, he swung the bucket under the pump and cranked the handle. Then he took the bucket back inside the outhouse and flushed the toilet. He let the empty bucket clang on the cobbled yard. "I'm living at Croker's Farm."

"I know," Mammy folded her arms. She was suddenly enjoying this.

"We all got sick. I was walking by your house, and I was caught short. I should have asked, but I was in a hurry."

"He's sweating, Mammy," I said.

"I can see that. Have you been drinking from the spring up there?"

"We have."

"It's contaminated by old slurry. You should have asked someone about it."

"Can it be put right?"

"Not unless you dig a big trench to take off the slurry and let the spring clear. In the meantime you shall have to fetch and carry your water, just as we always used to."

The man sniffed. "Can we use your pump then? To fetch water?"

Mammy stuck out a judicious bottom lip. "You can. Long as you understand it ain't right to barge into no one's home unasked."

He took out his tobacco and began rolling a cigarette and he did that same thing of looking at me while he licked the gummed paper. "Cool."

Mammy blinked. I don't think anyone had ever cooled her before. "Fern, go and get him some o' that riot. You planning to stay up there at Croker's?"

"I own it. Well, we all do now. We're going to farm it."

"Ha! You've got your work cut out," Mammy said.

When I returned to give him a bag with a mixture of dried herbs, he looked at it a bit suspicious. "Just make a tea o' that. Don't let it stew too long. It's meadowsweet and sage and other things if anyone wants to know. It'll stiffen your guts for you."

The man opened the bag and took a deep sniff of the contents. "That's so far out. By the way I'm Chas. Maybe we can be friends."

"Nonsense," Mammy said. "Be on your way."

Chas was taken aback by Mammy's bluntness. He shook his head slightly, turned to walk away and held a hand trailing through the air in a farewell gesture.

"Beatniks," Mammy said after he'd gone. "Can't be doing with them."

I wondered what there was in her history to give her any kind of opinion about beatniks. Mammy did have history. She was known in the town and in the villages. They even sent clever fools out from the universities to speak with her, though for what good it did them. It was just that Mammy didn't want her history known.

Jealously guarding all the details, she seemed to regard speaking of her personal experiences as a dangerous act. "Information is power," she would often say. Not that I was a blabbermouth, if she told me any of it. I'd learned caution from the old woman, and glad of it I was, too. But I'd had to piece together what little I knew about Mammy's past from stories told by others, from distant family members, from hearsay, from rumor; and from the rare moments when Mammy might slip into unexpected revelation. Mammy was the apostle of the Don't Tell, preaching the gospel of the Say Nothing.

It was like a passion trapped in the heart, all this secrecy. All this re-sistance to letting it spill. But Mammy had taught me that just like opening your legs, opening your mouth would get you into trouble one day. Whatever these beatniks or hippies were, they triggered some kind of sympathy for them in Mammy. This in turn released pictures in my own mind, images that were a close neighbor to imag-ination but with a different quality. They formed out of the wrinkle I had heard in Mammy's voice. Those wrinkles shook themselves out into an alphabet, a language of guesswork and insight. Not an exact science, but arriving with a jolt of confirmation, linking, the way coal trucks shunt up against each other on the railway sidings. A smack of truth. So clear that Mammy saw how it worked for me, too; which ac-counted for her momentary nastiness, because she couldn't stop it from being seen. After a lifetime of concealing, Mammy knew that in me she'd adopted a child who could sometimes shred the curtain.

After all, what would it matter if Mammy let go of a few details? If she said this or that happened, what would it matter, and isn't that how a young girl should learn, by being told by one who knows? And of course I wanted to know everything, warts and all and warts on the warts. Because it seems to me that some of the best fun in this world is in hearing a story and telling a story in turn; a whisper, a gossip, a tattle, a rumor, a breaking of news, the turning of a tale. Mammy was a tightwad, a skinflint, a miser with all the detail that gloried the garden. I resented it. I was determined not to grow up so defensive and wizened and dried-up, but I had to fight against my training as it were.

"Are we to walk all the way into town together with that frown on your face?" Mammy said to me. "Knock that devil off your shoulder."

We each carried a hated basket of completed sewing. It was all I could do to stop malice being stitched in the cotton at three shillings an hour. "You're the one who turned the morning sour," I retorted. "Being sharp when you sent that chap away this morning."

Mammy cracked a smile at that and took up her walking stick. "Liked the look of him, did you? That beatnik?"

"I never said that."

"Come on, my little vixen," Mammy said more tenderly, "let's get along before the day is vanished."

To change the subject, or maybe to make a point, Mammy told me she had recently been approached in the marketplace at Market Harborough by Jane Louth, the newsagent's daughter. "How far gone is she?" I wanted to know.

"Says she's only missed her first bleed, but she's sick, and she knows she's knocked up all right."

"Makes it easier. You going to help her?"

"Told her what I always tells 'em."

"Ask the mistress?"

"Ask the mistress. Though I don't know why I bother. I seen it in her eye, and she'll be back tomorrow. And I shall say, well did you ask the mistress, Jane Louth? Oh yes, Mammy, she'll say, I asked her ever so. And how did the mistress appear to you, Jane Louth? Eh, what's that, Mammy? And how did she appear when you asked her? Well she were just there, Mammy, when I asked her. Well was she on her back, or full o' water, or fighting west or east, or swollen belly? Oh, Mammy, I don't know of these things. And I shall say, Jane Louth, you didn't even look at the mistress, did you?"

"But you'll still help her."

"Daresay I shall. But I despair when it's done without thought. I shall help any girl, but not without thought."

"Mammy, if they don't come to you, they go down to Leamington, to see that dwarf with his knitting needles."

Mammy shuddered and clicked her tongue against her teeth. And I wished I hadn't said it.

four

The following day I heard a knock on the door from a timid hand. Jane Louth wore a pink miniskirt, tan-colored nylons and white patent-leather boots up to her knees. I know these girls think I'm a frump, but I couldn't help shaking my head. Her concession to stealth had been to pull a fake ermine white hood up around her ears. She'd made herself as well camouflaged as a pink rabbit.

Well, sometimes I'm glad I'm a frump, if that's what I am. I asked her in. Jane had a head of barley-colored hair and only a slightly pug nose. That and a hunched manner, by which she folded her arms and pressed her knees together when sitting, locking her ankles one around the other. What distracted me most was a set of huge fake eyelashes inexpertly glued to her eyelids. I mean, why wear those furry beasts when going to see another woman about a thing like this? I don't understand my own sex.

Though she was my elder by a year, I knew that Jane was afraid of me. After I'd told her that Mammy would be back within the hour, she settled to a cup of tea, glancing around at the herb bunches pinned to the rafters, and through the open curtain of the pantry, with all its jars and bottles and pots.

I had the transistor playing softly while Mammy was out. "Radio Caroline," she said.

"Yes."

"Is Mammy going to help me?" Jane blurted at last.

"She will. She'll ask you some things first."

Jane's clear blue eyes widened. "What things?"

"She'll ask you if you consulted the mistress about whether this is the right thing to do; and you must say that you did and that the moon was fighting east, which has nothing to do with where it was in the sky, but if Mammy should ask you what that means, you say it was a left-hand cup."

She held the teacup an inch from her lips. "Left hand?"

"Yes, and that will satisfy her that you looked properly, which I know you didn't but that's not my business; that's between you and your soul. And then Mammy will ask who is the father, and you should tell her."

"I can't tell her that!"

"You'd better, or she won't help you."

"But isn't that between me and my soul, for goodness sake?"

"You can try to keep it back, but Mammy will tap her nose and say *knowledge*. And if you lie, she can tell and she'll send you packing, and then you'll be off to that gnome in Leamington Spa with his spikes, so please yourself. Don't cry, Jane. Here, wipe away your tears because Mammy has no sympathy for tears. You've got to be strong, or she won't even consider helping you."

Jane sniffled and brushed back a tear with a knuckle. "What will she do?"

"She'll give you a tea and it will taste like peppermint, and you drink it as she tells you and that's it. And I know what you're thinking, and the answer is no, it's not a potion, it's not magic. It's a herbal is all, one that brings it on, and you'll get the sweats and you'll bleed and that's it."

"Oh God! Oh God!"

"Look, Jane, if your mind isn't made up, then take yourself off. Mammy definitely won't help you if she thinks your mind isn't made up. Go back to the man you did it with and see if there's another road out of this."

"No, I am made up. I am. I've brought this with me, look." Jane produced an envelope from the pocket of her miniskirt.

"Don't mention that, and don't try to give it to Mammy. Just leave it quietly on the mantelpiece and don't mention payment."

The hinge of the garden gate squealed, and we both knew Mammy had returned. I gave Jane a nod of encouragement and sat upright to model for her a better posture with which to greet Mammy.

Mammy bustled in, hung her walking stick on a coat peg and closed the door behind her. "Good morning, Jane."

"Good morning, Mammy."

I got up to help Mammy take off her coat.

"Ain't you cold with your skirt up the crack o' your bum like that? And did you ask the mistress about our matter?"

"I did Mammy, and she was fighting east, by which I mean she was in her left-hand cup."

Mammy turned and raised an eyebrow at me. I tried hard to fight the blush that came flooding up from my neck to my ears.

"What cobblers," Mammy said. "Let's get on with it."

After Jane Louth had scurried away with her herb tea Mammy sat down to her snuff. She took it every day, and she mixed the commercial stuff with the gray-green leaves of sneezewort from the woods. She had a silver snuffbox someone had given to her out of a deep gratitude. Engraved with flower heads, the snuffbox curved to her hand, so much time had it spent there. Mammy could flip the lid open with her thumb, dip, and bring the snuff to her nostril at the same moment as clasping the lid shut. And as the snuff hit the back of her nasal cavity, I noticed—though I detested the habit and would never partake—how it always made Mammy's eyes gleam. Mammy avowed that it put a fresh complexion on the moment.

"A silly wench," Mammy said, her eyes watering with pleasure as she tossed back her head to relieve the trickle in her sinuses. "She wasn't listening to what I said. She were too keen to get away from here."

"You scare 'em, Mammy. They're frit."

"So they should be frit. If they gave a little more thought to what lay under things, then they would be frit. But she told me she'd only missed the one flow, and I thought she was lying."

"Why would she lie?"

"The poor things always lie, my pigeon." The snuff stimulated and softened Mammy at the same time, and when she softened she always called me her pigeon or her leveret or her flower. "They hang on thinking it can't be right, then another flow is missed and then another and they tell themselves it's the first. They lie to themselves. And anyway in all things there is generally more lies told than truth."

"That can't be so."

"You're very young."

"You gave her the birdlime and the pennyroyal, though."

Mammy didn't answer, which was answer enough. She seemed to be thinking of other things. In any case I knew exactly what Mammy had pressed into Jane Louth's hand, and in what proportions, and could prepare it myself, though Mammy wouldn't allow me ever to administer it. The berry of the mistletoe, which we called birdlime, is too dangerous. One of the best abortifacients, it stimulates both bleeding and uterine contraction. The pennyroyal does more than cloud the tea with the taste of mint; it also stimulates heavy contractions. The herbs excite the active ingredients of each other, but in the case of the brilliant pearl of the mistletoe berry the quantities need to be exact. A small miscalculation in the dose might cause giddiness, hallucinations, paralysis and eventually death. In the prescription of abortifacients, Mammy called it the devil's game, and kept me from it at arm's length.

Mammy had warned Jane Louth of the ravages of the prescription: she would sweat; she would vomit; she would feel aches and giddiness. Mammy instructed her to disguise these symptoms. She told the girl to let everyone know she had collected morels or St. George's mushrooms from the field the next morning, and to blame her sickness on a harmful fungus.

"When would I go collecting mushrooms?" Jane had said. "I'm not some kind of a nun singing in the meadow. I mean it's a bit out of character!"

"That's why you'd make a mistake then, isn't it? Get yourself up and go one morning as if you've come over all giddy like one of them beatniks up the road. And tell everyone you're full o' the joys of spring."

When Mammy's back was turned, Jane had laid her payment on the shelf without a word, took her jar of tea and left.

When I asked Mammy to confirm the contents of the herbal, it was only to see Mammy's intentions. If Mammy were certain of the course of action, she would offer the most effective abortifacients, as in the case of Jane Louth. If Mammy was uncertain, or if the girl herself seemed unresolved, she would prescribe a milder herb such as marjoram, beet or valerian, stimulators of bleeding but less reliable. Mammy explained to me that sometimes she preferred the river to choose her own course. This was Mammy's way. She said you couldn't push the river. It might do. It might not.

But there was another thing I knew about. A factor in this decision of which kind of abortifacient might—just occasionally—lie in what Mammy knew.

"She told you the father then? I thought she might not."

"They have to. They look in my eyes, and they can't help themselves. That's why it's good they're a bit afraid."

"Were you surprised?"

"No, that one's name has been spoken here before," Mammy said, looking cross. She picked up her poker and cracked at a log in the fire. "Likes to get the girls on their backs, does that one." Then she chuckled, laying down her poker. "And they likes to let him!"

five

A robin redbreast trilled from a branch, suddenly and with thrilling penetration. Sometimes I had a notion that it was the same robin following me over the rolling hills, bursting with excitement every time I disturbed the soil and helped him unearth a meal. For a moment I was caught up in his song, until Mammy's voice dragged me back.

"Are you listening to me?" Mammy said. "It's been playing on my mind, and I've got to speak or I'll burst."

It was three days later, and we were out getting some early colts-foot, which Mammy sometimes called horse-hoof and is good for asthma and bronchial complaints and coughs; and as a compress it's always good for ulcers and varicose veins. We would regularly get up early in the morning to ride the rolls of the green fields on shank's mare, collecting. That morning a fine mist came roiling out of the stream near where we gathered. Mammy said the herb was best taken before the flowers opened. Mammy was also fond of powdering the leaves—though they would come later—to make a snuff good for blocked sinuses. Sometime she even smoked it. Coltsfoot grew easily in our garden, but she could never get enough of it to dry and parcel out for the coughs and colds of winter or summer. "It's been playing on my mind about how much you ought to know. I mean, what if I were to drop down dead in my shoes?"

I wasn't paying attention. The scent of the morning carried my spirits away, as did the sound of the fast-running stream, as did the robin's song. I felt the chilly mist condensing on my cheeks and my nose; that and the sound my long coat made on the grasses, and the skid of my leather boots on the wet underfoot. I adored it all. Black slugs were out, ascending the green stalks, and snails, seduced upward by the damp.

"You're gone, gal!" Mammy cried. "Gone! You're like a fairy on a dandelion seed! You're lost to us!"

"What's that, Mammy?"

"All the things I know that you don't!"

Even if I was too easily seduced by a spring morning, I knew exactly what she meant. "Well, perhaps you'd better tell me the names, and I'll write them down."

"You'll write nothing down," Mammy said sharply, plucking the coltsfoot heads. They fell into her cupped hand with a slight popping. "Then no one can find the paper on which it's written."

"I can't argue with that."

"You'd better not. You must commit it to memory. Because it's important to know what's what."

There was another reason why I wasn't paying attention. It was that Mammy was always threatening to tell me what she knew, but then always drew back. I'd heard it so many times I'd stopped listening to her promises. She said the knowledge was too dangerous for me to carry.

Mammy would always tell me—as she did again over the collecting of coltsfoot that morning—what the information was *about*. She just wouldn't ever part with the details proper. It was what she referred to as the names of the fathers. This was a long list she kept in her head, comprising information divulged to her by every woman in the town and neighborhood, young and not so young, who had come to her for help. It included the names of fathers of illegitimate children whose mothers had come too late, or without firm intention; the names of fathers who weren't, because of Mammy's intervention, to be; the names of fathers who did not know their sons and daughters; and the names of fathers who could not father. It was, Mammy was fond of telling me, a great deal of knowledge for one woman to carry. Perhaps too much. But it was the kind of knowledge that could mean power, so Mammy impressed upon me the need for secrecy and reserve. "You never know when it will come in," she said. "You never know."

"Yes, Mammy," I said, "and you'll tell it all to me one day."

I gathered a lot of coltsfoot that morning, but not a lot of knowledge. It was amazing how much Mammy could talk about it without actually revealing anything. Some of the names were of people long dead and unknown to me, she said. Others I might guess from a weak chin or a high lip, but some would come as a complete surprise. As I listened to all this noninformation it did seem to me that fornication was a very popular activity in this dark corner of the English Midlands. More popular than the theater, or study, or football, or church.

"Are they at it all the time, Mammy?"

"Well, there's some as have a rest in between."

I supposed if they weren't all at it, there would be no past and no future either. But I remember saying, "But is everyone at it, Mammy? Everyone?"

"All except thee and me," Mammy said. "Thee and me." And this she seemed to find extraordinarily funny.

Gathering from the hedges—and from the ditches, streams, woodlands and rocky outcrops—was one of my favorite activities. Mammy had introduced me to the hedgerows from the moment she'd taken me in, carrying me at first in a sling made from a crochet blanket and later letting me toddle behind. Riding the rolls. My earliest memory was of the sweet odor of the elderberry. It had been an apprenticeship to the hedgerow of twenty years. Though I knew otherwise, Mammy often pretended there were very few things left for me to learn.

Dawn and dusk, Mammy said, were the proper times to gather, times when the door was open just a crack. *What door?* I often thought, but never dared ask. Perhaps because in my heart I knew what door, and it being ajar made me afraid. I sensed, too, that there was another important reason to go about gathering at dawn and dusk, and that was because there were fewer people around to notice what we were doing. Not that there was anything menacing or even illegal about the sight of two women gathering plants from the hedgerows, but it did blow in all that whispering, and I would sense the local comment: the Cullen woman and her girl is out there again I see.

Let them, I always thought. What did it matter? But Mammy was more circumspect. I was young, and didn't know what Mammy knew. About how fickle were the people you helped. Keep silent as the sacred oak, Mammy said, and don't you write things down.

But I was never ashamed to be seduced by mysteries of gathering. Where did it all go, all the plants and roots and berries? Dried and cured, bottled and pressed, shredded and steeped. Thrown away, much of it. All sorts of stuff never called for, lost its efficacy, deemed collected on the wrong quarter of the moon, or with an inch of dusk too settled. I parroted all that, followed it all faithfully, yet doubted often.

But the dawn in the damp fields with the mist piping from the earth! When just passing through the wet grass was like intruding on some other person's dream. And then at dusk when it seemed what we were gathering was not berries or leaves, but the cottony stuff of twilight itself. You could wind it on a spool, so thickly did it come in. White stuff in the morning, black stuff at night.

That morning as we made our way back to the cottage with our coltsfoot gold, Mammy stopped and leaned on her stick. "My arse is itching. What do you think that means?"

She was always saying that. "No idea."

Now as she leaned on her stick she only appeared to be looking across the field. "There's more."

There was always more. And why did I know this one would scare me? More even than when Mammy showed me to the mistress when I was thirteen. Maybe it was the way she leaned on her stick and would not look me in the eye but at the middle distance when she said there was more. "What have you got in mind for me, Mammy?"

"It's not what I've got in mind for you. It's fate. It's what fate has in mind for you."

"Sometimes they seem like the same thing."

"Do you know you're getting insolent, girl?"

"Just tell me what it is, Mammy."

"You've got to do the *Asking* one day. What if I were to die before you'd done that? And no me here to help you?"

"What's this talk of dying all of a sudden, Mammy? You're as fit as a flea."

"I feel like we were of a time, we few, and it's a time done."

"You're being morbid, Mammy."

"Maybe. But who's that at our door?"

I looked up and saw a woman waiting outside the cottage. She wore a cloche-style black straw hat pulled low over her head, as if she didn't want to be recognized, but I didn't know who it was. "No idea, Mammy. Wonder what she wants?"

"Oh! I think I know that, young lass. This doesn't bode well."

The woman shifted her weight from one foot to the other as we approached. "Mammy, Fern," she said. She looked anxious. "I'm Judith. Doll's daughter."

It was then that I realized I knew her vaguely after all, and Doll, too. Doll was one of the few, but she and Mammy had had a fall-out over something when I was a child, so over the years I'd seen almost nothing of either the mother or the daughter. Judith wore huge hoop earrings, a long corduroy skirt and spike-heeled boots. She nodded at me, as if she knew me. Her eyes seemed to be in a permanent state of flare, and I didn't know if this was her natural condition or caused by the predicament.

"Yes I know who you are," Mammy said. "What's going on?"

"I thought to go inside and wait, but I didn't know if you'd think it right. So I waited here until you got back."

Mammy never locked her door. Usually when she went outside she even left it ajar to indicate that she would be back soon. She pushed her way past Judith and beckoned us in behind her. "Stop your prattle and come inside. What is it? What have you come for?"

Judith couldn't meet Mammy's eyes. Instead she looked at me to deliver her news. "It's Jane Louth. Mammy, she's died."

six

Mammy sank heavily into her chair by the hearth. She let her stick clatter to the floor, but I recovered it and hooked it on a coat peg. Mammy's face was the color of the cold ash in the grate. She touched her temple with the middle finger of her left hand. Her other hand lay on her lap, bunched. I saw for the first time the frailty of Mammy's age. This woman who would stand up to anyone, who would fight men with her fists if need be, was made giddy by this news.

I looked into the startling honesty of Judith's eyes, noticing how the blue iris of her left eye was compromised by a cloud of green. "What's being said?" I asked her.

"That she ate mushrooms, that she must have found a poisoned one amongst them. She'd been collecting mushrooms from the field, and she'd made breakfast with them."

"And the doctor goes along with that? What's that quack's name? Bloom?"

Judith blinked and looked away. "So far. And that might be the end of it, but Jane had a sister who took some of the mushrooms for her own breakfast, and she's been blurting to everyone how *she* is all right."

"But if there was one bad mushroom, and only Jane ate it, it wouldn't affect the other girl would it?"

"No, but we know it likely there wasn't a bad mushroom, don't we?"

"Who knows that she came to Mammy?"

Judith shrugged.

I was thinking fast. My thoughts were rushing past me, too quick to apprehend. "We have to find a way to get Mammy's jar. It will be around there somewhere."

"That won't be easy. But I taught the younger brother at school. I could go. Express my sympathy."

I remembered Mammy mentioning there was one who was a schoolteacher. Judith had a way of looking at me like she was counting off the seconds as she waited for an answer. "Can you? Can you get in the house?"

"I don't know."

"Try for Mammy, Judith! Try. Anything you can do. And find some entoloma, to leave in the kitchen, to be found. It's easily confused with St. George's mushroom."

"You're asking a lot. It might blow over."

"It might."

I needed to look after Mammy, who'd not spoken a word. I opened the door for Judith and stepped outside with her. "Look, we'll say—if anyone asks—that she came to Mammy and that Mammy sent her away as being too far gone. That's what we shall say. But only if anyone asks."

Before leaving, Judith touched my cheek lightly with the nail of her finger. "Let me write down my address for you. Come round to me. We're alike. You might need a friend, you know." She rummaged in her handbag for a pen and a scrap of paper. Bent over her bag in her cloche hat, she looked like a flower in the woods. I wondered if nature really had come up with a friend for me. I watched her slip through the garden gate and break almost into a run as she got onto the lane. Then I went back inside and poured Mammy a tot of sloe gin.

"Flighty," Mammy said of Judith. "Flighty, that one."

"Yes, Mammy."

"Her eye trickles color."

"I noticed it, Mammy."

"Might make her hard to trust."

"Yes, Mammy."

But her mind returned over and over, like an obsession, to the same question. "I'm so careful," she said. "Always."

"I know that, Mammy. I've seen you. Drink up, because you've had a hard knock today."

"And I always err on the side of making it a light dose. I always think, well if it don't work, it was meant to be."

"Mammy, you've done nothing wrong. There'll be another explanation. Who knows, perhaps the stupid girl did mix up her mushrooms. Or maybe she didn't do exactly what you said. Or maybe she didn't trust you, and she took her problems to someone else. Maybe a hundred reasons for it."

"I wonder did she hemorrhage? Or could she not stop vomiting? If I'd known, if they'd sent for me, I could have helped. This has never happened in all my years."

"You have to stop thinking of that, Mammy. If anyone asks, you're to say you sent her away."

"I've brought a shadow to our door."

"Mammy! You were trying to help the girl! You've always helped these girls! Remember that!"

But Mammy was not easily consoled. And from that day forward, a slow decline set in. A dusk crept over her. She went about her daily chores as usual, but in a mechanical way and with none of the vigor or spirit I'd always observed in her. She was distracted, preoccupied with other thoughts, and though I could occasionally winkle a smile out of the old woman, it was only ever a forced grin, presented merely to make me feel better. She resorted to her sloe gin more than usual, and to her snuff without seeming to take the old pleasure in it.

This behavior being so out of character, I wondered if there was something else.

Wonderful Judith had done her work, having somehow got inside the house and recovered the jar—now empty of Mammy's herbal—from the mourning Louth household. It hadn't been possible to drop off the entoloma fungus, but generally the mushroom story stuck. There were rumors, though they never went near Mammy's ear. Judith reported them to me, and I decided not to pass them on.

Judith excited my curiosity, and I asked Mammy about her. She was one of seven children. Doll's first six had been boys, and Judith was a very late "mistake." Mammy had told me that Doll was one of the few, so it was inevitable that Judith was, too, and I understood this to be the reason why she might go out of her way to help us. I asked why we'd had so little contact with Judith and her mother, and Mammy said that they all had much more conviction than I had, and that I wouldn't get along with them. The explanation was inadequate, but I let it go. Meanwhile I learned that Judith taught primary school children in Market Harborough.

We received a visit from the village constable, Bill Myers. He arrived looking slightly ashamed of himself, with his helmet tucked under his arm and fiddling with a small notepad. Myers's mother, dead these twelve years, had always spoken highly of Mammy, saying how she'd been a big help to the family in times of trouble when they couldn't afford doctor's fees. Myers, fingering his collar, said he was obliged to ask if Jane Louth had been to see her; and in deference to Mammy he directed most of his questions at me.

"She came," I said, pouring him a glass of elderberry wine, "because she was expecting. But Mammy said she was too far gone and sent her packing."

"Is that right, Mammy?"

"I sent her packing." She sighed.

Myers started to make a note, then thought better of it. "Didn't tell you who was the father I suppose?"

"Why would she tell Mammy?" I blurted, too quickly.

"Shut up girl, I can answer for myself!" Mammy turned to Myers. "She thinks I'm senile, you know."

Myers tried to laugh at the idea. "No, Mammy, you ain't that. So she went away without you doing anything for her, and she didn't say who the father was."

Mammy had been at Myers's birth. She'd dipped the policeman in water when he was still greasy from the womb. She looked Myers directly in the eye. "That's the top and bottom of it, Bill."

"That'll do me, Mammy," Myers said, snapping his notebook shut and draining his glass. "I'll be on my way. You look after your old self."

"I shall Bill, I shall. Have they give you that car yet?" Bill's village-bobby bicycle was about to be upgraded to a patrol vehicle.

"Any day now."

"And what will you do with your bicycle clips?"

"I'll give 'em to you, Mammy."

The fake humor was agonizing. But though it beat Bill Myers, Mammy barely went outdoors for the next few days. She stayed at home fretting over the fate of Jane Louth. Over and over in her mind she prepared the tea, measuring out the quantities, hunting for error—I know she did. I attended to whatever errands needed taking care of. I grew anxious about how badly Mammy had taken it all. She looked pale and drawn.

When the weather brightened, I rallied Mammy and persuaded her to go with me into town. I knew Mammy was afraid of the talk, that she was ashamed to show her face.

"You've got to go to market and hold your head up, Mammy. Otherwise, they'll think you're hiding. Otherwise, they'll think you're guilty."

So Mammy relented. She heartened, washed, and put on a change of clothes. The hens were laying well, so we gathered up the eggs in a basket and put together the sewing and hauled on our coats to make the walk into the center of Keywell, where a regular Saturday market took place.

It was a fresh and blustery day. Puffs of brilliant white scurrying cloud speckled the sky, and it was possible, after all, to feel the surge of spring. The hedgerows vibrated with life, and I was almost succeeding in trying to lighten Mammy's mood when I turned my ankle on a divot in the grass verge by the roadside. I gave a little yelp and hopped to a boulder, where I sat down.

"That's a bad sign," Mammy said. "We should turn around."

"I'm all right. I'll take off my shoe for a moment and rub it a bit."

"I don't like it. I see something in it."

"It's nothing. I just twisted it slightly. Give me a moment."

Mammy looked back down the path, then up at the clouds. I massaged my ankle and made light of her attempt at foresight. I had to keep her going. Now she was looking into the trees and the bushes, and I knew if she saw a single magpie or a mistle thrush, we would have to return home.

I refitted my shoe. "There, Mammy, I'm fine. Let's get along now."

It was already midmorning by the time we reached Keywell High Street, and the marketplace was busy with backed-up trucks and open stalls. There was a dairy stall where we habitually off-loaded the eggs. The market trader was a stout, red-faced man in his sixties, called Trump. I'd never liked him. He would squint at me and compress his thin lips. A line of warts, like a constellation of dark stars, ran from his nose and across his cheek. I waited until his stall cleared before taking the basket to him. Mammy stood at my shoulder as Trump greeted us cheerily enough.

"Got a full basket for you," I said.

The market trader made himself busy, rearranging his cheeses. "I'm overstocked with eggs this time."

"Oh," Mammy said. I looked up and down the stall. There were eggs there, but few.

Trump wiped his finger under his nose. "Can't use them today. Sorry." Then he turned to attend to a new customer.

"That's the first time he's ever refused my eggs," Mammy said.

I said, "Well, if he's overstocked, he's overstocked and that's it."

"He's not overstocked. We should go home."

"Don't make more of it than it is, Mammy. We'll sell these farther on."

I found a greengrocer who was happy to relieve us of our eggs. After that we delivered the sewing and stopped for a moment to gossip with one old girl by the square, and though she did seem in a hurry to move on, I said nothing to Mammy about it. With our business finished quickly we turned for home, passing by the Bell public house.

The Bell was crowded and 'roustabout' on market day. A jukebox hammered out tunes I liked by the Yardbirds and the Kinks, and a warm haze of tobacco smoke and sour ale spilled through the open door and onto the street, along with the good-natured babble of voices. Sometimes Mammy took me in for a glass of stout, but today she showed no inclination to venture inside. She pressed on instead, but Mammy hadn't made three steps past the pub's open door before a shadow darted and someone gave her a fierce shove in the small of her back. It sent her stumbling into the road.

Two men had loomed out of the Bell, beery, vinegary louts both unknown to me. As Mammy stumbled and looked up to see her assailant, the second man stepped behind her and pushed her toward the doorway of the pub.

"Shouldn't show your face round here," the first said. And this time he pressed Mammy hard in the chest, pushing her back again. Mammy roared at her assailant, but as she did so she twisted and fell into the gutter, her ash stick clattering in the road. Mammy lay on her back, panting hard.

I recovered from my astonishment at the first assault and picked up Mammy's stick to thrash wildly at one of the men, but they'd already gone, perhaps inside the pub. A few people gathered, but no one offered to help me get Mammy to her feet, and her weight seemed overwhelming as I tried to lift her. At last someone came out of the pub to help. It was Arthur McCann in his black leather jacket. He stooped down beside me in the gutter, blinking with his delicate eyelashes. Then he helped Mammy up. He dusted her down and gave her back her stick without a word.

I heard a reedlike voice call Arthur from the doorway of the pub, "Arthur, I'd leave well alone if I were you."

The small crowd, hitherto silent, started muttering. I looked up and saw a figure I thought I recognized scrutinizing us from the doorway of the pub. Mammy was on her feet, but was breathing hard. Someone found her basket and gave it to her.

"Shall I get her a drink," Arthur said, indicating the Bell. "She's had a fall. Doesn't look too good."

"I'll take Mammy now," I said coldly. I don't know why.

"Arthur's not to blame," Mammy said. "Get me home, Fern."

It was a struggle. Mammy was a weight, and she had to lean on me. The onlookers watched us make slow progress along the street. From inside the pub came the sound of that song "Get Off My Cloud" by them scruffy Rolling Stones.

*　　*　　*

Mammy never entirely recovered from the attack. On our return to the cottage she took to her bed. I was dismayed to see the extent of her bruises, on her back and her hip and her arm. Mammy was old, and old skin didn't repair easily. Under Mammy's instructions I made a salve from oil and fresh elder leaves, heating it until the leaves went crisp, then straining the mash into a jar. I massaged the elder salve into the livid bruises, whispering comfort to Mammy, who lay with her eyes closed. Now and then she winced.

At dusk a screech owl settled in the ash tree in the garden and shrieked at intervals. I didn't like it at all, though Mammy said it was a good omen.

"It doesn't matter how much you try to help people," Mammy said to me. "They always turn on you one day. This is why we keep apart. They always turn."

"Go to sleep, Mammy." I'd given her a soothing tea made from valerian, which Mammy always called vandal root, and peppermint. The owl screeched from the ash tree. It sat there in the full light of the moon. I looked out of the window at it, trying to scare it away with my thoughts, but it just looked back at me.

The next day Mammy seemed even worse so I sent for Dr. Bloom, the local GP. Mammy had no time for him as a doctor, and he knew it. He came—eventually—with his leather bag and his stethoscope and his bustling, superior air. I noticed he had a ring on his little finger, which Mammy told me was the sign of a Freemason. I don't know if that's true.

Bloom, who always seemed to be in a massive hurry, took the stairs two at a time. Mammy gave no resistance to his examination, and he soon told me to follow him downstairs. "We'll have to have her in," he said, running a hand through a thatch of hair thick with Brylcream.

"Not a chance!" I said. I knew she would hate hospital, and with good reason.

"She's got abnormally high blood pressure. Plus I think she's cracked a rib or two." He stuffed his stethoscope in his bag and looked up at the herb bunches pinned to the roof beams. "And if I leave her here, she's bound to choke herself on all this rot."

They'd had differences about this before. "She's not going anywhere. I can give her better nursing here than in there."

"You're as bad as she is," Bloom said, clipping his case shut. "I'll come again tomorrow, but if she's no better, we'll have to whisk her in." Then he was gone, as if he couldn't get out of the cottage fast enough, leaving behind him a prescription for analgesic and a whiff of Brylcreem hair tonic.

That evening Judith arrived with an old man in tow. He was stooped with age. His ears were hairy, dressed with a soft, white down sprouting from both the shell and the large, fleshy lobes. He seemed to me like some kind of a troll, as he pushed past me and went directly upstairs to Mammy. I stood at the bottom of the stairs, not knowing whether to follow, but Mammy seemed to know him, because I heard her say, "William, look at me all laid up."

"Who is he?" I asked Judith.

"William said you and he met about ten years ago."

I thought about it, then I realized I did know William after all. Mammy had taken me to his cottage once. She'd said he kept bees, and she was going to show me the hives. The man I now recognized had been arthritic and ancient even then. It was a meeting strange and brief. William had been planting a row of leeks in his vegetable patch. Mammy had hailed him from the gate, and William had got up, knee joints cracking, wiping his hands on his rough brown trousers before reaching out to me. There was soil on his hands. I stupidly thought the old man was offering to shake hands, but instead he had reached past me and twined his fingers in my hair before withdrawing his muddy hand.

"So this is yourn?" William had said.

"This is her," Mammy had said.

William had gazed at me that day. I remember a blowfly buzzing past his face, and he'd waved it away lazily. "Good," he'd said. "Yes.

She might do." Then he'd turned back to his row of leeks. That was it. I never got to see the beehives.

I made tea for everyone and took it upstairs. Mammy was chattering away: the visit had clearly perked her up though William didn't seem to be listening. He'd drawn a chair up at the bottom of the bed and was playing a game of patience with a deck of almost completely effaced cards that he'd laid out on Mammy's blankets.

"I hear that apple-arse doctor's been in," he said without looking up."

"He says Mammy's got cracked ribs."

"I ain't got cracked ribs!" Mammy forced a chuckle. "It's a bruise is all it is."

"He wants her to go into hospital," I persisted.

At last William looked up from his cards. "You keep her away from there. If she goes in, she won't come out again."

"Surely it's not that bad!" I tried. I meant Mammy's condition. Or the hospital. Or both.

"Just keep her out of that bloody charnel house," William said. He seemed cross with me. "It's up to you to keep her out. Now where's that tea I was promised?" William gazed at me meaningfully, then went back to his cards.

seven

*A*fter the visitors had gone I climbed the creaking stairs to see Mammy, but she was sleeping. I went back down and tidied up, then took a book upstairs with me. I thought to sit with her a while and read. Even though she was sleeping, I felt she might be able to sense my presence watching over her.

The curtains were still open, and the sky was full of bright stars. I saw one star moving, and I took it to be a satellite, maybe a sputnik. If ever I saw one twinkling in the sky I thought of Valentina Tereshkova the Russian cosmonaut. The Russians had put a woman into space, so why hadn't the Americans? If they ever did successfully land on the moon, it was my dear hope that there would be a woman in the team. It would be only right wouldn't it? Valentina, perhaps, would volunteer to go in an American rocket. I even considered writing to someone in authority, but I couldn't imagine them paying much attention to my views on the matter.

Finally, I drew the curtains, switched on the bedside lamp and settled down with my book. I'd paid only sixpence at a second-hand store for the book. It was about another planet where the planet itself was making people mad. It was very good. I was engrossed in it and getting near to the end when Mammy popped awake. She sat up, and said, "He'll be wanting something hot. What shall we give him?"

"Mammy?"

"Well you can't just give him a sandwich, can you? Not after he's been through all that and come all this way."

"Would you like a drink of something, Mammy?" I got up and I touched her hand. The tips of her fingers were chilled. "Let me plump up your pillow for you."

"Never mind me. Ralph will be wanting something hot."

My hand flew to my hair grips, and I turned away for a moment.

Ralph was Mammy's son. He'd been killed at Mons at the end of the First World War. Mammy had told me he'd been killed after the Armistice had been signed, by an enemy soldier who hadn't accepted that it was all over. Mammy kept his regimental sword in a bottom drawer in her bedroom. I wondered if it were possible for a person to wake from a sleep, sit up, and still be dreaming.

"What about you? Are you hungry, Mammy?"

Mammy looked at me quizzically. Then she looked about the room, at the door, and then at the bedside table lamp as if seeing it for the first time. "Was William here?" she asked me.

"Yes. And Judith. They came to see you."

She smacked her lips. "Did William say anything about a horse?"

"You've been dreaming, Mammy. Here, drink some water."

Mammy had a sip of water, then let her head sink back. I felt so sad seeing her iron gray hair against the white pillow. At last she closed her eyes again. I sat watching her until I was sure she'd gone to sleep.

The next morning Mammy slept very late. I wasn't happy about her condition, not least the way her fingertips and her toes were so cold, no matter how many blankets I heaped on her. What's more, the bruise around her ribs was swelling. I put on my coat and walked to the telephone box in the village and made a call to Bloom's surgery. The receptionist said she would pass on the message.

It was nearly midday before Dr. Bloom arrived. He went straight up to her. Within a few minutes he was back down. "It's no good. I'm going to arrange for an ambulance to come and take her in."

"But that's the last thing she'd want!"

"She's barely coherent up there. She just asked me if I was the rat-catcher."

"But that's a joke! That's Mammy's sense of humor!"

He sat down at the table, took some papers out of his case and began writing. "I don't think so. She complained about rats in the rafters."

"But we have got rats! They get inside the roof!"

"She's got to go in. What are you going to do for her?" He pointed to the bunches of feverfew, vervain, ragwort, dill, St. John's wort, all the usual ones hanging from the crossbeam. "Give her this stuff, will you?"

I said I wouldn't allow it, and Bloom sighed. Then he said he wasn't prepared to come out here on a daily basis just to have his advice ignored. He said if I didn't want his advice, then I shouldn't have called him there. He told me that Mammy needed tests.

"Tests? Tests for what?"

"Tests so I can answer that very question. Look, you don't seem to realize that she's seventy-seven years old. You can please yourself: keep her here and stuff her full of stinkwort or batwing or whatever it is dripping from the roof of this cave of yours, or we'll have her in hospital. But I'm not running back and forth every day. So make up your mind." And he clicked shut the clasps on his bag.

Click-click.

Perhaps it was the worst day's work I ever did in letting Bloom put her in hospital. I don't know what else I could have done. Resisted maybe. And though I hadn't even convinced myself it was the right thing, Mammy allowed me to persuade her and the ambulance came and took her away. She looked at me as they carried her out on a stretcher: not accusingly or in a way that might make me think she was hurt or betrayed. Rather she just looked confused. They took her all the way into Leicester, where Bloom promised me she could get the special attention she needed. He still wasn't saying what that was.

I visited her every day and for as long as they would let me stay, even though the smell of antiseptic gave me a headache. To save money I hitchhiked into Leicester. Getting people to stop wasn't always easy, but I usually managed a ride. A strange thing started to happen. It seemed that no sooner was I in the passenger seat, with the driver having learned I was on my way to the Royal Infirmary, than would they pour out their history. I didn't have to say anything, or ask anything. The men—and the drivers were almost invariably men—told me about their health problems or the stresses of their job or even their marital disasters. And they would take me all the way to the hospital. Even if I said drop me here or let me out at the lights, they would insist on taking me all the way. Sometimes I would look back, and they would still be talking as I gently closed the passenger door.

Visiting time was restricted to late afternoon and early evening. Some days Mammy was coherent, chatting normally. She directed me to smuggle in concoctions she might administer to herself. Other days she didn't even recognize me. There were occasions again where she might recognize me but not the place she was in. She seemed to have come unstuck in time, and in those moments she was in another location altogether.

"Fern, untie my feet would you? There's no need for me to have my feet tied up like this."

"What, Mammy? Your feet aren't tied up. Look for yourself."

"I don't sleep well. The woman in the next bed keeps scratching the wall. She's made her fingernails bleed crying out for her baby."

I looked, but the bed next to Mammy's was empty, and had been so since she was admitted.

"I don't want to be here when the mistress is full and shining through the window, Fern. You should hear 'em howl. All night long it goes on. You should hear them. Could you just untie my feet?"

Then she might cry. And she would say that she had so many things to tell me which she'd held back and which I should know. At those times she would make me put my ear close to her lips and she would whisper. Everything she knew. An entire visiting period might pass with her whispering in my ear and my saying nothing. Mammy would only break off if a nurse or other member of the hospital staff approached. Then she would resume. Though it was a strain, I sat on a chair by the bed and let her talk in my ear.

It would be twilight when I came out after those sessions. It was always more tricky getting a ride back than it was in broad daylight. One evening it looked like rain and no one was stopping for me. I tried to use mental powers to pull them in, but it didn't work. Perhaps I was too exhausted from all of Mammy's talk, because they just wouldn't pull over. So I rolled my skirt up my leg a way and used my hair grips to pin it up so that it looked like one of these miniskirts these wild girls wear. I know Mammy would have been scandalized.

The very next car that came along stopped for me. I thought: heck, the power of these miniskirts. I got in and the driver zoomed off, tipping me back in my seat. He was a kind of teddy boy, with a premature widow's peak and bad acne. I knew something that would have cleared up his acne, but he didn't give me a chance to tell him. He cleared his throat. "How's it goin'?"

"It's going all right."

He smirked at me, though I kept my eyes fixed on the road. He cleared his throat again. "Where you off to?"

"Near Keywell."

"I go right through there."

"Great. Thanks."

He nudged the gearshift as we rounded bends and ascended inclines. It seemed to me he deliberately made his knuckles brush against my thigh. He cleared his throat a third time. "Where've you been then?"

"I've been to the hospital. I've got a yeast infection."

His fingers didn't brush my thigh anymore after that. He dropped me in Keywell without another word and roared off.

Later that night I sat outside the cottage in my coat, looking up at the stars for sputniks and drinking elderberry wine until I nearly passed out. Mammy would never have approved of heavy drinking, but I was beginning to see its advantages. For one thing it doubled the number of stars in the sky. I'd also heard that the Russians had put dogs and monkeys into orbit, but hadn't brought them down again as they had with Valentina. They were just left to die, then to go round and round the earth forever. I wondered if they would decompose; then I thought not, in space. Mummified dogs and apes, up there, going round. The thought made me take another gulp of elderberry wine.

I could never have guessed that Mammy's going into hospital would touch off a landslide of events. For almost twenty years she had been my shield and my pathway through the world. Just as she had shown me the footpaths up and down the swollen-belly pastures of the rolling countryside, Mammy had laid out the map of life. I talked like Mammy, dressed like her and even walked and held my body like Mammy.

In many ways Mammy had prevented me from being part of the changing times. I wasn't, like most girls of my age, pulled by 1960s' fashion fads; nor did I moon over mopheaded pop stars; I was insensitive to political changes going on and ill attuned to all the new social rhythms. The technology I could see advancing all around me and even in the skies overhead barely touched our lives, and the astonishing rising affluence passed us by. I knew that the kind of life I lived with Mammy had barely changed in fifty years. Maybe more.

There was only one thing that was at odds between Mammy's and my life. I didn't have Mammy's belief; not quite. But she knew that. Knew it and forgave me for it. And anyway, I thought, sipping my homemade wine and squinting up at the night sky for sputniks, Mammy had told me there were as many different beliefs as there were scattered stars. And I knew that the stars were without number.

eight

On the Sunday morning Bill Myers came to the cottage, out of police uniform. "Might I go in and see her? Take her some grapes?" he asked me.

"You don't have to ask me," I said. "It'll cheer her up if she sees you. She's in ward twelve. She likes the black grapes."

"Ward twelve is it?"

"Is that significant?"

"No," he said looking away. "No." And I wondered why he would lie.

Before he went I asked him, "Is anything to be done about the lout who pushed her over?"

"No one seems to know who it was," Myers said, smiling sadly. "A stranger by all accounts."

"Yes, it was someone who was put up to it, and we know why, don't we? Surely we can find out."

Myers's mood changed. "You don't want to open this up, Fern."

"But why should he get away with it?"

"You open this and other things will open up and that's not what you want."

Myers was warning me off. I didn't know how to reply.

His manner softened. "Look, there are some things as have to be taken care of above the table and some things below the table."

"You mean you're going to do something?"

"I have to go. I'll call on Mammy next time I'm over in Leicester."

I watched from the window as the policeman made strides down the garden path. Judith was arriving as he was leaving. He held the gate open for her. They exchanged a few words, and Judith laughed at some remark he made.

I told Judith what Myers had said. I wanted her opinion. "He's right," Judith said. "Leave it be. For now."

Then the hippie I now knew as Chas Devaney lurched up in his van. I heard the ratcheting sound as he levered his hand brake and knew he'd come to fill his battered old milk churns with water, since Mammy had granted him permission. He jumped out and saw me in the yard. He had that scuffed leather coat on, with no shirt underneath it this time. Oh, he thought he was the cat's miaow. "Still cool?" he shouted. "About the water I mean?"

Cool? I could be cool. "It's all right by me." I sniffed.

As he started pumping water Judith must come out to stick her nose in. She linked her arm with mine, familiar-like, and said, "Who's this?" Then she moistened her lips, and they shone with pink lipstick I swear she must have applied only a moment before. Her eyes shone, too, but for Chas. What's more, Chas stopped pumping and leaned on the pump. I felt cross. I wanted to say this isn't the time for all that, what with Mammy in hospital. This isn't the time for making faces and pouting and making your spaniel eyes go moist and large. This isn't the time to smirk and stop pumping in your leather coat with no shirt. Instead I heard myself say, "Chas, this is Judith. I think she's a bit of a hippie, like you."

He looked her up and down. "Schoolteacher, aren't you?"

"Take no notice of Fern's hippie talk. She wouldn't know a hippie if one bit her on the ankle."

"I recognized you from the school. I'm bringing my little boy in."

"Oooo," Judith went, hitting an infuriating note that somehow made us both sound foolish, "you're not against education, then? Not about to start your own dropout school at Croker's?"

"There's a big long list of things I'm not against."

"A list? So you can read and write, then?"

"Oh, write, yes, write, I can manage that," he said dryly. "I have a degree in philosophy."

"Well," Judith said, tightening her grip on my arm, "we'd love to hear you go on about your academic qualifications all day, but we have things to do, don't we, Fern?" And she expertly wheeled me away and back inside the cottage before I had time to protest.

"What are you doing?" I said once we were indoors.

"You don't stand there gawping, you walk away."

"What? Who was gawping?"

"You were. You'd gone all weak at the knees. It made us look naive."

"Us? How does *me* doing something make *us* look anything? And anyway I wasn't weak at the knees!"

She ignored me, watching him through the window, hanging in the shadow knowing he couldn't see in. "He looks dirty."

"They're all soap-dodgers. That's what Mammy calls 'em."

"Not that sort of dirty. I wonder what they do at Croker's."

I went across and stood next to her, to watch through the window. "He loves himself, doesn't he?" At that moment he happened to look up.

"For God's sake, Fern! Now he's seen us looking! That was your fault!"

After Chas had gone I went back to sorting. Judith was helping me. With Mammy in hospital I was using the opportunity to give the house a real good spring clean for when she came out. I wanted Mammy to come home and see that I could take care of her and the cottage both.

Though Judith said the place didn't need cleaning, it needed knocking down. At the bottom of the vegetable garden by the compost heap we made a fire and burned some very old clothes and other rags and rubbish. Judith put bistort root on the fire, goodness knows why.

There was a lot of white smoke, and where I stepped back, eyes watering, it didn't seem to affect Judith. She gazed into the smoke, almost transported by it. There was something waiflike about her, something fey, and her alert eyes would often cloud over with an inward stare. As the white smoke coiled around her, it seemed to me that there was also about Judith a frightening air of abandon.

"What do you see in all that smoke, Judith?"

"Passing over. Difficulty. Awe and wonder. Burning knickers." She tossed a pile of holed underwear onto the fire.

That evening I walked along the A47 trying to hitch a lift into Leicester and I wasn't having much luck. I had no intention of raising my skirt again, so instead I concentrated. I saw a blue Morris Minor come over the hill, so I lifted my thumb in the air and focused on getting the driver to stop, and he did. I climbed in. The driver told me he was a salesman. Before I had time to ask him what he sold he told me I was about the same age as his daughter, who wanted to emigrate to Australia, and this would mean he would rarely see her again. I could see he was hurting, but I didn't say anything. I just let him talk. At one point I saw him knuckle away a tear forming at the corner of his eye. It seemed only moments later that we were outside the hospital. Though I hadn't uttered a single word, he thanked me for our conversation, which he said had been a big help to him.

When I got to the ward where Mammy was I noticed there were screens round her bed and for a moment my heart scraped. I pushed the screen aside. A man in a suit lay on the bed beside Mammy. It stopped me in my tracks. It was William. He'd kicked off his shoes and there he was, cuddled up against her with his head on her breast. It looked like Mammy was comforting him. I didn't even know if this sort of thing was allowed on a hospital bed.

Mammy looked up. "Just give us a few minutes," she said, "then come back."

I went outside and sat on the grass near the admissions for Accident and Emergency. Two ambulance men and a nurse stood about sharing a joke and having a cigarette. Someone came out with yards of bandage round his head, all holding a bloody cotton swab in place. After the ambulance crew and the nurse had gone back inside I decided to return to the ward.

William had gone. Mammy was sitting upright, looking much better.

"Where's William? What was he doing?" What I meant was: who is he?

"We've known each other for a long, long time, Fern. A long, long time. What about you, are you coping at the cottage on your own?"

"Me? I'm fine! What are they doing with you in here? When will they let you out?"

"Nobody tells me anything. They poke me with this, they stick me with that. They've had my blood and my pee and my bone marrow. They've had their heads up my back passage, these doctors. I said it's no mystery what you'll find there. But they tell me nothing."

I apprised Mammy of everything I could think of to keep her entertained, though it wasn't easy, since my life consisted mainly of coming to visit her. I told her about the soap-dodger coming for his water and Judith making eyes at him.

"Flighty," she said of Judith again.

I didn't tell Mammy that she'd read the smoke, though Mammy probably knew that. I was telling her about my ride in when a staff nurse came by and whisked the screens open. "Who put these screens here?" she said to me, looking very cross.

I blinked at her.

nine

The following day I cleaned the house thoroughly. I scrubbed, I washed and I swept, in a thrilling kind of fever. I propped open the front and back doors and all the windows and let the breeze drive through. I said, Out imps! Out! I did all that daft stuff she would do. Shortly after midday someone rapped his knuckles on the open front door.

Coming through from the back of the house, I saw immediately that it was a bailiff from the Stokes estate. They have a uniform look, of a long raincoat and a cloth cap. But I had to look twice because inside the set of clothes was Arthur McCann. He looked like he wanted to run away. Instead he handed me a letter.

"Are you working for the Stokes estate now, Arthur?"

"Read that, Fern. You'll not like it."

I took the letter and tore it open. It contained a bill for unpaid rent. "But it's so much!"

"Rent's not been paid for over a year."

"But doesn't Mammy take care of it?"

"I know nothing about it. As it says there, you've four weeks to find it and pay it."

"Four weeks! But where will we find that sort of money? This can't be right."

"I'm sorry, Fern. When I heard about it I offered to bring it to you. But if you don't pay it, you shall be evicted."

"Four weeks."

"They seem to think that's generous up there at the house."

"Generous! They waited until Mammy was in hospital to do this, did they?"

"It stinks, Fern, and it's not my way of doing things, but that's how it stands. I don't know why, but I thought it would be better if I brought it. Seeing as how I know you. A bit." He puffed out his cheeks, then let the air pop: pffff. After that he touched the peak of his cloth cap in an old-fashioned gesture before retracing his path down the garden. The hinge on the garden gate sang out in protest, like a hurt thing as it opened and shut.

With the arrival of the letter I understood, possibly for the first time in my life, how unprotected I was without Mammy. Although I wasn't afraid and I had the capacity to work hard, Mammy had stood like a door of oak and iron between me and the outside world. I knew there was a rent to square on the cottage to the estate, but I didn't know how much, nor whether Mammy found it hard to pay, nor how often it should be paid. Moreover, I had little idea of the consequences of default. As a child I'd once seen bailiffs pile furniture outside another cottage on the estate, but had always assumed that to be the penalty paid by the feckless, not the hapless.

Mammy had always counted the pennies. If I wanted something, I asked Mammy for it, and if Mammy could do so, she granted it; if not, I learned not to ask again. Any small earnings that I made with the sewing were instantly turned over to Mammy. I knew the value of things: that wasn't the issue. I would never go shortchanged. But I'd never been put to manage what I had, or even to thinking about it. Until now.

I would have to ask Mammy how we stood eventually, but this was the worst possible time. This would come as a hammerblow. I resolved to see if I could fix the problem myself. On the shelf we kept a tin tea caddy with pictures of the Queen's coronation. I reached it down and spread out on the table four ten-shilling notes and what few coins were in there. I calculated what I might raise if I took in some extra sewing and some more washing. I looked again at the figures on the paper, but staring at them didn't make them come to any less.

Then I ransacked the house, looking for keepsakes I might sell if push came to shove. Of course I'd have to get Mammy's permission, but even then there wasn't much. There were the mementoes from the War. There was Mammy's gold locket chain and her silver snuffbox. Though there was very little else besides, I had a notion these things might fetch something at the pawnbroker's in Market Harborough.

Things looked up, just a little, when a lovely mouse of a girl with piercing brown eyes knocked on the door and asked me to bake her a cake. Her name was Emily Protheroe, though her name was soon to be Emily Cross, and what she wanted was her wedding cake.

Another of Mammy's skills was in baking, and in the baking of wedding cakes she was peerless. Not that any woman worth the name in the district was unable to bake a cake; but this was not just any cake. This was a wedding cake, this was the cake of life. And when it came to a wedding cake, everyone said, it was what went into it that counted, and not everyone had what was needed.

Word was that Mammy Cullen's cake got a young couple off to a good start on the winding road of a long marriage. It would sustain you in times of shortage and feed you in times of trial, it was said. At that time there were in the locality well over a hundred women who preserved, wrapped in paper and stored in a tin away from mice and weevils, a single slice of cake from their own wedding day to be halved and sewn into the grave clothes of the first in the partnership to go over. Because in those days one married not just for life, but for death, too.

That's all gone, that way of thinking.

But for the cake Mammy Cullen's rule of thumb still applied. One tier kept for the first christening party. Then to every guest at the wedding a slice. To the bride and groom each a slice. To any at the wedding who were not guests but who served at the table or who helped dress the bride, a slice. To the minister a slice, even if he were sour like most of them are. And one slice kept back, to be divided later, for the long journey into dark. Because, said Mammy's rule of thumb, where you have love to share it should be spread as far and as wide as it might go.

Mammy loved to be asked to bake a wedding cake. She was paid for her labors, but she poured all her love into the mix. So when Emily came knocking, even though I trembled at the challenge of matching one of Mammy's glorious cakes, I said Mammy will be back in a few days, and I said yes, we will.

"Only my mam had Mammy Cullen bake her cake when she were wed, and they have been 'appy and good to each other through some rough times," Emily said, sitting by the hearth, wringing her hands out of shyness and nervousness, "and it did upset me to hear Mammy being in hospital because I thought, well, no cake—oh! that sounds so selfish! Now you'll think I'm a terrible person! But then I thought of you and I thought well you may depend Mammy has taught her some if not all of what she knows and—"

I put a hand on the girl's arm, to stop her from chattering. "It'll be my very best one," I told her. I didn't add: it will—to date—be my only one.

I'd watched Mammy bake the wedding cakes often enough. If it were merely a matter of knowing the recipes, the quantities, the stirring, the mixing and the oven time then there wasn't much more I needed to know. But Mammy had never let me bake one. If the cake turned out badly, then the marriage might, too. The responsibility! And there's the matter of belief. Would my doubts run into the mix? Would a bit of scepticism make the cake too light or too heavy?

Emily brought me out of my thoughts. "There's a little one, too," she said.

"Oh! How far gone are you?"

"Not long. I wondered if you'd give me something to feel less sick."

"Ginger, have some ginger, and I'll give you avens to make a decoction."

"Avens is good. Mammy used to call it haresfoot."

That made me smile as I got to my feet. "She did." I shook a little twist of ground ginger into a packet and the same for the powdered root of avens.

"Will you knit the first booties? Mammy did mine, and my mam says I was walking at one."

Goodness, I thought, she believes in it all more than I do. "I'll do 'em for you." I handed the small packets to Emily, but the girl wouldn't take them.

"No," she said. "Mammy always says you must pay before you accept the package. That's what Mammy says."

I felt an unaccountable flush of anger. It was true that Mammy had complicated rules for how they were to pay for different things, upfront, afterward, backhand. All nonsense. "I do things a bit different to Mammy, understand?" The girl looked down at her feet. It made me soften, so I said, "Not much different, just a bit. I find it works better." I held out the packets again.

This time Emily took them. "I'm sure you know. How much shall I pay you then?"

"For the cake I shall have to reckon on it. Two tiers? I'll tell you next time I see you. For the other things it's just as before. Leave what you can afford on the mantel."

At this Emily looked pleased. Then she said, showing me her thumb, "There's another little thing. I'd be so pleased if I could get rid of this before my wedding day."

Hell in a bucket, I thought. I nearly told Emily I didn't do those, but she would have only said that Mammy did them. "Did you bring a bean?"

"Of course!" Emily twinkled with pride and produced a haricot bean from her pocket.

I shuddered inside but I didn't let her see that. "Hold up to the light, then." She angled her thumb and I touched the wart on it with my index finger for a count of three; then I took the bean from her and touched the bean for a count; then I took the bean outside and buried it and told it to perish with the wart. Emily came out, and I walked her to the garden gate before she remembered anything else. I promised to stitch her a charm bag, which is a little magical sachet with herbs inside it, to guard her unborn. She seemed pleased with that, chattering away nervously, but my mind was on the cake. I was going to have to ask for help. Returning inside, the first thing I did was to check the mantelpiece.

Emily had left a two-shilling piece. I sighed, and tossed the coin in the caddy.

I liked the chime on Judith's doorbell at her terraced house in Market Harborough. There seemed an age between the dying of the first note and the fall of the second. I could hear the motor of a vacuum cleaner, so I rang again. Finally, Judith answered. Her eyes flared on seeing me, and I was glad. The door admitted directly into her sitting room. The television was running.

Judith took my coat. She lived alone, and I was amazed at how spotless her house was. She made me tea and gave me some Garibaldi biscuits. I always think Garibaldis look as though dead flies have been baked into the biscuit, and I feel queasy when I see people eating them. "I have to finish vacuuming," she said, and proceeded to switch the machine on, running it painstakingly along a carpet on which I swear there was not a particle of dust.

I didn't mind. I sat down. Since we didn't have a television I found it mesmerizing, and I listened above the sound of the vacuum cleaner. There was a hospital drama playing. The hospital looked spotless, too, unlike the one where Mammy was.

Eventually, after Judith had slowly passed back and forth in front of my vision vacuuming with a kind of passionate focus, she switched the machine off. It was as she wound up the flex that she said, "William thinks you shouldn't have let her go in."

"I couldn't do anything else."

"He thinks she won't come out."

"He doesn't know that," I said sharply.

She put the vacuum cleaner away in a cupboard and came to sit beside me. We watched the television in silence. A nurse was in love with a doctor. You could hear if one of us blinked. Then I announced—as if it were nothing—that the estate was going to evict us from the cottage. Judith turned to look at me. I told her about the back rent.

"Well," Judith said at length, "you have to do what we do, and work. Women alone can't have it easy." She snapped a Garibaldi in two and dunked her dead-fly half biscuit in her tea with such vigor that the tea splashed over the rim of her cup and into her saucer. It was then that I thought: *Judith I could slap your face for a whole day and not stop even for lunch.*

"I work. I do everything. I wash, I sew, I bake."

"You'll find that's not enough." Judith said. "In the meantime we're going to have to think how we can help you."

I looked back at the drama on the television screen and pursed my lips. "Anyway," I said, not wanting her to think I was flinging myself on her mercy, "I was asked to bake a wedding cake, and that will earn a little, though the girl is poor—"

"They always are," Judith put in, "or otherwise they go to the baker."

"I'm afraid I won't be a patch on Mammy."

"A wedding cake is it?" Judith interrupted. "Do you know what you're doing?"

"I have to do it myself. It's another way of earning for one thing. I just want to be as good as Mammy."

"Okay. But you don't want to take chances on someone's wedding cake. It's a responsibility. Though you must have seen Mammy do it enough times."

"Yes," I said, "but it's what's unseen, isn't it? It's the whisper."

Easy. Too easy. But Judith went silent at that. Then she said, "You know, it's a pity that it all isn't written down somewhere. Then when someone dies it isn't lost with them. Wouldn't that be the thing?"

I don't know why but I heard myself mouthing Mammy's words. "What's only in our heads they can't take away from us." I told her about that chap Bennett from Cambridge University, who'd come to our door with a feather up his arse.

"Really?" Judith said. "What did you tell him?"

"Oh, we chased him away."

Judith returned to her idea that things should be written down, and I let her talk. Then the thing between the nurse and the doctor came to a head so we abandoned the conversation. Not having a television myself I didn't mind. You could just watch it and your head would empty, and what with all the anxieties I had at the time I didn't mind that either. Then the news came on and there was an item about the Gemini rockets and an astronaut making a space walk.

"I'd like to do that," I said.

"What?" said Judith.

After the news was over we watched a program called *The Outer Limits*. There were small plants like a clump of sage but from another planet, and these plants leaped onto people's faces. It didn't spell out exactly how these plants leaped: that was left unexplained. Then the people would be somehow changed, but no one would know.

It was very good.

ten

*The next day brought a hard-*driving rain clattering on the roof, and with it a knock on the door from Arthur McCann. The rain, stinging, silvery and bone-chilling struck at such a harsh angle that it ran between the slates of the cottage roof and coursed down the corner of the room. I was setting a saucepan to catch the drips.

"Let me in, Fern!" I heard him shout. "I'm getting a leathering."

I hurried to the door and opened it. He slammed the door behind him, falling back against it, blowing out his cheeks as if he'd been chased in by a bull. He took off his cloth cap and wiped water from his brow. His face was a riot of freckles and water droplets, like a freshwater trout.

"Stand by the fire," I said.

Arthur shook the water from his waxed coat, and some of the drops landed on me. Then he stood with his back to the fire, steam rising from him, his face flushed. I took his saturated cloth cap from his hands. "Not on that blooming motorbike in this weather, are you?"

"I walked here."

"What for? Is that Lord Stokes up in his big warm mansion still in a hurry to get my leaky cottage?"

"Lord Stokes is gaga, Fern. It's the Norfolk Eel who is after you."

The Norfolk Eel was everybody's name for Venables, the estate manager, a sleek and slippery character with a pink complexion and soft, rosy cheeks. I suddenly recalled his face looking at me from the doorway of the Bell the day Mammy was pushed into the gutter. "Makes no odds who it is wants me out."

"I feel bad," Arthur said. "I wish there was a way I could help you."

And for a second I looked at him with an expression of hope, but he met my eyes steadily, his coat steaming around him. Then I let the hope die. I didn't know whether there was much if anything he could do in his position. The rain was pinging into the saucepan, and it drew his attention away from me. "The roof's a sieve," I said.

"I'll get up there and fix it for you when the rain gives over."

"Before you throw me out you mean? Why would you do that?" But I knew why.

"Eh?" he said, as if he hadn't heard. Arthur stuck his forefinger in his ear and jiggled it about, as if trying to dislodge a plug of water and wax. He stepped under the leak, gazing up at it. "You should have a chap to take care of these things for you, Fern."

"Chaps eat too much," I said.

He looked at me sideways, then went back to conducting his survey of the roof. "I wonder if I can swing another few weeks for you. Hold them off a bit."

"How?"

He seemed to be talking to the leaking roof. "Norfolk Eel's got a lot on his mind right now. Got his attention on other things. Not promising I *could* do anything, mind. But I could try."

I sensed he might know something he didn't want to reveal. "Why would you do that for me?"

Arthur finally stopped regarding the leak and looked instead at me. "Stop it, Fern! You know why!"

I looked at him and thought, well it isn't fair what we get away with; how we can make men dance and pretend we don't see them hop and skip, making out we know nothing about it. And I felt sorry for Arthur. "I'm grateful for anything you can do."

I got him to take off his coat. I made him a cup of tea and laid out the exact details of my money situation. He whistled and scratched the underside of his chin for an inspiration that didn't come. We had a laugh about the day Mammy had stung his backside with her stick and I tried to thank him for the time he'd stuck up for us in Keywell but he didn't even want to talk about it. "It was a disgrace," is all he said, and the subject trailed a silence behind it, and that gave him a cue to get up to leave.

"There's another thing." He shuffled his arms into his wet coat.

"Those hippies from Croker's. They've been drawing water from the pump here."

"What of it?"

"I've been told to tell you they can't."

"But that's just mean!"

"I know. They're doing no harm. But the Norfolk Eel admitted he couldn't stop you from giving them water, so I've told you that as well. Up to you, Fern, but you ain't doing yourself any favors with the estate by going against them. Up to you."

Arthur put his soggy cap on his head, though much good it would do him since outside it was still raining hammer and nails. But he had other things to do. I let him go and shut the door behind him a fraction too quickly. Then I turned and thought for a minute, and a drop of rain from the leaking roof went plop in the pan.

That morning the rain curved in the gray air and set in hard until after midday, and though it didn't blow over completely, it fell back, and later the day brightened a little. I put on my thick woollen coat and my boots and decided to go for a walk in Pikehorn Woods, to think things through. I wrapped a black scarf around my head to save my ears from the stinging wind, and I didn't give a damn, frump or not.

The efforts of the estate to evict us from the cottage were not merely about the rent. They wanted the cottage, perhaps to install one of the estate laborers, and now that Mammy was off the scene the power that held them back from merely seizing it was away with her. I was a girl with little experience and no protection. I thought about Arthur again, but it seemed to me that the rush to find a man to help me—any available man—was a kind of weakness.

The electricity lines carried across the fields by giant pylons were hissing with water. I got off the road and went into the woods all heavy from the downpour. The black path—a rich compost of bracken root and moldering leaf—was waterlogged. But the green ferns were springy, and the trees and the thicket were rinsed clean, singing with water. I found in the dripping outdoors a crackle and a power fizzing on leaf and frond and branch. The rain had charged the air. It smelled good.

I knew the woods as well as I knew the land. The earth and its delivery of plants and bushes and herbs was a consistent calendar. In fact it was better than a calendar. What use was it to know that it was the fifth or the tenth day in March if the earth told you that the year was loitering? The days might pass, but if the land wasn't ready, you couldn't trot it on. No good collecting camomile in May if you've had a lot of rain or the blackthorn sloe in autumn if you've not had a frost. Only the leaves of the field turning make a calendar, a leafy almanac telling us the true time of year. We charted their constellations in the hedgerow; and they told us where to walk.

In the woods I was often in the condition (Mammy would complain) of being seduced. Even as I walked I felt myself going, drifting, but this time I didn't call myself back, and there came to me a kind of vision. The beads of rainwater on each branch tip or bud and on every bracken leaf began to expand; perfect, light-refracting silver spheres inflating until they were pregnant globes of light. The bracken became heavy under their new weight, tilting back until the fleshy spring of the green stems snapped back and triggered like catapults, firing the globes into the air; so did the budded branch tips of the trees, flinging iridescent baubles of light into the air.

I knew I could ride these baubles of light. Get right inside them, and drift free over the houses, where I would hear folk talking. The moment was a gift. If only I could calculate its meaning I would have been beyond the reach of this world, but at that moment I was soaring, soaring in the spaces between the trees. I felt in no need of help. I felt I could answer anything.

"What are you doing?"

The question brought me crashing to earth, a moment of panic, a clumsy descent in which I couldn't find my voice to answer; a moment in which I had to reassemble my person, to find the throat, the tongue, the words that might not arouse suspicion. But suspicion against what?

"Did I startle you?"

I was startled indeed. It was none other than Venables, the estate manager. The Norfolk Eel himself, and I could do nothing but stare at him stupidly. He looked back at me with spaniel eyes. His cheeks were so soft and rosy you wanted to stroke them with a finger. And though he smiled gently at me, there was an aura of sadness, of personal tragedy about the man that made me want to protect him.

Ridiculous really, when this was the man getting ready to evict me. I dared him to say anything about my walking in the woods. The Stokes estate liked to pretend they owned these woods, but I knew they were owned by a trust and that estate land merely abutted the tree line. But he didn't.

"I was admiring you. You seemed so lost in thought," he said.

"I was," I countered.

"I do that. Come here to lose myself I mean." He took a step toward me but folded his arms, which was a clever way of advancing and stepping back at the same time. "But you know what's odd? I was on my way to your house. To visit you."

"To visit me?"

Mammy once told me that in the woods she could make whatever she wanted to appear. Yet I hadn't wanted this soft-talking man to appear. I hadn't called *him*.

"Yes! Were you thinking of going back? We could walk together. I've got some news. Something that might cheer you up."

I hesitated. I was intrigued, because in all of my years with Mammy no one from the estate had ever visited the cottage, and I'd never thought it strange. But I was annoyed, too, because my bubble-moment in the woods had been popped, and I would never know where it was leading me. He seemed to read my thoughts.

"Hope I didn't spoil a perfect moment for you."

We walked back to the cottage. On the way he held up a spiny branch in an arch over my head so I might pass safely through it. He even offered his hand as we climbed the stile, and against all my instincts I took it. He refused to tell me his bit of news until we were installed in the cottage.

Once there I made up the fire. Venables was a tall man, and I sensed his eyes on me constantly. He politely refused tea, sloe gin and elderberry wine but accepted a glass of water. I stripped off my wet coat and pulled my chair closer to the smoky fire.

"I hear Mammy's in the Royal. You must miss her."

"I do," I said. "Now what's this news you have for me?"

"It's about you leaving this house."

"I'm not leaving the house. You're throwing us out."

"Here's the amazing thing. It's your good luck that Amy English is leaving the service of Lady Stokes to get married, and they want to replace her at the house. So there's an opportunity for you, if you fancy it, to be trained."

Service. I heard the word tinkle like a bell in my head. It sounded antique even to me. "Do they still do that up there?"

"Personal maid. A respected position. I spoke up for you."

"But you don't know the first thing about me!"

"Look, Fern, Mammy has her critics in this parish, as you well know, and there are a lot of people who are full of prejudice. But I'm not one of them. And there are others who speak up for you. I simply reported that at the house. The position is yours if you want it. Accommodation, everything."

"What about Mammy?"

He sniffed. "We're prepared to help with that, too." He emptied his tumbler of water, leaned across to place the glass on the table and let his voice go low. It had the effect of making me lean closer toward him. I almost felt he was trying to seduce me with his voice. "Sometimes events have a habit of arriving together. Like meeting in the woods. Sometimes these things are not accidents. They are meant to happen. Sorry if that sounds a bit mystical, but I do believe life has a way of shaping a path for us."

I admit I giggled. I tilted my head back and laughed. He smiled and nodded enthusiastically, pleased with his engineering.

Sobering, I said, "I'd rather cut my throat."

His rosy cheeks took on a deeper shade. "But it's an opportunity. It would solve your predicament."

"My predicament? I'd rather be a hermit in the woods than go into service waiting on the so-called quality. Those people you work for: haven't you looked at their hands? They're reptiles. Anyway it's mediaeval. Didn't it occur to you to ask whether I might like it before volunteering my services? And what clever scheme have you got lined up for Mammy in all of this?"

He tilted his head and arched a single eyebrow very high, still smiling, but with a far-fetched tolerance. "Fern, you don't have the luxury of this attitude. You've no education to speak of and no resources. I've done my homework on you. Don't think you'll be allowed to follow Mammy's line."

"I have a mind to get a diploma."

"You're the one who's mediaeval, Fern. With your history, they won't let you practice. Midwifery is a proper profession, and I'm afraid you're tainted by association."

"What do you mean 'tainted'?" I looked him in the eye. "This is Mammy's house we're in."

"I know that. And I don't want to show any disrespect. But while she's away I'm just trying to steer you to a better path. You can see that, can't you, Fern?"

Now I understood why they had never come to our door in all these years. It was because Mammy would have chased them away with her stick, and they knew it. "You've come to save me, haven't you?"

He smiled. He knew what I meant. "You're very beautiful, actually. Underneath. Everyone agrees. But that doesn't change anything."

Get him out of here now, said a voice in my ear. *Get him out.* I stood up. "I'll consider it."

Venables took his cue and got to his feet. "I can be a good friend, Fern." He paused at the threshold. *Get him out,* said the strident voice, *get him out of here.* "By the way, what were you doing? In the woods?"

"I was giving thanks and praise for all the things I have," I said.

"Really!" He smiled feebly at me and made an odd little punch in the air, in front of his nose. I don't know why. Then he turned to go. The gate whined on its hinge, and the spring snapped it back into place after he passed through.

Evil to your black heart, I thought, watching him walk away. "Was that you, Mammy?" I asked in a whisper. "Was that your voice telling me to get him out?"

I was still muttering to myself when a boy stepped from behind the bushes. He wore an anorak with the hood pulled so tight around his face only a tiny oval of mouth, nose and eyes was left exposed. He came up the garden path, sidling like a crab.

"I hung back while I saw the Norfolk Eel," he said, casting around him. "Only my mam sent me to tell you Bunch Cormell, her waters have gone, and she says if it's not to be Mammy, it's to be you. Did I do right to dodge the Eel?"

I flicked at his hood, this sweet little boy. "You did well. I'll get my coat and follow you down the road."

eleven

That sound, when they suck the very first draft of life. It's a click, a key turning in a tiny lock before the eerie ripple of knowing, the awesome shudder of recognition. Then they wail it out again! Oh I love that first sound.

It was Bunch Cormell's fifth, and her first four could not have been any easier than this one. Wait, Mammy had taught me, standing at the foot of the bed with her hands lightly clasped as she waited for time to round the corner; and if in doubt wait a little longer. All I had to do beyond putting my hands on Bunch's belly, and after inspecting the dilation, was to wait on nature. The boy, so he was, slipped out as easily as a fish. I checked him over and stroked his tiny nose to get rid of some mucus; I cleaned the child and laid him on Bunch's belly; I helped latch him on to Bunch's huge, expert breast; and then I delivered the afterbirth, cut the cord, and within the half hour I had my coat on. Oh, this job of life: you wouldn't want any other.

"You've got the touch, Fern," Bunch said happily. "You have." Bunch's husband was a farrier, but her own biceps were bigger than his, and she would put her fists up to anyone. Her sleek black hair was plastered to her rosy face. Her dark eyes were liquid with happiness. Otherwise, she looked like she'd done nothing more than run to catch a bus. "Just like Mammy, you are. Better than. But don't tell 'er I said that."

"If they were all that easy, you shouldn't need me. Now, you've four wide-eyed sprats outside the door. Shall I send them in?"

"Send them. Will you be burying that?"

I took some old newspaper out of my bag and wrapped up the afterbirth. "In your garden?"

"Up by the rhubarb patch, Fern. Please."

I opened the door. Bunch's husband and their four children were gathered on the landing. The children filed in, all with eyes like sloe berries, but averted, and stepping clear of me as if I were not merely a midwife but a frightening herald from another world. The farrier let them go ahead of him, and touched my arm. Then he pressed two folded banknotes into my hand.

"It's too much," I protested.

It did seem such a lot when the state offered the help for free. The man looked at me with the same sloe eyes as his children. "Heard you had some bother with the estate. Bunch will have my hide if you don't take it."

I felt the fluid gathering at the back of my eyes. I almost couldn't stand this big, brawny man's kindness. But I said, "Go and see your strapping new lad. He's a pretty one."

Dusk was falling on the small vegetable garden in the backyard. A halogen lamp had come on in the street behind the house, and it cast a dim light on the garden, enough for me to see by. I took my small trowel from the bag and buried the afterbirth in the earth near where the young crowns of rhubarb had pushed through the mulch. The soil was black and damp and turned easily. Mammy always told me to bury it deep enough so that a fox might not unearth it but not so deep that the bees might not know about it. Though I knew the difference between Mammy's practical common sense in midwifery and her rampant superstitions, I was always faithful to her instruction and to the needs of women like Bunch, who wouldn't be satisfied if I didn't do these things.

Mammy said we did this to dig into the world from where the baby had come, to return to the earth the vessel in which the baby had arrived. For this reason she said you should always be careful to shake the soil loose from your fingers, because you had plunged your hand into that other world. When I looked up from the job, I saw in the corner of the garden a hare, and it was looking directly at me. And I knew.

I knew because my skin flushed, almost as if it wanted to peel itself off my bones. A terrible fear rippled behind the flush of my skin. The hare was a big one. It gazed at me with large eyes, yellow and lunar. Its grizzled, reddish brown fur had a sheen, a luster. The creature was immobile, but its massive hind legs were compressed: hard-packed muscle waiting to spring. Long black-tipped ears stood erect, listening.

I was astonished to hear myself speak to it, as if it were human, as if it might reply. "What are you doing here? So far away from the fields?" Or perhaps I only thought these words. The moonlike yellow eyes gazed back at me and for a second time I felt a frisson, a prickle almost like a fur along the length of my own spine. My stomach squeezed and I felt paralyzed by this unreasonable terror—not of the hare, but of the quivering air around it, and of this numbing of my senses—and I still had my knees locked in the dirt where I knelt. Then came a warm stench, the sudden odor of the animal, like a signature flourished at the foot of a message as it turned and moved through the hedge, and was gone.

I recovered, and the fear had gone, too. After all it was only a hare. I cast about to see if anyone else had seen. I got up and went to the downstairs window and looked in. There was no one, only the flickering blue light of the television broadcasting to an empty room. The Cormells were busy upstairs admiring the new addition to the family. I felt a little foolish. I went back and finished tamping down the earth with my trowel before dropping the tool in my bag.

Then I remembered Mammy. What with Venables's distressing visit in the afternoon, and with this job at the Cormells', I'd neglected Mammy. I thought of her in hospital, alone, unvisited.

The next day was a Saturday, and Judith called. We discussed the pressing problem of my rent. Judith must have heard dismay in my voice. "Make some tea," she said. "We'll think again."

I stepped outside to draw water from the pump in the yard, but the handle found no resistance. When it wants to dry, I thought. Bad luck pulls more bad luck. "It needs priming," I shouted. "I'll go to the well."

"For God's sake!" Judith shouted, emerging from the house. "Isn't it time the estate piped water into this place? They've got men orbiting the moon, and you're drawing water from a bloody well! It doesn't seem right. Are they too bloody mean? Come on, we'll go together."

I grabbed the metal bucket upended against the wall. On the way I told Judith about the hare I'd seen in the dusk of Bunch's garden.

Judith stopped in her tracks. "Have you *Asked*?"

"Mammy said I should know when it was right. But I don't like to think of it. She told me stories, and they scared me. I'm not going to invite it in. I'm too scared, and I don't mind who knows it. There's a lot of it I just don't care for."

"You might not have a choice about it."

"You've done it, haven't you? What's yours?"

"Never tell. But I'll help you, if ever you decide to do it."

"I'm not going to."

"All right. Now shut up about it."

Keywell had an ancient well in the village square. It had been bricked round in Victorian times so that the cold, pellucid springwater trickled and refreshed the shallow well and drained through a pebble floor. Very few people used it at all now for practical purposes, but its preservation was a matter of village pride. The amber pebbles shone like gold coins in the well, and the water was always sweet and clear.

Two laborers in donkey jackets and with newspapers rolled under their arms were chatting near the well. They stopped talking, watching as I lowered my bucket into the water. Then they both turned their attention to Judith. One lit a cigarette. Their gaze wasn't at all lewd. It was an almost unconscious moment when their talk had been broken, midsentence, midword, even by the intercession of an attractive woman, and they barely knew that their communion had been abducted. I looked up slyly and saw Judith stretch her neck, basking under the scrutiny of the men.

Look how she pulls them in, I thought. And how she rides it. And I loved her female power. Then I dipped my bucket in the water, but a shadow or a reflection I saw there made me yelp, and the bucket went clanging into the water.

"Are you all right?" Judith came over and reached in to grab the bucket from the shallow well. "What happened?"

"I slipped."

I took the handle to share the weight and together we carried the bucket back to the cottage. I was still thinking of the shadow that reared at me from the well. It made me fear for Mammy, and for myself.

As we walked, Judith said, "They look at you, too, and it's not vain to enjoy that."

I was puzzled for a moment, then realized she was talking about the men. "I said nothing of the sort!"

"You didn't *say* it."

"Do you read every thought another person has?"

"Like you: not *every* thought."

Back in the cottage yard I primed while Judith pumped. She held the pump handle suggestively between her fingers and raised it up and down. "What does this remind you of?" I narrowed my eyes at her, and she said, "Oh, you're such a bloody virgin!"

"What has that to do with anything?"

The water began to spit from the spout. Judith pumped harder, and the water flowed. "This young man. The bailiff. Is he a bit of all right?"

I filled the kettle from the pump and took it inside. "I shan't even answer that," I said over my shoulder.

Judith hurried in after me. "All I'm asking is how much could he help you."

"I don't know. I think he knows something he's keeping back. In fact I'm certain of it. Why?"

"Well, there are things you can do to get him on your side."

I was slow to get her drift. "But that would be wrong! Wouldn't it?"

"Wrong? He likes you, and though you haven't said it, I think you like him. You have to make these things work for you for a change."

"Judith, I've never had a man. I don't have your experience."

I meant it as a reproach, but it only drew a smile. Then she said,

"Know what? Your virginity is the most overvalued thing you'll ever own."

"Well I'm not about to give it away cheap. When I give it I'll give it to someone I want to have it."

"What if I said there was a way in which he could have you and not have you. What if I told you that? Would you go along?"

"Uh?"

"There is a way. But you'd have to play it out."

"What are you on about?"

"Kettle's boiling, Fern," said Judith.

twelve

I heard the swing doors crash open and looked up as the flame-haired specialist entered the ward at speed. He was trailed by junior doctors and medical students all in flapping white coats. Somehow he seemed like a big boat making a wake in the water of the hospital ward and surrounded by tugs.

Mammy grabbed my hand. This is him," she whispered. "He's the one. The *Mason*." Mammy couldn't help drawing back her teeth at this last word. She had a hatred of Freemasons for reasons I only dimly understood.

The specialist pulled up short at the foot of Mammy's bed, as if at the last minute. There was something comical about the students and the juniors having to skid to a halt behind him. They, too, gathered round the foot of Mammy's bed. The specialist wore a three-piece tweed suit and a scarlet bow tie that didn't go well with his hair. "Good afternoon, Mrs. Cullen! How are we today?" He said this to Mammy, but his genial smile was addressed at me.

"Am I to be on show again?" Mammy said. "And I don't know what you're teaching these young doctors. They don't even warm their hands before they touch you."

The specialist lifted Mammy's chart from the hook on the bed. As he studied it I noticed the silver ring on his little finger. Mammy told me to look out for that. "Mrs. Cullen hasn't been sleeping too well, have you, Mrs. Cullen?" He attracted the attention of one of the junior doctors and tapped at some figure on the chart. The junior raised his eyebrows and nodded. Then the specialist passed the chart round for others to see.

"This is how they treat you here," Mammy said to me, but in a loud voice. "They talk about you without you knowing what they're saying."

"I was looking at your blood pressure, Mrs. Cullen." He took out his penlight. "Do you mind if I shine this in your eye again? You won't get cross with me this time?" He looked over his shoulder at his students. "Mrs. Cullen must have had a nasty experience with someone shining a light in her eyes, so we have to be very careful. Not going to bite me, eh?"

I looked at Mammy. I couldn't tell if the specialist was joking. I thought not. He angled his light beam and gently pulled down the skin below her eye with his forefinger and began to murmur a kind of incantation. "Marrow aspiration results pending slight macular degeneration probably AMD no obvious Drusen but new nerve distension indicates possible cerebrospinal? We'll see." He clicked off his penlight. "Thank you, Mrs. Cullen." And with that he swept away with his tugs, the white coattails flapping at his flanks and in his rear. The group proceeded along the ward, then skidded to a halt again at the far end as the specialist snatched up another patient's chart.

"Monster," said Mammy. "The monster. Did you hear that? Deliberate that was. Just to set my teeth on edge."

"I think that's how they talk about everyone, Mammy. It's not just you."

"Don't you believe it. They could talk sense if they wanted to. He's a monster. A *Mason*. Did you mark the ring? Did you mark it?"

I looked up the ward. The specialist had finished debasing his next patient and was about to exit the ward by the doors at the far end. I got up and went after him.

One of the juniors almost let the doors swing into my face but saved it at the last moment. "Excuse me!" I cried. The specialist stopped and turned. His entourage all stopped and turned, half a second behind him in everything. "Can I ask you something? Can I ask why Mammy is wandering? Why sometimes she's clear as a bell and sometimes she doesn't seem to know which hospital she's in? Can I ask that? Because no one seems to want to tell us anything."

The juniors and the students all went very still. I was conscious of several pairs of eyes peering at me as we all waited for the specialist to answer. I know he was taken aback. I know this because he made that motion of retracting his head and shoulders slightly, but theatrically, in a way that says: see how you have taken me aback? Then he opened his eyes very wide, as if to apprehend my question better.

"Are you Mrs. Cullen's daughter?"

"I am."

"Miss Cullen, I know your mother thinks we've been injecting her with potions to make her ill, but what we've been doing is draining fluids from her bone, so that we can make tests, and we won't be able to say for sure until those test results come back."

"But why is her mind wandering?"

"She cracked her ribs when she fell, and this was because her ribs were weak. I suspect her bone is crumbling, and the calcium from the bone is getting into her bloodstream; from there it is circulating in her brain and causing this drifting."

"Yes, but what's making the bone crumble?"

All the heads turned to the specialist to see how he'd answer. "You're asking, aren't you, Miss Cullen?"

"Yes, I'm asking."

He sucked in his cheeks. "I won't know for sure until I see the results, but I suspect your mother has cancer at an advanced level."

I felt a pricking behind my eyes. I saw a shadow in the water in the well. I saw the thing that had settled on Mammy. I saw why the fight had gone out of her. "Thank you," I said.

"You can ask me anything anytime," he said. "Anytime." I don't know if it was because he saw my eyes on it, but he unconsciously fingered the silver ring on his little finger. He dropped his hands to his side, turned and marched on, drawing his entourage with him.

One of the junior doctors hung back slightly, offering me a small smile and a quick levitation of the eyebrows. Perhaps this was meant to be sympathetic or a gesture of completion, but I gave him a look that said: *and you can fuck off.* Anyway, he did, hurrying to catch the migration from ward twelve. Then I went back to Mammy.

"Did he tell you anything?" she said.

"No, Mammy."

After I left the hospital I got up to the A47 and stuck out my thumb for a ride. A motorcyclist pulled up. He had to take his helmet off before I realized it was Arthur. "Fern!" he shouted. "What a coincidence!"

"Oh," I said.

"Well, get on the back then!"

I didn't much fancy it. His motorbike I mean. It was a heavy, dirty-looking thing, apart from the chrome that was polished to a wink and the badge on the petrol tank proclaiming a *Triumph*. Arthur saw my hesitation. "Hang on," he said. He dismounted, lifting his long leg over the saddle and coming round to the rear of the bike. He had a pannier at the back, and he opened it to pull out a black leather jacket like his own and a spare crash helmet. He offered them to me. "That's you sorted."

Still none too keen I took the leather jacket from him. There was something on the back. In a white gothic scripted arch it read "Ratae Motorcycle Club," and underneath that was a death's-head in a crash helmet. I held it up in front of me. "I can't wear that!"

"Why not?"

"Why hasn't yours got a silly skull?"

"I don't ride with that club anymore. But it won't matter for you."

"What's Ratae?"

"It's Roman. It was the Roman name for Leicester. Are you getting on or not?"

"I'm not wearing that. I've just come from the hospital. You can't go home from a hospital wearing a skull on your back. It wouldn't be right."

Arthur's jaw fell open. He looked down the road, as if he wished he hadn't got into this. "Okay, you have mine, and I'll wear that one."

But then I felt foolish, so I relented and put on the death's-head jacket. Arthur said the helmet had been there for an old girlfriend of his. It fitted well enough. I told Arthur I was afraid I'd fall off, but he said if I wanted I could put my arms around him, so I did that. We went speeding away down the A47, so fast that the wind squeezed tears from my eyes, so fast that I thought that this must be what it's like to fly. I folded my arms around Arthur, and I could smell the petrol and the oil of the engine and the warm skin of the nape of his neck. My grip on him was so tight that when he drew up outside my cottage he had to prise my arms free. He lifted me off the bike, and my knees knocked together. I'd never been so afraid. I went through the gate without a word of thanks to Arthur.

"Fern!" he shouted. "I want the jacket back. And the helmet."

I turned round and took off the jacket. The death's-head grinned at me. I took off the helmet and my head was aching where the helmet had dug the hair grips into me when I'd pressed my head against Arthur's back. My neck dripped with sweat. I handed the gear back to Arthur, still without a word.

"You all right, Fern?"

"Mmm," I said, nodding. "Mmmm."

Then I went inside and drank two huge glasses of water.

thirteen

Those few days I remember as endless shuttling to and from the hospital, afternoons and evenings fanning out like a deck of cards, interchangeable days, so that when I looked back I couldn't tell one from another. The only marker I had was the ride to and fro. Arthur on his motorbike would keep turning up by coincidence. He would drive me in, and I would arrive at the hospital looking like someone shot out of a circus cannon; and then he would insist on hanging around until he could rocket me, wide-eyed, home.

I was amazed he kept up the pretense of "just passing." I don't know why he didn't come out with it and offer to take me in on a regular basis, but no, we had to keep up this game where I would be on the soft, grassy shoulder of the A47 with my thumb in the air and he would cruise to a halt on his popping and gurgling Triumph going, "Here we are again, Fern!" and I would go, "Gosh, here we are again." After a while I stopped handing back the helmet and the black leather death's-head jacket and just kept them. He didn't object. In fact one evening I got halfway down ward twelve still wearing my grinning death's-head on my back. Then I remembered to take it off. It didn't seem appropriate, what with the state of some of the people on the ward. I mean it looked like some of the patients.

Mammy sometimes seemed to think that the nurses in the hospital were keeping her there against her will. Their starched uniforms reminded her of another place. The institutional hospital beds did, too. As did the all-pervasive smell of antiseptic.

I arrived every day determined to cheer up Mammy with some little piece of news, but it was exhausting since my time was spent traveling back and forth to see her and worrying about the rent. I did everything I could to help pass the time. I washed her, and I groomed her. I even cut her hair for her, and carefully trimmed her fingernails and her toenails, but even that caused a panic in her mind about how I might dispose of the clippings. She became terrified that "enemies" or "Masons" might get hold of the clippings and use them against her. I had to ask a nurse to find me a jar to keep the hair trimmings and the nail clippings. Mammy made me promise to take the jar home to the cottage and keep it on a hidden shelf, which I did.

Sometimes Mammy was clear: "Have you made that gal her wedding cake?"

"Not yet."

"Pull your chair up. Closer, that's it. Put your ear to my mouth. I want to whisper because I don't want all these fools hearing everything I've got to say. Now then, this is how you bake lots of love into a cake . . ."

And sometimes Mammy was rambling, and either way it was easier for me just to pull my chair up and lay my head on her bed and listen.

"All your life, Fern, it's been there all your life, only you don't know it. Though you shall know it on the day you ask; because when you look back you'll see it was listening, listening from the very edge of your life.

"And we few don't talk of it. One doesn't tell another. That's the way of it. Talking it out will *offen* kill a thing, you must know that, Fern. Listening is what you do. You will listen to yours and yours will listen to you. You'll see, my pigeon, you'll see. Can you loosen these straps for me, Fern?"

I would lift my head, and say, "There are no straps, Mammy."

She might look down and move her feet a little under the bedsheets. Then she would seem confused. But would then resume, and though she rambled, I never thought to stop her. "You can believe it or not, you'll come to know it whatever you or I have to say. One day you will *Ask* of it, and if it recognizes you, well, there's an end to it. Though it may also turn you down flat, and there's no use sighing, for if you can't, you can't.

"Though you'll pay. Oh yes, you will pay. I've paid in my time. I've been sick. I've had the terrors. I've shat my pants and I've suffered. But I wouldn't want it any other way. There's not a one who would. When you've seen, you won't want to breathe for fear of losing the glory of it. You would die tomorrow and say, well, I've seen that.

"But you do it for the help, and the help must come. Something's worrying you isn't it, Fern? Something you're not telling me? You must be ready to *Ask*. That's how we get help. Oh, there are so many things I haven't told you! An' I've left it too late!"

"No you haven't, Mammy. You haven't left it too late."

"Three times, maybe, if you're lucky. I never heard of a call more than three times, because it nearly kills you, and it's worse each time. But then you need most help, when you're caged around, that's when you do it. When you must.

"And when you're ready, Fern, I'll be there. I'll make the way straight. I know how. Don't you worry. Mammy will be there for you. Mammy will make the path straight.

"You must also attend to the mistress. Though you should know some have gone mad and some died. It's not for the weak-minded. In any event, you'll want to choose the cusp of the first or last quarter. I was attacked in my bed last night, Fern."

"What, Mammy?"

"One of those men got in here from the other ward. I fought him off. They came and trussed him up in a straitjacket. Then they strapped me down again because they said I'd let him in. This is what they're saying. To make out that I led him in here. They're making out it was all me. The doctor is a Mason. I'd get out, Fern, I'd leave by the windows, but look at the bars."

The window by her bed stood slightly open to the spring air. There were no bars. "Mammy, I love you so much."

"Have I give you the list?"

"The list?"

"That's why they put me here, isn't it?

"Don't forget to prepare an incense for burning the night before if you favor a dawn path, or for burning through the day should you go for the dusk. Though you may have to walk the same path many times, because yours will not always come on the first time of *Asking*, unless you're lucky. Patience, patience, Fern."

I don't know when she stopped talking like that, because I must have drifted off to sleep myself. I might even have dreamed half of these things she said. I was stirred by a nurse who shook my arm. "Visiting time's over," she said gently.

Mammy was snoring. I stroked her fingertips. The hospital light aged and yellowed her skin. The lines in her face appeared to run deeper than ever, and the dewlaps sagged at her throat. She used to say each crease in her face was a babe delivered safely: a joke that, not a belief. Even though I rejected so many of her wild beliefs, I somehow always felt that she was strong enough in her powers to cheat death. Now I doubted it altogether. I leaned across her and kissed her weathered brow.

I gathered up my leather jacket and the crash helmet. "I'm ready, Mammy," I said before leaving. "I'm ready to *Ask*."

fourteen

A *crow woke me, cawing out-*
side the window, so I got up early to do some essential gathering of
meadowsweet, which Mammy always called queenie and which
works the same as aspirin amongst other things. I pulled on my coat
to go out, then took it off and put on Arthur's leather jacket instead. I
was getting to like the way the soft, battered leather shaped itself to
my curves. It was warmer than my own coat and, anyway, I didn't
have to look at what was grinning on the back of it.

A fine mist hovered above the grass of the meadow, torn from the
land like scraps of chiffon. I was raking the hedgerows when I stumbled across some birthwort—Mammy wouldn't grow it in the garden
not just because it is poisonous but also because it points the finger
back, with its midwifery uses so well known. With meadowsweet you
collect the leaves before it flowers, but the birthwort is of course no
use until the little yellow flower winks. I was making a mental note of
the spot—birthwort being rare in the county—when I heard voices. I
scrambled to hide in the hedge, something Mammy and I often did
when we didn't want to be seen, and I was surprised to see it was Chas
and two of his friends from Croker's. They were trawling the field,
just as I was, looking for something in the grass.

Were they rival gatherers, these people? Surely not, I thought. I
stepped out of the hedge, and on sighting me they made straight for
me.

Chas called out from twenty yards away though I could barely understand him. "Fern it is! Letta-me intro the juice to Greta. Here is.
And this fine champion the wonder horse rides the nimrod Luke."

Either I had hedge cobwebs stuffed in my ears or he was drunk.
When he drew up close his eyes were boiling in his head. This friend
Luke he pointed at was a sleepy giant of a man with an astonishing

mass of tightly permed hair and a wispy beard dyed blue. Or maybe purple. His trousers were striped like pajamas, and he had a huge brass buckle on the belt to hold them up. I felt like I'd seen him before in a nursery-tale book I'd had when I was a child. His eyes, too, were boiling. He put his hands on his hips and treated me to the most wide-mouthed smile I'd ever seen in my life.

This Greta was also out to dazzle me with a sunbeam of smiles. She was some kind of Spanish gypsy, with a cotton head scarf and long, lacy skirts. She danced up to me—and I mean danced—and stroked my arm without saying a word. It was all very queer.

"You're up early," I said.

"Haven't been to bed, old bean!" Chas said, way too loud. "Up up up all night busy bee been!"

The other two laughed heartily as if this was funny. When they stopped laughing they all beamed at me, full-on, but as if it was my turn to speak or say something funny. I suspected they must be drunk, but it was six o'clock in the morning, which is a fine time for it. The expression on their faces—but for the smiles—was like that of sailors struggling against a high wind, but there was no wind. Greta continued to stare at me with an imbecile grin painted on her face. Luke stroked his beard now, looking toward the rising sun, but with an expression suggesting he'd mislaid something important. Then he said, "Later." Or perhaps it was, "Letter."

"Oh," Chas said, rolling slightly on his ship-in-a-storm. "Those bar star hards? Sense me a postie man up the path a-whistling, good morning says, plop on the mat. Reads. Hmm: can't use of your pump sayeth he. Or writeth rather. For water, get me?"

I gazed at him, trying to muddle it out. "What? The estate told you not to use my pump?"

Chas nodded, seeming to find my reaction a matter of mirth. He giggled. "Out-bloody-rageous!"

"While it's still our pump you can ignore 'em, can't you."

"Swat Luke says." Chas laughed. Then Luke and Greta laughed, too. But a barking laugh, like hyenas. I began to suspect it was me they were laughing at.

I noticed that Greta had with her a cotton bag. "What are you collecting there?" I asked her.

Greta opened her bag for me to see, but with great and delicate ceremony as if she were unwrapping collected fragments of the Holy Grail. Inside the bag was a sorry mess of fungi. There were field mushrooms, St. George's, ink caps, morels and, to my utter astonishment a vivid red fly. Way, way out of season.

"You can't eat that!" I shouted at her. "You shouldn't even pick it!"

"Yes," Greta said. She had a husky voice, like someone who has smoked too many cigarettes. "But scrape off his white spots and eat the red meat you can have a yummy fine old time."

I couldn't believe they had one of these. At this time of the year. Today of all days. "You'll still be sick. You'll get the shits."

"Oh," Luke said, nodding vigorously. "Yes. By crikey."

I turned to Chas. "Was that what was wrong with you when I found you in the outhouse?"

"In the shout house. Yes. Maybe. No." Chas laughed again.

"The red one you should put back where you found it," I said to Greta sharply. I was cross. "And I don't mean throw it away. I mean exactly where you found it. It's not a joke."

"What?" Luke said, running his fingers through his massive, wiry crown. "What?"

The smile vanished from Greta's face. She nodded solemnly. "Know what? I am so tuned in to this lady. Going to do exactly what she says." Greta turned with her bag and made long loping strides toward the woods.

"Where going, Greta?" Chas shouted. "Hey, nice jacket, Fern. Swear that skull just blinked at me. Ha."

"What?" Luke said.

Suddenly Luke and Chas looked like two naughty schoolboys. "Phew!" Chas said, as if he had just run a race. Now his face looked very flushed. He ground his teeth.

"What?" went Luke.

I wanted to get away from them. I know it was the kind of thing Mammy would say, but they each had some kind of a shadow, a spirit mounted on their back. Whenever I was afraid I retreated into think-ing like her. "Beware the toadstool," I said, and I swept away. Either they were drunk or insane, but I wasn't staying. I felt disturbed and upset. I'd gone about thirty yards before I heard Luke's voice calling after me:

"That is so fucking far out!"

On the same afternoon I was planting late sets. I turned a trench with my spade, composted it from the heap in the corner of the garden and dropped my sets in a line, eighteen inches apart. Then I raked soil over them. I looked up and saw a figure hovering at the gate. It was Greta, the hippie woman I'd met in the field that morning.

I leaned on my garden fork. "Come for water?"

"No," Greta said shyly. "To see you. Can I come in?"

"Nothing stopping you, is there?"

The gate snapped back after Greta passed through it. "What you doing?"

"Planting taters."

"Is it the time? Maybe we should be doing that at the farm."

"You're a bit slow. These are lates. You should have put 'em to bed before."

"So why are you putting them in now, then?"

"Well if you plant 'em at the same time, they all come at the same time, don't they? You can't eat them all at the same time. Anybody knows that. Who don't know about planting potatoes?"

Greta admitted she didn't know the first thing about planting pota-toes. They hadn't taught her that at university, she said. Greta was a talker. She told me how she'd been to study law at Durham Univer-sity. Law, my word. Greta also explained that after that she'd worked in an office but she hated it and then she'd met Chas and the others and they'd all come to Croker's Farm to live off the land. Except that none of them knew anything about the land. Nothing in all those law books about it, apparently.

"Then you'd better find out about her," I said, "if you expect to live off her."

"That's why I'm here, really."

"Is it?" I turned away, tidying up my gardening tools and making myself busy, because I didn't like where this was leading.

"I think you're a wisewoman," Greta said.

"A what now?"

"You're younger than I am, and yet there's something about you. I think we could learn a lot from you."

"And listen to you! From the University of Durham! Well I'll not be here much longer because I'm being thrown out of this cottage. So that's not very wise, is it?"

"So why are you planting potatoes? If you won't be here much longer?"

Sharp enough, I thought, this one. "Because it's what I've always done. It's what Mammy showed me. So I keep doing it."

"Next Saturday," Greta said, "is Chas's birthday. We're having a party at the farm. Will you come?"

I nearly dropped my rake as my hand flew up to the three iron grips in my hair. "I've no party dress," I said. It wasn't a joke, but Greta laughed. When Greta realized her error she covered her mouth. She had a slight overbite, and I could see it made her self-conscious.

"It's a come-as-you-are party. We don't dress up. We'll have a big dinner. Then a bit of music. We've got some good musicians. I'll come and fetch you at six o'clock if you like."

I had no intention of being the butt of their party jokes, or going along there as the village idiot just so they could make remarks about my clothes or about the way I parted my hair. "No, I'm not one for parties. I've too much to do." I clattered my tools into the lean-to and retreated inside the cottage, slamming the door behind me.

I was angry and upset by this invitation. Perhaps it was all too much, what with Mammy in hospital and the estate trying to evict us from the cottage. But I sat down in Mammy's old chair by the fireside with my arms folded. Then after a good while I found myself crying, and calling for Mammy as I did so, but knowing that she couldn't help me.

Rarely was I invited to parties as a child. Living with Mammy had put me on the edge, and other children shrank from me. Not dramatically, not as a torment, but in a tiny hesitation, in the briefest of pauses before they quietly rejected any overtures of friendship. It was never done with name-calling, nor with a scene, but their withdrawal, their quiet and firm rejection slowly and surely made a stone out of me.

I attended school, but my main education there became mastering the art of invisibility. I saw that the teachers only ever responded to the clever, the dull or the depraved, so I resolved to be none of these and in that way went unnoticed. Occasionally I suffered agonies if teased by other girls over the shabby quality of my school clothes. So I learned quickly how to dye and to shorten or otherwise disguise the poverty of these garments. It almost worked. I saw that any deviance from standard, however small, marked me out for attention. So whenever a teacher asked me a question I always had the answer, though I never volunteered it.

Neither did I offer surplus information about my life at home, and when called upon I hid behind the blandest of accounts, the thinnest of reports. I stopped seeking out friends, and they never sought out me. In life's lesson of going unnoticed I was top of the form. In the eternal playground wars I took no sides between bullies and their victims, and discovered a bearing and body posture that would avoid me ever becoming one of the latter. Perhaps they feared me, a little.

Thus the party invitation was a rare bird winging in. Mammy had been my only childhood friend, and celebration had been confined to the experience of Mammy's way of doing things, or contact with the few. When I slammed the door on Greta it was fear I was trying to shut out. Had I genuinely not wanted to accept Greta's surprising invitation, I might simply have said so. But the idea of being asked to go along and have some fun in the company of people my own age excited and terrified me; because after all these years without I was in sore need of company; and because after all these years without I didn't know if I was worthy of it.

After a while I got up and went to the window. Greta had gone, and

I felt ashamed. Whatever are you doing? Mammy would have said. Come away from that window and stop making a fool of yourself while yourself is watching. Because if you don't know your own mind, your own mind will want to find a home somewhere else.

"I've no party dress," I said again, but this time to myself. And I cried again.

fifteen

*A*re you going to Ask?" *Judith* persisted. "Are you or not?"

Still bothered by Greta's invitation, I had called in at Judith's tiny terraced house one evening after visiting the hospital. I had found Judith marking school exercise books while watching television. Her vacuum cleaner stood upright in the corner as if permanently at the ready, but it was the television screen that pulled me in again. It hypnotized me; it was like sitting watching a stream of water, and when called upon to say what you'd just seen you almost couldn't answer. The only distraction was in Judith's repeated sighs of exasperation as she corrected the blotched schoolwork of the terminally thick.

There were reasons, though, why I resisted answering Judith. Firstly, I wasn't taken in by her trick of asking me while she was doing two other things at the same time. I knew my answer was important to her. Secondly, I didn't want to confess that I had so little in common with her in the way of belief. It would have seemed a betrayal not only of her but of many other people, too, and worst of all to have made it concrete would have seemed a betrayal of Mammy.

Thirdly, I was afraid.

Some contradiction, yes. If I didn't believe, then what was I afraid of? But it was not so simple as that. To do the *Asking* demands preparation, mental preparation. It also requires the use of certain decoctions. Whatever I believed or didn't believe, I was afraid that going into this with negative thoughts or doubt in my heart might cause me harm. Whatever is done should be done with a pure heart. By which I mean a committed heart, a wholly committed heart. An act of war or even of malice can be done with a pure heart. But it must have no trace of doubt.

And doubt I had, and purity of heart, not. "Judith, I can't be thinking of these things when I'm about to get slung out of my home!"

She knew it was true. To do something so radical required a time of no distraction. "You're right," she conceded. And that was when Judith started up again with her plan for me to seduce Arthur McCann.

Had I known more about men, and about their ways, I would never have agreed to the idea. But I allowed her to talk me into it. She was confident it would buy me a few more weeks. "It's simple. He's got influence up there. Let's find out what he knows. He just needs a bit of pressure on him. Plus it's all you've got going," she said pointedly. "That Arthur McCann is your only hope."

Her idea wasn't subtle. I should allow Arthur to get me into bed in the hope that he might feel beholden, or "pressured" as she put it, and that might buy me some time with his employers. Outrageous and whoring as it at first sounds, according to Judith I wouldn't have to give up anything. That was the trick of it.

"Saltpeter," Judith said. "And to make certain, a decoction of black willow buds is mighty powerful. And there's sweet water lily."

"What are you talking about?"

"And hops, of course. We'll get him to drink beer."

"Beer?"

"Brewer's droop on top of the other stuff. It's just a matter of disguising all of it. You can bake him an egg-and-bacon pie. He's a bloke, isn't he? Beer and bacon pie: he'll think his ship has come home."

"You're completely mad, Judith."

"Please yourself, don't do it. But you've only got two weeks left." And she went back to marking her schoolbooks with her red pencil, suddenly doling out—with effortless largesse—sensuous, long-stemmed ticks to the slow and the obtuse alike.

I gazed glumly at the flickering television screen. Then I muttered something about my invitation to a party at Croker's Farm. This news made Judith break the lead in her red pencil. She gazed at me as if I'd shown her a hole in the wall of a prison cell we'd shared for twenty years.

"Take me with you or you're dead meat."

"I said no."

Judith flung herself facedown on the rug, thumping the floor, kicking her feet and shrieking. "She said no! She said no! Keywell's first promise of a wild party in over a millennium, and she said no!"

Anyway, I had other, more serious plans. Though it wouldn't serve to deal with my immediate housing problem, I had taken steps to secure a longer-term income by enrolling for a diploma in midwifery.

Certification of midwives had been around since the turn of the century, but many poor and working people had ignored the regulations. If an unlicensed midwife was no good, word of mouth gave her warts or stinking breath or otherwise killed her off. Mammy's services, by contrast, were highly prized by the women who reported to each other on her abilities. But now the state provided free, trained midwives, and in that way women like Mammy lost most of their livelihood. I knew if I was going to recover the work for myself, I would have to get what Mammy called the damned ticket. "That damned ticket has been the ruin of me," she would rail. "They'll not give me a ticket."

An act of law prohibited midwifery by the untrained "handy-women"—and that's how Mammy found herself described—on whom many poorer women had formerly relied. By putting my hand on Bunch Cormell's belly that night I'd acted illegally and could even be prosecuted. So in search of the *damned ticket* I went to visit the offices of the Royal College of Midwives in Leicester.

The floor of the small reception area was stiff with gleaming wax polish, and the floorboards creaked under my feet. A huge grandfather clock ticked loudly and the place reeked with the hateful odor of potpourri. A superior lady with a white starched collar sat behind a desk. From her I picked up an application form and took it away with me to a table in a cafe on the London Road, where, with the shiny chrome espresso machine roaring in my ears, I began to fill it in.

There was a place on the form to enter any previous experience, so I wrote that I'd assisted at perhaps fifty births. Then I crossed that out and wrote fifty-five. I didn't mention the births I'd done on my own, like Bunch's or on the few occasions when Mammy wasn't able to get there. Then there was a place where I was to name any midwife who had given me instruction, and I started to write Mammy's name before I remembered it would work against me, so I scratched it out.

By the time I finished it the form looked a bit like it was filled in by one of Judith's dense schoolchildren, but I took it back to the reception and handed it in to the lady with the starched collar. I tried to creep out, but she summoned me back.

"You *hiven't* completed this *kestionaire*," she called out.

I went back to her desk, the floorboards creaking under my nervous step. She had an elegant fountain pen and she was tapping the box where you had to say which local authority you had worked for. I explained that I hadn't worked for any local authority. The clock ticked loudly as she examined the form again.

"But you've put *hya* that you've had all this experience. Look. Fifty-five births it says *hya*."

"Yes."

The lady looked over her glasses at me. "It doesn't do to fib, you know."

I colored instantly. I wanted to spit in her eye. "I'm not fibbing!"

"But . . . how old are you? When did you start this . . . assisting?"

"When I was thirteen." It was true. As soon as my first period arrived, Mammy told me it was time I knew what it was all about.

She looked over her glasses again. "What about the name of the midwife you were helping?"

My fingers fluttered to my hairgrips. The ticking of the clock got louder and the odour of the potpourri grew more sickening as I tried to frame a reply. I stammered something about working with different ones. Then I rushed out of the building. Once outside I ran up toward Victoria Park, not stopping until I was out of breath. Then I let down my hair and went and sat in the park by the white war memorial arch, where I stayed for two hours.

When I got back to my cottage Chas was helping himself to water from the pump. He was filling the old milk churns. "Hey Fern!" he called. "Don't mind, do you?"

"Why should I mind?" I wanted to sound a little sour with him after the way he and his friends had mocked me in the field, but I found it hard to stay in a munk with him.

"Still got trouble with the lord of the manor?"

"They're throwing us out of the cottage anyway." I explained to him about my back rent and about the estate owning the cottage.

"Fucking feudalism is what it is," Chas said cheerfully. "It's nineteen sixty-six and you still have to grind your flour in that bastard's mill. Out-bloody-rageous. Anyway, fuck him: if they turf you out, you'll come and live with us at the farm."

"I will?"

"If you want to. Greta thinks you're a fucking oracle. Luke thinks you're gorgeous. You'll fit in all right." Chas rolled the heavy water-filled milk churn to his van and hoisted it in the back. He was strong. I could smell the fresh sweat of his exertion.

"Can't see Mammy fitting in," I said, "not with your band of gypsies." And not with all this foul-mouthed cussing, I thought.

"You and the old lady got somewhere better to go?"

We hadn't. Judith hadn't offered, and I wouldn't ask, and time was closing in. But though I could see he was entirely serious, there was no way Mammy could rub along with Chas's lot.

"We're living off the land, and up there the land is owned by anyone who wants to stay on it." He rolled the last churn away, and I followed him out of the garden.

"Thought it was you that owned it."

"No," he said. "Property is theft."

"Is it?" I said. "Why's that then?"

He ignored my question, which was meant seriously. He was about to swing himself into his driving seat, when he said, "Want to jump in the van? Have a look up there? Come on, Fern. You know you're curious about us."

And he smiled at me, and he made a single eyebrow curve like a bird's wing, and I felt something very deep in me let go, something deep in my womb, just for a second.

sixteen

*C*has *would keep taking his eyes* off the road ahead to smile at me as we bumped along the lane in the van. My hands started to behave as if I didn't own them. They touched the dashboard, they brushed the door handle, they stroked the three grips in my hair. He noticed and turned his smile on me again. "You okay?"

"Pay attention to where you're going," I said.

"You're funny."

"Funny? That's rich coming from a bloomin' hippie."

The van lurched to a stop in the yard at Croker's Farm. Chas jumped out, ran round and slid open the passenger door for me, as if I were royalty. "I can do it," I said.

If this was supposed to be a working farm there, was no one about. A few Rhode Island Reds pecked at the muddy ground and a sorry-looking cock eyed me from the top of an old muck heap. Two sleepy greyhounds and a whippet cross came to have a sniff at me. The farm buildings were being slowly sucked into the ground, and any pieces of farm machinery I saw were held together by orange rust. There was little evidence of anyone "living off the land."

"Come inside," Chas said. I folded my arms. I didn't want to go in. But he held the door open for me.

In the kitchen a woodstove was burning, and the place was warm enough, though empty. A strange music floated into the kitchen from another room. It was a music I'd never heard before, and I wasn't sure I liked it. It made me think of sunlight on thin strands of dripping molasses. But it also went in my ear like a crawling insect. "What's that sound?" I asked.

"Come on," he said, and he led me through the house.

Though it was broad daylight outside, the room he took me into had curtains drawn, and low-burning candles were placed all about. A number of people slouched against the walls on mattresses, smoking cigarettes. There were three or four small children there, too. Everybody was half-asleep, taking little notice of me. Luke was there—I recognized him, and he gave me a sleepy wave. The music was coming from a record player by my feet. I looked down and saw the disc spinning. All I could think as I looked at these folk sitting in the dark listening to this odd music in the middle of the day was: what a waste of candles!

A figure stirred in the corner and blinked at me from the shadows with badger eyes. It was Greta. She extricated herself from one of the children and came over, hugging me like I was a long-lost sister. I didn't know where to look, though I did my best not to wince. She could see I felt uncomfortable so she led me back into the kitchen, with the promise of a cup of tea and a slice of Battenberg cake. Chas followed us.

"What's that awful noise?" I asked, when we were sat around the kitchen table.

"Oh that's a sitar. Indian music, Fern, from India."

"Well you can bloomin' well keep it," I said. I wouldn't fancy that going on in my ears all day.

Chas laughed. "It's very difficult to play."

"I've no doubt," I said. Then I turned to Greta. "Was that your child there in the room?"

"No," she said, stirring the teapot, "that was Forest. Chas's little boy."

"Forest? I never heard of a boy called Forest."

"I haven't heard of too many girls called Fern," Chas said.

"Where's his mam, then?"

"Oops," went Greta, "Chas don't talk about Forest's mum."

"Why's that then?"

"Cos she's a witch," Chas said.

"A witch?" I said. "You mean she casts spells?"

"Do you want sugar? She wants sugar in that tea, Greta," said Chas. "No, not that sort of a witch."

"How many sorts are there?" I wanted to know.

"I mean she's vicious and selfish, so we don't have anything to do with her."

"So you mean she's a bitch, not a witch."

Chas rubbed his face with a large leathery hand, then said lazily, "You know exactly what I mean, Fern, so why are you picking on me?"

"He don't like to talk about her," Greta said.

"I'm not picking on you," I said. "What are they all smoking in there? Smells like old wet dog."

After finishing my tea and my slice of Battenberg cake I walked home. Chas offered to drive me, but I declined, seeing as how it was only fifteen minutes, though I wished I'd accepted because Greta insisted on walking with me instead: why, I don't know. It occurred to me I'd never met such a happy person as Greta in my life. Always grinning she was. Maddening, in a way.

"How's the old lady?"

"Middlin' " I said.

As we walked she mentioned the party again. I said I didn't want to go to a party if they had that bloomin' Hindu music going, and she said no they play their own music; and then as we walked she burst into song. It was an old whaling song I'd never heard, she being from Yarmouth she said, and it was a good one, and I got it in one, though I didn't tell her. So when she was done I gave her "John Barleycorn" in return. She wanted to stop and listen, but I felt stupid standing in the lane like that so I insisted we should keep walking.

When I was done she told me what a voice I had, and asked me how many songs I knew.

"Dozens and dozens," I said.

"But where did you collect them from?"

"Collect? I didn't collect them. Mammy taught them to me when we were gathering in the fields." And this time I had to stop and turn my head away from Greta. It wasn't because she was still grinning at me like a gargoyle, it was because I had the shocking thought that Mammy might never teach me another song.

After I'd recovered I said to Greta, "So are you standing in for the boy's mother, then?" I was intrigued by the setup at Croker's Farm. I used Greta's clinging attachment to me as an excuse to poke my nose in as far as it would go.

"No, we all take responsibility for the children. We all act as parents to all the children."

"And who acts as Chas's wife?"

"Oh," Greta said, cottoning on. "We're easy about that. Everybody loves everybody."

I was shocked. "Well I don't think I'd like that! How does it work?"

"I sometimes have my doubts," she confessed. "Sometimes I think it suits the men more than it suits the women."

I stopped in my tracks. "You mean you're forced?"

"No," she said, laughing. "We choose who and when, of course. But the arrangement sounds all right as an idea, but when it comes to living it . . . Well!"

I searched her eyes. She blushed, then giggled again, and I began to wonder what sort of people I'd fallen among.

A few days later a letter arrived at the cottage. It was from the College of Midwives. It pointed out that there were some gaps on the application form I'd filled in and there were discrepancies, but that a new course was about to commence that very week and in view of the urgent demand for midwives I should enroll. I'd been accepted.

The course was to take place in Leicester, and was for one evening per week for two terms. That was no hardship, since I could visit Mammy, then go on to my class. It was a special course, an accelerated course for women with some experience of midwifery and those returning to the profession after a period of absence. I tried to think whether I'd lied about anything that might get me a place on this course, but I thought I'd been truthful enough. Though the course didn't lead to full qualification, it did offer a diploma, from where I might go on.

I looked at the date on the letter, and I checked the calendar. The first class was in two evenings' time. After all my woes of the past few weeks it was a sudden spilling of light. I wanted to tell somebody. My first thoughts were to tell Judith, or I would have even been glad to tell Chas, or Greta. But as I hugged the letter to my heart I had to make do with a quiet word to Mammy, who wouldn't have disapproved.

The following day Venables appeared in a bowler hat and raincoat, with Arthur McCann and another chap. I looked out of the window and saw Arthur hanging back, and I could tell he didn't want to be there. Venables came to the door and knocked gently. When I opened the door Venables stood back and took his bowler hat off to talk to me.

Venables got straight to the point. "Look," he said politely, "you don't have to let us in if you don't want to. But we'd like to make a survey if that's all right." He had a very refined way of speaking. He was the sort of man who used his voice to stroke you. "To be honest with you, we need to make a decision about whether to pull the old place down."

"The cottage? Pull it down?"

"But it won't make any difference to you," he said. "You'll be gone."

I was so shocked by the prospect of them demolishing the cottage that I went back inside and took my seat by the fire, leaving them all standing there. Mammy was still everywhere in that house. It was the only home I'd ever known. My thoughts had always been that even if we had to leave it for a while, I might later be able to devise some way of getting it back.

I saw Venables make a motion to the other men, then he followed me inside. "I don't want to add to your distress. But the plain fact is you're in arrears with the rent for over a year, and you've shown no sign to me that you can find it."

I shook my head. I tried so hard not to let him see the tears that were like lime in my eyes. How could someone be like that? How could they be so polite and well-mannered and take off their hat and speak with a beautiful voice when they were really behaving like a dog?

He gazed down at me. I could tell his thoughts floated somewhere between pity and contempt. At last he said, "We'll leave you be." Then he made his way out.

Arthur hung back after the other two had gone. I felt sorry for his shame. "You okay, Fern?"

"Arthur," I blurted, hardly believing myself, "come on Friday . . ."

"Friday? What, have you found some rent? I could come in the morning."

"No, not the morning," I said, holding his gaze. "And not for rent either. I'd rather you came in the evening."

"Evening?"

"I wanted some company. Someone to talk to. Perhaps I could offer you a bit of dinner."

He seemed thunderstruck. Then he drew himself up to his full height. "Dinner?"

When I nodded he looked around the cottage as if seeing it for the first time.

"McCann!" Venables shouted from the gate

"Seven o'clock, Arthur? On Friday?"

He nodded, then he was gone, and I still couldn't quite come to believe what I'd done. But all I could think was how Mammy would not have approved, even had it been the last option available in the history of the world. And then I wondered if that was true.

seventeen

Gulp. You did it. Gulp." Judith, by her own admission, had more experience in beguiling men than in discouraging them. Now that I'd taken her advice, now that I'd baited the hook, now that I'd run dangerously near to whoring myself, she had little to offer except to pipe up with these comic-cuts noises.

"Stop saying gulp."

"Gulp is what I feel," she said. "But look at it this way: what's the worst that can happen? That he'll fuck you."

The weather had turned out very warm, and that evening we sat on the grassy mound of the old motte-and-bailey castle, overlooking the few lights twinkling on in the village of Hallaton. The day's sun had warmed the earth, and I could scent it in my nostrils, knowing we were in for a hot summer even though we were still at the gate of spring. The earthworks mound was raised on a high natural point, from where it was possible to survey the county all around. It was a locus of strange energy, a charged and mysterious place about which I always felt ambivalent. I looked up. Stars were coming out and in that magnificent way where one moment there are none, then you blink and there are many.

"You're so crude, Judith," I said evenly. "And I don't want him to fuck me."

"You say he's not awful-looking." Judith started plucking stalks of grass.

"You come and offer yourself in my place, then," I said.

She pretended to think about it for a moment; and then, as if I were offering her flat beer, she said, "Nah."

I gazed southward to the darkened hill they call Hare Pie Bank and to the rolling lands beyond and had cause to think of whether Arthur might be a prospect. Firstly, with a man there is always the question of his smell. They have to smell right. It's not necessarily about hygiene. Arthur always looked well scrubbed and passionately groomed. Chas the hippie by contrast didn't always look too clean, but his male odor didn't offend the nostrils, either. There were probably many women who would find Chas's smell a pleasing one. I think to love someone you have to first have a conversation through the nose.

And then, quite apart from his looks, there is the matter of his carriage: if he holds himself wrong, or leans too far forward or back, or lists to one side, or slumps at the front. All of these things can be mighty discouraging. But after those things comes, for me, the way that a man sounds.

How does his voice enter the ear? And if Arthur smelled good enough, I'm not sure he sounded quite right. There was a reedy quality to his voice, a slight trilling. Is it possible that one could ever be relaxed in the company of a man who trills, even slightly? There was another thing: his elbows flapped against his jacket. That was a noise and a distraction.

Was I being too picky? I wondered. Would anyone, anywhere, ever measure up? It was no good. Every time I tried to think of Arthur in the best possible light, I found myself heaping more and more objections up against him. And I had more or less invited him to take away my virginity.

Then, traveling at seemingly great altitude amongst the stars I saw what I knew to be a satellite. "Look," I said to Judith. "Maybe it's a sputnik. Like the one that once carried Valentina Tereshkova."

"Who?"

I had to explain who Valentina was. Shouldn't every woman know?

Judith squinted up at the steadily moving satellite. "How do you know this stuff?"

"I know where to look. It comes round every night at almost the same time. Maybe it's one of those with a dead dog in it."

"What?"

"The Russians sent dogs and monkeys up there. They died of course. They're still going round."

"What, with dead monkeys inside them?" Her mouth open, Judith continued to track the silent passage of the satellite in the sky.

I regretted telling her this. There are some things you tell people, and it changes their world forever. I switched subjects. "After this is over, this thing with Arthur I mean, I'll be ready to *Ask*."

Judith turned her gaze from the skies and squinted at me. She was about to speak, but I was ready for her with a look that said, don't you dare.

For Judith, as it would have been for Mammy, my willingness to *Ask* was an article of faith. It was as if—despite all my protestations to the contrary—I lived, like her, within a belief. But I did not. I did not believe. Not all, at any rate. Not in the way that she and Mammy and the other few believed.

The truth is I was prompted by desperation. I had lost Mammy's guidance for a while, and now I was about to lose my home and my way of life. And who knew what else besides? I could retreat behind the skirts of what Mammy wanted me to be; or I could reject all of it and start out on a new way of life, in a scrubbed place of antiseptic and diplomas where illumination and imagination had no part. Though my brain shuttled between those two extreme venues, my heart remained with Mammy, and blind loyalty was winning out over rational objection.

All this time, the thing I was agreeing to do was not something to be treated lightly.

The *Asking*.

I would need at least one helper, possibly two. In matters such as these it is important to have those around who will, as it were, hold your coat. By now Judith was someone on whom I felt I could rely.

The next evening I had other things to keep my mind occupied: namely my first evening class at the College of Midwives. I went out somewhat sooner than usual, planning to visit Mammy earlier and leave her in good time for my class. As it happened I couldn't seem to get a ride, so I used willpower to stop a car.

It's not as difficult as people think. I'd often practiced from behind my school desk or on a bus. All you do is concentrate on someone's neck to get them to look round at you. Eventually they have to. In a similar manner I succeeded in getting a driver to stop for me and I was just climbing in the passenger seat when I saw Arthur roaring up behind on his motorbike at my normal time. He zoomed by, but not without my seeing the look of collapse and anguish on his face.

The driver, a middle-aged man who smelled of a metalworks factory told me about his disappointment over a missed job promotion. Perhaps I wasn't listening hard enough to him, but he dropped me outside of town, and I had to walk the last mile. It was a fresh spring evening, and dusk was falling on the city as I approached. Lights were pricking on all over the town, and I felt a thrill at taking control of my new life. As I came down the London Road a flag on a pole flapped happily, and a man in a car tooted his horn.

"Did you bring the gin?" Mammy said.

"Yes. Another pint." We had gallons of it. Mammy used to make it in the bathtub. Then she'd use sloe berries to disguise the awful taste.

"Tip it in that vase. No one will see. Bring another pint in tomorrow."

"Another? Are you getting through it that fast?"

Mammy giggled. "I'm selling it."

I looked across the ward. Two old girls with white hair and powdered faces made a thumbs-up sign to me. At the bedside there was a red vase containing three long-stemmed plastic roses. The ward was clear of nurses, so I did as I was told and emptied the sloe gin I'd smuggled in with me into the vase. Then I replaced the plastic roses. "Them girls run it to the men's ward for me. Here." She pushed a pound note and a few shillings—the profit from her unlicensed trade—into my hand, and I wondered if she knew.

But Mammy was very tired. She didn't seem to be listening as I told her about the antics of the hippies at Croker's. I left out the thing about the mushrooms and the out-of-season fly because it would disturb her. She didn't seem to object when I left a few minutes before official visiting time was over.

*　　*　　*

Including myself, the class was made up of nine women, and I seemed to be one of the youngest. Called thither by the baby boom, some of the ladies were returning to the profession after a long absence; though they were made to feel they had even more to learn than the rest of us. The class was tutored by Mrs. Marlene Mitchell, a stern lady of senior years who wore her nursing uniform in which to teach and stood like a plaster saint on a raised dais at the front of the class. Mrs. Marlene Mitchell sensed her elevation keenly. I was instantly plunged back into the shrinking shyness of my school years.

Fortunately it was easy to remain invisible even in so small a class. Mrs. Mitchell liked to talk and did not like to be interrupted for anything. And since I could listen for all the world, that was exactly how I liked it; I calculated early that I could flap my ears through two terms of instruction, collect my diploma in silence and continue to practice midwifery but still according to Mammy's tested precepts.

MMM, as we pretty soon came to call her, addressed us from the front on that first evening. I remember a vase of daffodils stood on a table at the side of the classroom, beneath a window open to the spring evening air. MMM had a shocking overbite, even worse than Greta's, and this was a shame because one of her front teeth was chocolate brown. I remember thinking, *imagine that looking at you as you pop out of the womb.* The first thing you see on this earth. A cruel thought, unworthy Mammy might have said, and I tried not to keep it in mind, but it would keep coming back.

She addressed us from a stiff, standing position, hands clasped lightly in front of her. She would break this pose only occasionally, lifting her heavy, black spectacles off her nose to inspect the watch pinned to the breast pocket of her starched, midnight blue uniform. These moments created the only break in her monologue in which someone—not I—might interrupt.

"Can I ask something?" said the fidgeting lady next to me, whom I came to know as Biddy, during one of these pauses.

MMM didn't exactly say yes, but she made a small gesture with her open hand, as if to say: the floor is all yours but briefly please.

"You said that in the course we were going to be talking about formula. Well I have to say I don't hold with formula, so where does that leave the likes of us who don't hold with it?" Biddy was a stocky woman with a kindly, ruddy face. She looked around the class for support; most kept their heads down.

Before answering, Mrs. Marlene Mitchell checked her list of names. "Mrs. Carter. You are with us this evening to learn that some major changes have taken place over the last fifteen years. Major changes. I'm afraid you'll find it's not a question of what you or I hold with, it's a question of nursing policy. That's a phrase you'll come to hear more and more over the next few weeks. *Nursing policy.*"

"So am I to tell women what I don't believe in myself?" Biddy said jovially, folding her arms.

MMM wasn't jovial. "This we'll discuss in the fullness of time. Meanwhile you've committed yourself to come to an understanding of what's best for mothers. That's the point of these classes. Not you. Not I. Mothers." And when she said *mothers* she tapped the air in front of her with her index finger. Satisfied, she lifted her glasses from her nose and consulted her watch again. "Now time is against us, so let me run through what will be expected of you."

MMM swung back into her monologue. Biddy turned to me and made cross-eyes.

As I came out of the College of Midwives building I saw Biddy swinging her large bottom over the seat of a bicycle. She called out to me. "Not much change out of her, eh? Lot of air. No hardship though, eh? Stick with us old broilers, you'll be fine. See you next week!" And she was away, pedaling her bike unsteadily before I had a chance to reply with a single word.

But I was too flooded with the moment to be concerned with Biddy's opinion of our teacher. I'd come prepared to listen hard, and to measure everything that was said against what I knew and what Mammy had taught me. To be learning again, I felt, brought me to the wall of life; and even though I'd not fitted in at school, I realized that evening how badly I still wanted to learn, and how learning from Mammy always made the world anew. Learning refreshed the roots of life, it seemed to me. Or perhaps it was like peeling a layer of skin from an onion, to find another, brightly colored skin underneath, then one golden or glittering or iridescent beneath that. And as I thought these things I saw that the city itself had grown a new skin of darkness illuminated by neon and sodium electrical light as I walked away hugging my exercise book. I managed to thumb a lift easily enough, and I barely noticed the driver or heard his story, so entranced was I by the prospect of learning. I was ready for anything.

"I can't carry this off," I said to Judith.

"Keep still! How do you expect me to fix your hair when you keep tugging away from me? And leave those hair grips alone. You don't need them."

"But why do I have to have my hair pushed around at all? I thought the idea was to discourage him! Ouch!" I felt Judith was deliberately being mean with the brush. She was parting my hair in the middle when I'd parted my hair at the side all my life and it felt like she was removing my scalp in order to do it.

"He needs to find something worth going after before he can be discouraged. When did you last put a brush through this lot? You look like some kind of hedgerow witch."

I'd gone to Judith's house immediately after the school day had finished. She wanted to "prepare" me for my evening with Arthur. She had a bath with proper taps, so much more luxurious than my zinc tub filled from pans boiled on the stove. I soaked in the bath, listening to the sound of Judith's obsessive vacuuming downstairs. But after having me bathe she now wanted me sweetened, like a suckling pig with honey sauce for a gala dinner. She'd got her lipstick and her mascara and her blusher and all those things that make a painted clown of a woman, and I wasn't standing for it.

"I don't want to be too attractive to him!"

"Don't bloody well flatter yourself, girlie! We won't get a silk purse out of it!"

"Ow! Stop yanking my hair! We're not all sluts, Judith! We're not all loose."

By way of reply, and quite deliberately, Judith dragged the brush really hard on a knot of hair. I screamed, turned, and slapped her face. She dropped the brush and put a hand to her cheek. I'd imprinted five red finger-mark welts there. They were already fading before she flushed red with anger. She lifted her own hand and slapped me back, hard, and with double the stinging force. It was my turn to hold my face. I tried to return the slap again, but she danced backward out of my reach, and I nearly toppled forward.

Then we were overcome with the ridiculous spectacle of each other, and we both started cackling. Judith picked up the brush and gently resumed the grooming of my hair.

"Slut," I said softly.

"Vixen," she answered.

"Tart."

"Witch."

I put my hand out to stop the brush-strokes. "Judith, I'm scared of doing this."

"Look, little mouse, it will be all right. After what we're going to give him he'll be lucky to even find it in his trousers never mind stick it inside you. I'll make it disappear."

"But what if it doesn't work?"

"If that happens—and it won't—then you just make him pop with your hand. Have you never done that, really?"

I shook my head.

"Every girl should know that. If you're under pressure, just bring him in with your hand. Unless he's a swine; most men just want to go off pop, and they don't much care how. Use your hand, or if it gets too hot, then use your mouth."

"What?"

"Give it a suck. He'll be so busy writhing about he won't want to put it anywhere else, I tell you. I know men."

I was horrified! "But won't it taste of piss?"

"Not unless he's weeing on you it won't. Don't you know anything about blokes?"

"No," I wailed. The idea of sucking one of those things made me want to gag.

"Come on," Judith said. "It won't come to that. Now turn your head. Won't you let me put just a little makeup on you?"

I was sick with anticipation. Not simply apprehensive, not tummy butterflies, but sick as a dog. I vomited when she'd finished preening me. Then when she'd cleaned me up again she made me close my eyes. Carefully, she led me to her dressing table mirror.

"Open," she said.

I opened my eyes and a music-hall stranger peered back at me. Most shocking of all was not the small amount of blusher I'd allowed Judith to dust on my cheeks, nor the eyeliner that emphasized the whites of my eyes, nor the touch of shadow that drew attention to my eyelids, nor the delicate pink lipstick that budded my lips. It was the white parting down the center of my head. It split me in two. I turned my face sideways, so I could see only my profile. Could I be this other person? I thought.

"You look gorgeous," Judith said. "Come on. We've got lots to do."

eighteen

*W*e *got back to the cottage, and* the first thing we did was to prepare the egg-and-bacon pie and slam that in the oven. Then Judith wanted to dress up the table with a fresh cloth and candles. I did complain that she was making a whore's boudoir of the place, and she retorted that I'd never seen a whore's boudoir, which was true. We got two flagons of beer at the ready, and Judith got busy with the saltpeter and the other things. I sipped at the ale, trying to assess whether you could get the tang of it, and Judith kept sprinkling the stuff in until I felt we'd hit the point. As for the egg-and-bacon pie, we wouldn't know until it was cooked and we got to taste it. I shook in plenty of pepper to disguise. There was a fruit crumble for pudding, and that would be easy to mask with all the sugar.

"He might not get what he wants, but he won't go away hungry," Judith said.

Apart from that, Judith had also whisked up a salad dressing. "Isn't that a bit fancy?" I asked her.

"It's nothing," she said airily. Judith had once spent some time in France, where I think she may have found a Frenchman to give her these racy culinary ideas. "Just make sure it goes on his lettuce and not his dick."

It would be easy to hate Judith.

When the meal was prepared I vomited again, but there was nothing left for me to bring up. Judith said I should settle my stomach with some beer.

"What, with all that stuff in it? You're joking! I'll have a drop of sloe gin."

"Come on now, Fern. We've got half an hour to get you dressed."

I was the same size as Judith in all respects, and she had a complete outfit for me to go with my painted face. There was a figure-hugging neat white satin blouse that I loved, but the skirt she'd brought me showed far too much of my legs.

"I can't wear this!"

"It's a Mary Quant miniskirt. Just put it on."

"No."

"Okay then, slip your old dress back on. Never mind that it was sewn in a prison cell."

I sighed and donned the miniskirt. "But I look ridiculous!"

"It's what I wear all the time, dammit!"

"Exactly."

"Shut up and put these nylons on."

I'd never worn nylons before in my life. Judith had to show me how to take the black tights and roll them so as not to pop the nylon, starting at my toe, along the foot, up my calf and to the knees before stepping in with the other foot. I wanted to know how anyone was supposed to piss with these things on.

"You just hoik them down, stupid. Why are you being so difficult? And anyway, if things are working out, he'll have them off you before you get to the fruit crumble. I'm joking, Fern! Don't look like that!"

Though there was something about the dark nylon that I liked. It was like a soft breath on my leg as it rolled on. It whispered to my skin and made me want to press my legs together at the thigh or at the calf. I liked the way the nylon swished. It talked. And it made my legs look long and shapely.

"See," Judith said. "Now put these on. They're not too high."

She handed me a pair of black patent-leather shoes. The heels lifted me an inch and instantly pushed my hips and thighs forward. My balance changed.

"There. Let me look at you." Judith lifted a strand of my hair and parked it behind my ear. "Fern, you're gorgeous. I could almost fancy you myself."

I blinked at her. "Couldn't you take my place? Please?"

"For God's sake this is a date! You don't substitute for a friend! Is that pie burning?"

The pastry on the egg-and-bacon pie had caught and was smoking. Though it wasn't too bad, and Judith said if he complained that the pie was bitter, I was to say it had burned slightly in the oven.

Everything was ready except me. I couldn't stop myself from trembling. I made Judith promise to come back at nine o'clock to check on things. She was to look through the window and knock on the door on the pretext of having forgotten something. She promised me I would be fine, kissed me on the lips, then reapplied some lipstick before leaving.

Arthur McCann was punctual enough. He knocked on the door on the stroke of seven.

I took a breath and opened the door. "Hello," I said, "have some pie."

"Christ! went Arthur. He faltered, looking like he might have come to the wrong house. He looked at my hair, then at my legs, then he peered over my shoulder at the candles burning and the table all laid. "Christ," he said again, "you've been busy."

My cheeks burned, and my hand went up to touch the hair grips, which were gone. My head felt as though it were swelling. Arthur had ditched his motorbike gear and had turned up in a neat gray suit and wearing a thin blue tie. He swayed slightly on the step, and I caught a whiff of vinegary ale. It hadn't occurred to me that he might have gone drinking before showing up. I stepped aside to let him in and slammed the door shut behind him, too hard. He looked alarmed, so I opened it again and left it ajar to the evening air. Then I told him to sit in Mammy's chair while I poured him a glass of beer. He was about to say something but I felt my gorge rising so I slammed the beer down on the hearth for him and stepped outside, where I leaned against the wall to calm myself.

I needed a moment just to look up at the first stars twinkling out. It helped me to think of Valentina, my cosmonaut heroine, all alone in her shiny satellite. She would know what to do with Arthur. I called myself a ridiculous little virgin, and after a moment I felt my heart begin to slow again. Finally, I went back inside.

"Are you all right?" he said.

"Of course I'm all right! Do you think you're the first man I've ever cooked a pie for and got dressed up like this for and entertained in my own cottage without anyone else being present? Is that it?"

Arthur put his forefinger in his ear and shook his head. "Well, no."

I saw his ale untouched on the hearth. "Drink some beer, will you? Just drink it." My voice was shrill. It didn't sound like me at all.

"I think I've had enough beer tonight."

"What? You can't have!"

He blinked sleepy eyes at me. "I'm pickled already. I've been in the Bewicke Arms. If I have any more, I'll fall over."

"But you can't be!"

"Well if you insist!" He picked up the beer and drank halfway down the glass. "It's flat."

I sank slowly into the chair across the hearth, staring at him, wondering how I might liven up his beer for him.

"You look fabulous, Fern. Fabulous."

"Never mind that, drink some more."

"That beer's off I tell you." Then he belched silently.

"Right," I snapped. "You'll just have to eat something."

I pulled a chair from under the table, like a waiter in a restaurant, waiting for him to sit. Puzzled, Arthur scratched his head, came over and obediently lowered himself into the chair. Then I lifted out the pie, still warm in the cooling oven, cut him an overgenerous slice and served it up on a plate with a salad.

I was about to set it on the table before him when he said, "What's this then?"

"Egg-and-bacon pie."

Arthur sucked air through his teeth. "Sorry. I should have said. I'm a vegetarian."

"You're a what now?"

"Vegetarian. Have been for some years."

"You can't be!"

"I can be!"

"Vegetarian!" I cried. "But in God's name why?"

"Well," Arthur said in a reasonable tone, "I don't think it's right to eat animals, that's all. Not that I force my views on anyone else. If you want to eat meat, that's your business. I happen to think it's not necessary." He was slurring a little already. It never occurred to me that he'd had to find his own Dutch courage to be there.

I stood openmouthed, still holding the plate in my two hands, stooped in the act of setting it on the table and thinking how could it be that the entire district might have only one vegetarian, and I'd found him. I slammed the plate down on the table and picked up his knife. He winced a little, as if I was about to use it on him, but I set to work cutting the bacon out of his pie. I fished the bacon strips out with my fingers and made a little pile of them on my side of the table. "There," I said, "no meat in that now."

"Look, Fern—" he started.

"Don't say anything, Arthur McCann. I've spent all afternoon baking that pie for you, and you'll bloody well eat it." I couldn't keep the shrillness out of my voice.

He laughed and hiccuped. "All right! Calm down."

"I'm perfectly calm."

"Aren't you going to join me?"

I remembered the salad dressing. "I've no appetite," I said, fetching the dressing. I returned and spread it liberally on his salad.

"Hold on!" he said. "What's that?"

"French dressing. Very fancy. No meat in it either. Not going to object to that, are you?"

"No."

"Good, have some more then." I soaked his plate with the stuff. Then, under the pretext of opening a new bottle of beer for him, I went away from the table and poured him more from the flagon. Then I decided to strengthen it with a good measure of sloe gin.

"That one's better," he avowed, after sampling his freshened drink. "Though you could stand your spoon up in it."

"Are you going to complain at me all night about everything I put before you?"

Arthur chewed grimly on the charred crust of his pie. Then he blinked at me again with eyelids drooping over bloodshot eyes. He smiled sleepily. "This is turning out to be quite an evening."

The pudding went down rather better, I'm very glad to say, though I had to keep exhorting him to drink. At least my pulse rate was settling by the time he'd had two helpings of dessert. He even complimented me on my fruit crumble, which was a little unnecessary. Then, just as I was working up to asking him one or two probing questions about what he might know about Venables, I twigged that he was getting ready for what Judith warned me would be *the pounce*.

Judith had told me I might expect one of only two kinds of pounces. The first she said is so blindingly obvious that it is telegraphed a long way ahead, in which men move into a kind of lumbering and distracted slow-motion world, as if their feet and their thoughts are caught in deep river mud. These she said are easy to dodge, since you see the event coming a quarter of an hour ahead of its delivery. The other kind, she had told me, was an onslaught so fast and so out of nowhere that even the man can appear somewhat startled by it.

So I thought I had the measure of Arthur when he started yattering about fruit crumble. But I was mistaken. I took Arthur's dish to the sink and I was rinsing it when I heard a rushing sound behind me. Arthur fastened his arms around my waist and started kissing my neck. I supposed this to be a Type Two. The thing is I didn't know what to do with his crumble dish. Instinctively I flapped at Arthur with the wet cloth, and it caught his eye.

He staggered back, rubbing his sore eye, then seemed to collapse on one knee. He groaned. Feeling bad, I rushed to him to see if his eye was all right and the next thing I knew was that he folded his arms around my bottom and sank his face into my thighs.

I didn't know when he'd last shaved but I could feel the rough of his chin snagging on the nylon as he went, "Fernfernfern. You're fabulous." That's all he was saying: "Fernfernfern."

I thought for a moment he'd fallen asleep with his face between my thighs, but he hauled himself to his feet and kissed me, pushing me back against the kitchen sink. I wasn't averse to the kiss, but I could taste beer, saltpeter and sloe gin on his breath, not to mention Judith's garlicky salad dressing. They didn't blend well. What's more I could feel what was inside his trousers, pushing against my thigh. After a while I tried to shove him away, but he laughed and picked me up in his arms.

I admit I screamed—more in fun than in fear—and he carried me through to the parlor and flung me down on the old sofa. Mammy's lace doily on the back of the sofa was dislodged. I wanted to giggle until he reached up under my ridiculously short skirt, hooked his fingers around the elasticized top of my nylons and my knickers and hoiked them all the way down to my shoes. I screamed again.

"Arthur! Get off me! What do you think you're doing? I want to hear what you know about Venables!"

"Eh? What? I'm on fire I am! Got to have you, Fern."

"Get off me, you pig!"

But I couldn't get myself from beneath his weight and he had already loosened his own trousers and had them down round his knees. The next thing he reared up and all I saw was his long pink cock bobbing in the air, and it seemed less like it belonged to him than something that had got loose from the exotic animals' tent at the annual county show, and I thought dammit he's going to stick it in me.

So I grabbed it.

Arthur yelped, and then froze, and then shuddered. Next he collapsed on top of me in a spasm, going Fernfernfern in my ear, Fernfernfern, and I felt his fetch in my hand. At last his spasms got gentler and his voice in my ear got quieter, and after a moment I realized he'd gone to sleep on top of me.

I tried to get out from under him, but he was too heavy. I looked at the palm of my hand. His fetch was all in my hand, gleaming like the vernix on a newborn baby. I held it up to the candlelight, and the light raced over it like it was mother-of-pearl, or the berry of the mistletoe. It was beautiful, a kind of magical substance hot and messy and curving to the lifeline of my hand, and I thought that's all it takes, some of that, a bit of that in the mix of inside you and the whole howling laughing crying screaming thing begins again for another soul, and I thought, what brilliant, dangerous stuff!

He started snoring gently. I had to force myself from under him before some demon inside me wanted to push some of that stuff where it wanted to go. I shouted in Arthur's ear. I hammered on his shoulders to let me out, but he snored on and there was no waking him. At last I managed to maneuver my leg from beneath his great weight and roll him off me, whereupon he flipped over on his back, smacked his lips a couple of times and continued to snore. I dashed to the sink, where I washed the magic starlike stuff off my hands so that it could do no mischief.

When I went back to him I was shocked to see his thing still stuck up in the air. I was always led to believe that these things went down again after a man had fetched. But there it was, standing proud, like the last stubborn ninepin in the cave of the skittle alley, or like a stinkhorn fungus on the forest floor.

I had a closer look. It didn't smell bad like a stinkhorn—a fungus I wouldn't even like to touch—in fact the smell coming from it, musty and cloying, put me in mind of the May blossom. Now that Arthur was snoring away this thing that moments earlier had been like a thrashing, snapping ferret now looked quite comical. I was wondering what would happen were I to touch it again when I heard a tapping on the door.

Nine o'clock! It was Judith, come to see if I was all right.

"Where is he?" she said, standing on tiptoes to look over my shoulder after I'd got the door open.

"Back room, sleeping."

"What?" She pushed past me. "What's he doing there?"

"He was already completely drunk when he got here. Then I gave him four pints of beer and gin mixed."

Judith looked at me as if I were slightly mad. Then she bustled through to the parlor. "Good God! What's that?"

"It's what it looks like." I watched Judith approach the snoring

Arthur very slowly. Her eyes were fixed on his tent pole. "Don't worry, you won't wake him. I've tried."

"You might at least have covered it up."

"Oh pardon me, your ladyship! I'll throw a handkerchief over it! Never mind that: what about your saltpeter and black willow buds and sweet water lily? All useless! Completely hopeless. You said he wouldn't even get a stand!"

"Heck. Did he eat the pie?"

"Of course he ate the pie. But look at him now! The opposite! I'll never listen to you again, Judith!"

She got down on her knees and leaned against the sofa, fascinated. "Look at it! Shows no sign of flagging, does it?"

"What shall we do about it?"

Judith thought for a minute. "We could tie a little bow to it."

"This is serious, Judith! I don't want him to wake up and try to stab me with that thing."

Judith made a spring of her thumb and forefinger, reached out and flicked the head lightly. It vibrated and returned to position. Judith flicked it again.

"Judith!"

Judith opened one of Arthur's eyes between forefinger and thumb. It was all white. Then she pulled Arthur's hair. Harder. Then she slapped his face. He snored on happily. "Right. We'll get him outside. The cold air at least might bring him round."

"Then what?"

"I don't know! I'm thinking as I go, Fern! Get a leg and an arm, will you?"

"Let's put that away first."

We tried to tug his trousers up around it but the thing wouldn't lie flat and we couldn't button him up. "How the hell do men go around with one of these in their trousers?" Judith said. She reached for something black that was hanging on a peg behind the door and covered it with that.

"That's Mammy's best hat! Get it off him!"

Judith sighed and replaced the hat with a tea towel. Then she snorted.

I didn't find it so funny. "I'm not using that for the dishes again," I said.

"Shut up and let's get him outside."

It was a huge effort dragging Arthur from the sofa, through the parlor and to the kitchen door. He was a big man. His head cracked on the doorstep as we got him out. Judith wanted to just dump him on the lawn and bolt the door against him, but it hardly seemed fair. Then I had another idea. I suggested we drag him to the outhouse and set him up on the toilet so that when he came round he'd think he went outside of his own volition and fell asleep. So we dragged him to the outhouse. We had to stop once to replace the tea towel, but he slid pretty sweetly along the damp cobblestones of the yard. Setting him upright on the throne was tricky, but after a struggle we left him slumped there with his trousers round his ankles, still snoring and smacking his lips in deep sleep. We left the tea towel to give him something to think about when he woke up.

Back inside we bolted the door against him. I was exhausted, but Judith made me recount everything that had happened. In the end I persuaded her to sleep over with me in case he came back raging, so we climbed into my bed together and lay talking in the dark.

"He fetched into my hand," I told her. "Then he turned to mush."

"They do that, men," she said. Wistfully, so I thought.

After an hour or so Arthur came rapping on the door, calling my name. Judith and I hugged each other and stayed silent as mice. He knocked and called again. Soon he gave up and went away.

"I'll never go along with your ideas again," I said.

"Shut up," Judith said. "Go to sleep."

nineteen

I doubted if the evening's events had advanced my cause or helped me in my predicament. The idea had been for me to quiz Arthur about my prospects and to butter him up so that he might use his influence to help me. All Judith would say about that was, "Wait and see."

The next day being the Saturday of the party at Croker's Farm, Judith hung around all day prevailing upon me to take her along. She also spread out the *Old Moore's Almanac* on the kitchen table, but only after I'd got her to scrub the table down and otherwise extinguish all sign of the previous evening's dinner. The *Old Moore's Almanac,* in addition to its precise lists of positions of the moon and information about the stars and the tides, was littered with advertisements for a lucky rabbit's foot and a pixie charm and the like, along with written testaments as to how cash had fallen to various after obtaining such as talisman. "We ought to go in for selling this tripe," Judith said.

"Yes," I said, scraping egg-and-bacon pie leftovers into the bin. "We could sell anaphrodisiacs as well."

I was more comfortable back in my own clothes, and in my own hair as it were, with three comforting iron grips pinned high above my right ear. I told Judith if that's what tarting it up does for men, she could keep it.

She ignored me and continued to pore over the small-print charts. "You've only got two full moons before midsummer's day, and you won't want to do it after; and you won't want to do it waxing; and you won't want to do it when you're on the curse." She wet the tip of her index finger to leaf through the pages of the almanac. "It's amazing how the time is eaten up if you don't plan ahead."

"Don't badger me!"

"Please yourself. But if you really are going to *Ask,* you'll want to do it while you're still here in the cottage, with easy access to the woods and the meadows. That's all I'm saying."

"I know that," I said, and I poured what was left of her wickedly ineffective salad dressing down the drain.

I made my visit to Mammy earlier in the afternoon that day, and Judith came with me. The visit didn't go well. Perhaps it was the leather jacket, or that I'd arrived there along with Judith, but Mammy was confused. She didn't seem to recognize me at all. Seeing how this upset me, Judith left me alone with Mammy and waited outside. I plumped up Mammy's pillow and combed her hair. She looked at me glassy-eyed. "Why are you plaguing me? Have you asked the mistress?" she said.

I wondered if she'd guessed what I was about to do. I never underestimated Mammy's intuition in anything. "I always do, Mammy."

"Stop tormenting me, Jane Louth," she retorted. "How far gone are you?"

"I'm not gone at all, Mammy."

"I know what you want, Jane. You girls come to me for help and you don't want to be straight with me. And you're all blabbermouths. I ask you to keep quiet, but you go shooting off your mouths and I'm the one who has to suffer." She seemed unusually angry.

"Yes, Mammy."

"They're out to get me, you know that, don't you?"

"Yes, Mammy."

"If you go blabbermouthing everywhere, I shall be the one to pay. I don't see why I should help any of you. Who's the father?"

"I can't say, Mammy."

"Well if you can't say, I can't help you. There, that's got you, hasn't it? It's part of what you pay me. Knowledge. It's my protection, that knowledge, that's why I have to have it. Was it him up at the big house?"

"No, Mammy."

Mammy let me give her a bed bath all over, but then she seemed to think I was one of the nurses, and she cried and said her feet were cold.

I left the hospital feeling lower than I ever had after a visit. Mammy hadn't identified me for a single second. Judith saw my distress and looked after me. She got me home, and she was determined that I needed cheering up, so I let her have her way about the party that evening.

Though I'd already had enough of Judith flapping round the place when it came time to get ready to walk to Croker's. She irritated me by asking questions like who would be there, and what was so-and-so like. Then she challenged me about my hair all over again and asked me was I going to get dressed up. I said I was going just as I was, and that seemed to infuriate her.

"I'll look dull just by association," she said.

"And I'll look a tart by being with you."

And we didn't speak a word to each other for the next hour, which suited me down to the ground. Judith had a fashionable maxiskirt with buttons shaped like blackberries all the way down the front that invited everyone to pick them off like fruit from the hedgerow. And under that skirt she wore white patent-leather boots up to her knees. She went upstairs and was quiet for a long time. When I went up I found her poised in front of Mammy's old dressing-table mirror. "What on earth are you doing with those?" I said.

"Don't distract me. One slip, and you have to start all over again. It's a lot of trouble, but it's worth it."

She was gluing huge false eyelashes into place. I watched as she ran a line of gum across her eyelids and carefully applied the things to her eyes. "There. Are they on straight?"

"You can't go out looking like that! They'll just laugh at us!"

"I swear I will *clout* you, Fern, before this evening is out."

We were about to start another shouting match when I heard a male voice calling from outside. I looked down from the window and saw a ginger-top stooped at the door. "Oh God, it's Arthur," I said.

"Go and talk to him," Judith urged. "Make out it was all his doing."

I let Arthur in. He'd sloughed off his suit and was back in his biker's gear, which I liked better. He blinked at me, maybe at my clothes. Then he shook his head slightly, as if beating off some outrageous notion passing across his mind, or as if a fairy had reversed some spell. He was agitated enough, and said he'd come to see if I was all right. I told him that *I* was all right, but that I'd wondered if *he* was all right. I made out that I was dismayed when he'd upped and left me after dinner to go to the outhouse, after which I'd seen no more of him.

"Woke up this morning with the worst headache of my life, I did, Fern. Hit with an anvil. Felt a bit silly really. Cut my ear I did, too. Don't know how I did that."

I remembered his head thumping on our granite doorstep, but I said nothing. Then Judith came down. She stood at the foot of the stairs with her knee swinging inside her maxiskirt and her white boots, leaning against the wall, one hand on her hip. She had her tongue poked in her cheek and was smirking at him. "Hello Arthur," she said.

"Oh," Arthur said, never having met Judith before.

I introduced them. "Pleased to meet you, Arthur," she said, and she deliberately let her gaze settle on his crotch before twinkling at him again from beneath those ridiculous eyelashes.

"Oh," he said again. "Anyway I came to apologize. I drank too much afore I got here. Remember you picking the bacon out of my pie and next thing I know I was in your shithouse with a thumping headache. So I thought I'd better go home."

"Yes," Judith said, "Fern mentioned that you came over a bit forceful."

"It's all right, Arthur," I said quickly.

"Bit of a wild thing you are, Arthur!" She flared her eyes at him.

"I hope I didn't—"

I cut him off. "It's all right, really. Ignore her."

Arthur dug his hand under the back of his collar, as if chasing a small insect. Then he looked at me from head to toe again. Something was clearly bothering him but he was unsure what it was. "Right, I'll be off then. Long as you're all right."

"Bye, Arthur!" Judith said, still smirking and swinging her knee.

Arthur retreated down the garden path, fingering the small cut on his ear.

Perhaps I'm out of touch, but when people say "a party" I assume they mean they might go to some trouble, maybe spruce up the place a bit, buy a few balloons or somehow indicate that the day is not the same as every other day. Even the dullest churchgoer pulls on a clean set of clothes. But there was nothing at Croker's Farm to indicate that any attempt had been made to mark the occasion out as in any way special. It looked exactly the same as it did on the day I'd made my first visit.

I mean exactly. There was no more evidence of work around the farm, and though something savory and garlicky bubbled away in a huge pan on the stove, the kitchen was empty. Music drifted through from another part of the house—not that bloomin' Hindu music but some scruffy wild vamp thing that fashioned a strange mood.

"Are you sure this is all right?" Judith said, her confidence faltering for a moment.

The kitchen door had stood open, so we'd ventured inside. "Well, we are invited. Come on." It was true: I was invited. Though after my behavior I doubted they would be expecting me.

I led her through to the room I'd been in before, where I was confronted by a scene identical to the one I'd seen earlier. Folk slouched around on mattresses in a fog of cigarette smoke and flickering candlelight. Half-asleep in the gloom. Kiddies lying in their laps. A strong smell of incense. Maybe no one had moved in all that time. Either the party wasn't happening, after all, or this was the party, and I'd stumbled on a similar celebration on my first visit. Chas hauled himself to his feet out of the tangle of bodies.

"Hey, look who's here! This is amazing. Incredible. Did you know it's my birthday?"

I was confused. "Yes. That's why we came."

Chas looked at me as though I were a Greek oracle. "That is so far out! Look everybody! They knew it was my birthday!"

Judith and I exchanged glances. There were a lot of smiles. Luke, interrupted in the task of rolling a cigarette, jiggled his eyebrows at us. Some people waved lazily. Greta stood up and embraced me, and when I introduced them Judith got a hug, too. "Welcome to the party. Have a seat."

There weren't any seats. It was like the opposite of *Alice in Wonderland* where there are lots of seats and the Mad Hatter says there's no room. There wasn't even much space on the bare wood floor, but Judith and I managed to kneel down and we sat back on our ankles. A cute little boy with hair as long as a girl was sent into the kitchen to fetch us each a glass of warm beer. Chas was still exercising his imagination as to how we knew it was his birthday. I heard him say to someone, "Either it's the most amazing coincidence or . . ."

I noticed a few guitars and hand drums and a fiddle leaning against the wall in the corner. Greta followed my eyes. "We're having food and music later on." This, at least, was as I'd been promised.

"Don't you usually have food, then?" Judith said. Greta laughed out loud and clapped her thighs, as if this was outrageously funny. But Judith just blinked at her with those long stick-on eyelashes.

Chas joined us again, forcing himself a space between Judith and myself by stepping between us and wedging his bottom against ours. Greta sank back into the room somewhere. Chas put an arm around each of us. Judith looked at me again, and I decided I was going to avoid eye contact with her for the rest of the evening. "I'm so happy you both came here on *this day*," Chas said.

I actually thought he was going to cry with happiness, the way he went on about it.

"What's this music?" I said. I couldn't decide whether I loved it or hated it. Yes, it was what I call vamp, but it got inside you, deep down. It tickled. I wasn't sure I wanted to let it.

" 'Green Onions.' "

" 'Green Onions'? That's a funny name for a record."

"Yeh, funny. So good though, ahey?" He said this to me but he looked at Judith, bobbing his head in time to the music. " 'Green Onions.' "

"I hate it," I said.

"No, you don't," he said.

I listened to it some more. He was right. I did like it. I just had to let myself. "Yes," I said at last. "I do like it. I like it a lot."

"She likes 'Green Onions' a lot," Chas told Judith. Then he shouted to the whole room, "Fern likes 'Green Onions' a lot!" Everyone blinked and smiled at me, as if to say well, that proves you're a good person after all.

"Actually, I love it," I said, but I don't think he heard me. His attention was elsewhere.

"We had three other parties to go to," Judith said, "but we plumped for this one."

Chas looked at her soulfully. "Plumped," he said.

Judith gazed right back at him. "Yes, plumped."

Just when I thought this soulful staring was going to go on forever, Chas leaned over and kissed Judith full on the lips. I thought she'd leap back, but instead she kissed him. The kiss went on. And on.

If I'd had a watch I would have timed the kiss. I looked around the room to see if anyone else was witnessing this, but no one seemed to take much notice. Greta looked over at me and grinned, a little unhappily I thought. I looked back at the kissing pair and I thought they must be going for a world record. Chas still had his arm lightly trailed around my shoulder as he stretched toward Judith. I felt like folding my arms.

Slut.

After a lifetime, just as the music stopped, the kiss stopped, and I thought I heard dogs barking in the yard. Chas leaned back, but their eyes remained locked. Judith was actually licking her lips as she gazed steadily back at him. Chas reached for a home-rolled cigarette from behind his ear and lit it. He inhaled almost theatrically before passing it to Judith, who also inhaled deeply, theatrically. Then she held out the cigarette for me to take.

"I don't want that," I said. "It's pot."

Even more distasteful than what was in the cigarette was the residual kiss bubbling on the end of it.

"I know it's pot," Judith said. She waved the thing at me again.

"Get it out from under my nose. It stinks."

Judith shrugged and took another draw. Chas looked from one to the other of us, and smirked.

I was provoked by this smirk, but I didn't show it. I got up and moved away from them. Greta saw me and also stood up. "Fern, I hope you don't mind, but I told them you could sing."

"What?"

"Oh go on! It would be a great birthday present for Chas. It would blow him away."

I looked at Chas. He was blowing smoke rings for Judith, and she was puncturing them with her finger. I didn't know how to answer, because even though I knew I had a good voice—better than good—I rarely performed. I didn't want the attention. I said something about wanting a glass of water and went out to the kitchen.

Greta followed me out, but as I stepped into the kitchen three men and a very tall woman passed us on their way into the room. "Hi," said one of the men genially, but something didn't feel right. "Who are they?" I asked Greta.

"No idea," she said. "Go on, Fern, I'm going to sing, and I would love it if you would, too."

"Do you let complete strangers come in and out of your house then?" My intuition was firing. There was definitely something amiss with those men.

"People are always in and out of here." Then Greta glanced out of the window. "Oh dear," she said, and she rushed back into the other room.

I looked out into the yard. There were two police cars. Leaning against one of them was Bill Myers. He must have graduated from police bicycle to police car because he'd traded in his helmet for a soft, flat policeman's peaked cap. He was talking to three other uniformed officers, one of whom was fussing the dogs to quiet them.

I went back into the other room. The music had stopped, and everyone was on their feet. One of the men who had passed me in the kitchen had a plastic bag in his hand. The others were plucking cigarette stubs from ashtrays and collecting them in another bag. The tall woman apologized to me and said she'd have to search me, but all she did was pat my pockets before moving on to another girl. I guess they'd got much of what they needed already.

"What's going on?" I said to Chas.

He smiled, but his brow was wrinkled at the same time. "We're busted," he said.

Then Luke picked up his guitar and started improvising a song called "The Birthday Bust," and I marveled at how calm everyone was, though one of the small children was crying. But Luke was singing about pigs, and I realized he meant the police.

> *Oh it's so mean, oh it's unjust*
> *When the little piggies do the Birthday Bust*

"You can shut your mouth right now," bawled one of the policemen aggressively, but Luke didn't stop.

Greta tried to leave the room, but she was hauled back by the woman who said everyone had to stay where they were. The policeman told Luke if he didn't stop, he would bloody well make him stop, but Luke carried on singing about pigs. The policeman with the plastic bags left the room, and with everyone's attention focused on Luke, I followed. He went out to the police cars and handed the plastic bags to Bill Myers. Bill put the two bags on the passenger seat of his car, then when he closed the door he saw me.

"Fern! What the bloody hell are you doing here?"

"It was just a party. They invited me."

"Fern, sweetheart, you don't want to be mixing with these people. They're druggies, Fern, druggies. They deal in drugs, do you know what that means?"

I said I thought I did.

"These are not good people, Fern. I can't believe you're here today!"

I explained I'd never been there before. Which was of course untrue.

"Look, why don't you slip off?" Bill said. "I'll square it. This is nothing to do with you. You don't want to get caught up in this lot."

He'd hardly finished saying this when there came the sound of a window smashing and a lot of screaming and shouting from the house. The rest of the uniformed policemen ran inside, and Bill went tearing in after them.

"Clear off, Fern!" were his last words to me.

I was left standing outside in the yard, all alone. I looked about me. Then I looked through the car window. The two plastic bags were resting on the passenger seat. I opened the door of the police car, took out the plastic bags and stuffed them in my pocket. Then I closed the car door and walked away from the farm.

twenty

*U*ltrasound. *You've heard this* old wives' tale and you've heard that old wives' tale, and I'm here today to tell you there is no way of knowing the gender of a baby unless you have one of these."

MMM had a machine plugged in at the front of the class. It was a huge evil-looking cabinet with a screen and dials and switches, and trailing leads and wires like it hatched out writhing snakes just for fun. It looked like a nasty piece of science fiction. It had taken two caretakers to wheel it into the room and set it up for us to see. MMM said it was a great boon to obstetrics. She patted the machine as if she'd wired it together herself, or as if it were a capsule that had brought her safely back from space.

"We're going to need a good bicycle," Biddy said loudly, "if we're to take one of these contraptions out and about with us."

MMM did what she always did with Biddy's remarks, and that was to squint through her glasses, scrape her bottom lip with her prominent front teeth, and pretend Biddy was slightly simple. "No, Biddy. Midwives will not be expected to carry one of these around. One day, and that day is still a long way off, one of these will be set up at every hospital. This one we have here at the college is for teaching purposes."

I say she pretended. Sometimes MMM seemed so short of irony that maybe she actually thought Biddy had contemplated putting the machine in the wicker basket mounted on the handlebars of her bike. Biddy, though, was never thrown by this manner. "So we're learning about a machine we'll never get to use, then. I see."

It was only the second week of the course and already I could see the war shaping up between Biddy and MMM. Whenever Biddy spoke it was always with humor or arched, so that you took what she meant indirectly. MMM always said what she wanted to say with no room for margin nor skew, nor space for misunderstanding, deliberate or otherwise. These two women couldn't possibly inhabit the same room or breathe the same air. They shouldn't even have been put in the same lifetime together. It was a mistake.

"Well, Biddy, it's crucially important to keep abreast of technical developments. A modern midwife should know of the resources available to support any difficult diagnosis. That's why I'm showing it to you, here, this evening."

I could see the alliances forming, too. Some of the women on the course were irritated by Biddy's interjections. They just wanted to blink at the sci-fi equipment and go home to make their husbands' suppers. Others supported Biddy with a well-timed chuckle directed against our teacher's squinting superiority. As for me, I wanted to side with Biddy: I wanted to challenge MMM, to speak up for Mammy and say there is indeed a way of knowing a child's gender long before it sees the light of day, but that only we few know of it. But I didn't. I shrank. And anyway, MMM was already introducing Gloria Tranter, a spectacularly pregnant lady well into her third trimester. The radiant Mrs. Tranter had agreed to be the subject of a demonstration and was already taking her place on the examination couch while we crowded around the screen.

MMM rolled up Mrs. Tranter's clothes, then she smeared a kind of jelly over Mrs. Tranter's hugely distended belly.

"Is it a Geiger counter?" Biddy asked.

"No it's not a Geiger counter, Biddy. It's an ultrasound monitor. Very technical. Are you ready, Mrs. Tranter?"

"Yes," said Mrs. Tranter, smiling at us as if she'd been handed a bouquet of spring flowers.

MMM flicked some switches, and the screen fizzed. Then she moved a small, wired suction cup over the lady's belly. And there on the screen was the outline, clearly visible in all the fuzzy gray lines, of the unborn baby. MMM pointed out the baby's beating heart and its male genitals.

But it wasn't what I could *see* that had me nailed to the wall. It was what I could *hear*. Because that machine had allowed me to see not an image of the baby in the womb, but to see exactly what I was hearing. And in a way it was a sound I had heard before, but fabulously enhanced. Now, with all the switches and dials of MMM's infernal machine turned up, I could hear that baby. There was an amplified shucking, like someone pulling air in through the teeth and blowing out again, but in a slow, steady, articulate pulse. I was utterly lost to that miraculous and awesome sound.

So lost I had to be called back. When I looked up, all the other women had taken their seats again, and MMM was disconnecting the equipment and calling to me. And even though the machine was switched off and Mrs. Tranter was climbing off the table, I could still hear it, shucking and blowing. And I didn't want to stop listening, because I could hear the baby, and he was telling me all his plans for this life.

"Are you with us, Miss Cullen? I know it's all rather marvelous but could you retake your seat with the others?"

Afterward, as we left the college, Biddy came up to me, wheeling her bike. "Gone, weren't you? For a minute there. Listening to that contraption. Completely gone."

I was anxious to change the subject so I blurted, "She's wrong. You can tell the gender by the heartbeat. A boy's heartbeat is faster."

Biddy looked at me strangely. "Well we all know that," she said. Then she climbed on her bike and pedaled away.

"Have you heard about the miracle?"

The following morning I was bent over my vegetable garden with a rake, and when Greta called like that from the gate it startled me. My hand flew to my three hairgrips. "What miracle?"

Greta let herself in through the gate. It whined before it snapped back shut, and I thought: someone ought to put some oil on that gate. "We got away with it."

I leaned on my rake. "Got away with what?"

"The evidence. It vanished. They couldn't charge us."

Greta was grinning at me, and I saw how one large front tooth slightly crossed the other. Like the gate, it made me want to fix it. Greta went on about how the police had taken Chas and Luke down to the police station but they hadn't been able to charge the pair—or anyone else—because the evidence they'd collected from the house had gone missing. Greta described it as a miracle that they'd kept all the gear together and that even though the police had made a diligent search, they hadn't found anything else. "Not even a roach. Not even a grain," Greta said. "Don't you think that's a miracle?"

"A miracle?"

"Yes. It's destiny. We're protected, our little family up there on the farm. We're watched over. We're special."

Oh dear, I thought. "What happened to Judith?"

"I thought she'd left with you. Then she came back on Sunday. She and Chas seemed to have hit it off."

Vixen. Tart. Slut. Then Greta pulled a face. "What's up?" I asked her.

"Nothing. Just period pains."

I let my rake fall to the soil. "Come inside. I'll give you something for that."

"Lady's mantle?"

"Tshh. Mugwort and sage."

Sometime in the afternoon I heard a vehicle stop outside the cottage and I also heard the ratchet of a handbrake, but I was busy steeping herbs in vinegar, so I didn't look up, even when I heard a scuffle at the door. When I did eventually go out, there on the doorstep was a box record player. I identified it as the one they'd had at Croker's on the night of the party. I opened the box and on the turntable was a record. The record label read "Green Onions" by Booker T. & the MG's. There was also a tiny handwritten note, saying, *"Thanks!"*

I immediately took the record player indoors and plugged it in. I'd never used a record player in my life, never had such a treasure as this. I saw the disc spinning and my hand trembled as I tried to lower the stylus on the vinyl. I didn't know there was an automatic switch and I made a terrible scratching sound as I dropped the stylus onto the spinning disc. Then came the music I'd remembered from the party. It starts off with deep throbbing notes and a heavy beat, then it cuts with that jagged guitar and I found myself staring at the disc rotating on the turntable and disappearing into the music and not having to think about anything, and I tell you I was *gone*.

Later that day I was on my way to Bunch Cormell's house. Her baby was thriving, but she had cracked nipples from the boy's enthusiastic mouthing, and I had some lanolin for her. As I walked down the street a car drew alongside, engine purring, keeping up with my walking pace. It was a police car. I stopped.

The police car stopped. Bill Myers leaned over and wound down the passenger window. "Want a lift somewhere, Fern?"

"Bill! No, I'm just off to the Cormells'."

He opened the door. "Jump in. I'll take you."

"But it's only two minutes!" He smiled at me and held open the door. I got in. The upholstery inside the car smelled new. "This is nice, Bill. Better than your bike, anyway."

Myers put the car into gear and moved down the street. "How's Mammy then?"

"She's middlin', Bill. Didn't recognize me the other day."

He nodded. "Was surprised to see you at Croker's the other night."

"Just as I was surprised to see you!"

He paused at the road junction and his indicator was going tick tick tick.

"Quite a night of it, we had." The car moved off again.

"I didn't know all that stuff was going on."

"Don't expect you did. They don't work for a living, that lot, Fern. Deal in drugs, they do. That's how they make a penny. Other people's misery." He stopped the car outside Bunch's house. It was a ridiculously short ride. I didn't feel I could get out. "Not that we got what we went for."

"No?"

"Even the bit of evidence we got I managed to lose, somehow, Fern."

"Oh?"

"Can't think how I did it, Fern. Landed me in hot water it did. On my way to promotion I was. Sergeant. Buggered that up, it has."

"That's a nuisance, Bill."

"You know if you've got cause to go to Croker's again, it would help me if you kept your eyes open. They do all sorts up there. Pills. Needles. The works. If you see anything, like."

"I'll keep my eyes open, Bill."

"Don't put yourself in a spot, though, Fern."

"No."

He leaned across and opened the passenger door for me. "Go and see that nursing mother, then."

I got out of the car and I waved at him as he pulled away. The bottle of lanolin I had for Bunch was sweating in my palm.

twenty-one

You have to. *It was like a voice* whispering in my head, getting louder all the time. *You have to* Ask. *You must.*

It was a watershed moment in my beliefs. If it worked for me, then I would know forever. If it didn't, then my scepticism would be confirmed. Quite apart from that I was running out of options, and I was running out of time. Judith was correct, in that if I was going to *Ask*, then I had to do it while I was still in possession of the cottage, and if I was going to do it at a time when the moon was with me, then I had to make immediate preparation.

The fiasco with Arthur McCann hadn't helped me in the slightest. In fact he hadn't shown his face since the morning after. Moreover I had no prospect of finding the wherewithal to pay off the estate.

I took off my clothes and sat in Mammy's room, at her old dressing table, gazing at my reflection in the foxed mirror. Did I have the courage? A sorry figure looked back at me. I don't know how long I stayed like that, staring. After a while I came to, and my hand automatically fluttered to my hairgrips, and the grips released themselves into my hand. I picked up Mammy's hairbrush. It still smelled faintly of her sebum. I began to brush my hair forward, then I took a comb and parted my hair in the middle, the way Judith had for Arthur McCann.

I lit some incense, one of my own. Bistort, valerian, lavender. The extravagance. The intention. Mammy would be furious, oh. I went outside, naked, knelt down on one knee and smeared some incense oil on the gate.

I returned inside. The incense smoked the room and clouded my reflection in the mirror. Judith had still not collected all her things from that night. The clothes, the nylons, the cosmetics, the face paints. I spread them out before me on the dressing table. The tiny brushes, the miniature pots, the tidy little cauldron of it all. First my eyes. Then my eyebrows, nut brown. My cheeks, a hint of rose flush. The buds of my lips. I loved myself in that mirror. It almost wasn't me. Then I rolled on the nylons, smoothed them over my shins and along the sheen of my thighs. Slipped on the little skirt, the other clothes. Finally, the wicked cologne. A spray, a burdened puff of air.

And then I willed him to come.

He was a long time coming, but I knew he would have to. And sure enough after a while I heard his van outside the gate. I heard the ring of the great metal churns as he bounced them out of the van and onto the road and rolled them one at a time into the garden, and each time I heard the hinges on the gate complaining. I heard him drag at the pump and then curse when the dry pump wheezed and spat. So I went outside.

"You have to prime it," I said.

"Good God," Chas said. "I was looking for Fern."

"Oh, Fern stepped out for a while. You do know how to prime a pump?" I asked.

I leaned over to drag the half-full pail of water, but I paused, looked back to see his eyes on me, on my legs, on my bent back. I could almost see a blue fire leaping around him, paralyzing him. I lifted the pail to the pump. "You pump, I'll prime."

He was wary. He grabbed the handle of the pump and started to work it as I tipped the water in. Though I watched where I was pouring, I knew he hadn't taken his eyes from me. He couldn't. Then the pump handle found some resistance, and that slowed him as he pumped. "So where did Fern get to?" he said.

"Oh, she's around here, somewhere."

With the pump flowing he dragged a churn into place and held it there. "Are you sisters, you and Fern?"

"In a manner of speaking."

Then he stopped pumping and let the churn clang back on its bottom. "You know what, you nearly had me for a minute there, Fern."

"I did?"

"Oh yes. Nearly had me."

"Then you're easily had."

He looked at me as if calculating what I might mean by that. Then he stepped toward me, too close, though I didn't step back. He was near enough for me to smell him; his manly scent strong but not unpleasant. He stood close enough for me to feel his breath on my cheek. He reached up a hand and gently lifted my hair above my ear and held it there for a moment. Then I put my hand on his and firmly pushed it away.

He looked confused for a moment. Then he smiled, turned, and dragged another churn under the pump. I went back inside while he completed his chore. From the window I watched him roll his churns to his van, watched him hoist them in the back before driving away.

After he'd gone I put on my coat and I went out to the woods. I'd done my calculations. As I saw it—and going by the *Old Moore's Almanac*—the moon, or *the mistress* as Mammy called her, would be hatching anew at 4:32 A.M. three days after the Friday, and if I was correct, my period should have finished three days before that, which was perfect. Auspicious, even. It was just that it was running things up close to the date of my eviction. After my *Ask*, not counting the day of reckoning itself, I would have three days before being turfed out. That meant three days for an answer to present itself.

I trudged the path through the trees, taking the short cut toward the A47 and cursing the stupid shoes of Judith's I was still wearing. A blackbird called out in alarm and went winging in front of me, trying to draw me off. The woods were in the headlong rush of spring and the trees were full of birdsong. I could hear insects busy in the tree bark. You could almost see the lush green fern inching higher by the second. I set my back against the great old oak and asked Mammy, in hospital in the town, if my calculations were correct and if I was doing the right thing.

A breeze played in the creaking upper branches of the oak. Wood pigeons cooed in mating nearby. I could hear a cuckoo in the depth of the woods. Gradually the sound of the cuckoo and the pigeons went away. Soon all birdsong had stopped. The sound I imagined to be the labor of insects seemed to go, and it left me listening only to the wind in the trees and the pulse of the growing things in the earth. Finally, the wind dropped.

The woods became silent and still. Only the pulse, the rhythm of the growing cycle of life, remained. And then quite naturally that stopped, too. I listened hard, and then I heard Mammy's voice speak to me.

She said, "Why are you all dressed up like that?"

"Why are you all dressed up like that?" Mammy was sitting up in bed, eating black grapes. Bill Myers sat beside the bed. He was in uniform, and his police cap was on the bedside cabinet.

"Good lord, Fern, I wouldn't have recognized you," he said. "Would have passed you by in the street."

I was glad to see Mammy was coherent this time, but I had mixed feelings about seeing Bill there. He'd messed up my plans. I'd gone expecting Mammy to mistake me for one of the girls again. One of the girls needing help. I'd thought it might answer a few questions.

But I felt slightly dizzy. I didn't remember the journey into Leicester that afternoon. I recalled leaning my back against an oak in the woods, but then I was there, in ward twelve, with no intervening journey. That is, I must have hitched a ride from someone but I couldn't remember it. Neither did I feel tired, so I couldn't have walked the distance.

"Are you all right, Fern?" Bill was saying. "You look a bit queer."

"I'm all right."

"Are you looking after yourself?" Mammy said. "Are you eating properly?"

Bill surrendered the bedside chair to me. He picked up his cap. He said he'd got some business to sort out at the police station in Charles Street, but that he'd come back and give me a ride home.

"You look thinner," Mammy said. "Here, have a grape."

"Why are you all dressed up like that?" It was also what Judith said when I knocked on her door that evening. At first I thought she wasn't going to let me inside. She took a long time to answer the door, and I couldn't hear the sound of her distracting vacuuming.

As I looked over her shoulder I could see why. Chas was relaxing on her couch, watching TV. He had his boots off and was picking at his toenails with a penknife. "I can come back another time."

"No, come in."

I went inside and Chas looked up. He winked at me and went back to picking at his toenails. Judith chased me through to the kitchen, where I told her about my plans, my calculations, the dates and the rest of it. "Good for you," she said.

I could see she was uncomfortable with my being there. I said, "We'll talk about it another time. He was round at my place earlier."

"Was he?" she said, too lightly.

"He made a pass."

She turned away and filled a kettle from her tap. "You going to have some tea?"

"There's something not right about him. I don't think he's a good man."

"Why? Because he made a pass at you?"

"No, not that."

"Who wants good men?" Judith said. "Good men are dull."

I should have gone then. I wanted to go. But I stayed and drank tea with the two of them. I sat in the living room while the TV was running. I thought if I stayed long enough, I might catch an episode of *Outer Limits*. Judith and I chatted, but somehow without real engagement. Chas spoke barely a word to us. I knew he was listening to everything I said. Apart from the moment when I'd come in the door, he never once made eye contact with me. But I knew he was watching me, too. Watching me. Constantly.

I got up suddenly and put my coat on without a word. I opened the door onto the street. "See you," I said, and I closed the door on their dumbfounded faces.

When I knocked on the door of William's cottage, he answered in his socks. He didn't have much of a greeting for me, just thrust out his bottom lip. "Thought you'd have been here before now," he said. "Mammy send you, did she?"

He wore a scarf even though he was indoors. Unbelievably, he returned to a game of patience, as if not five minutes had passed since I last saw him. His cottage had a downcast air. The place badly needed a dusting. "Would you like me to come do a bit of cleaning now and again, William?"

Without looking up from his cards, he showed me his bottom lip again. "Everybody wants to do me a bit o' cleaning. That Judith wants to bring her bloody vacuum cleaner. What is it with you girls?"

"Well, I don't want to, really. Mammy mentioned I might. She was mithering about you, and I was just offering."

"Well don't."

I pulled a chair from under the table and sat down. "I'm ready to *Ask*."

"I know."

"You know?"

"Yes, I know. And I don't think you should."

"Why say that?"

He stopped turning cards and looked directly at me. "Cos you ain't full-on."

"Not full-on? What does that mean?"

"It means you don't believe it. You know you don't, and there's no need to argue. You think it's tripe. That's fair enough. Nobody will bother to persuade you. Not even Mammy."

"Not all of it!" I protested. "I don't disbelieve all of it!"

"But it adds up to the fact as you ain't strong enough, and he tapped the side of his head, "up here." He went back to turning his cards.

"I'm going ahead," I insisted.

"I know that, too. So you will. Agin my advice."

"Any other advice for me?"

"Empty your mind. Don't force it. Wait like a bloody midwife, ha! That's it."

"But how should I know what to ask?"

William let a little gasp of air shoot from between his teeth. *"What to ask,"* he muttered, but remained focused on his cards. I waited a while, but he never did answer my question. I could see nothing worthwhile coming from the old man, so I got up to leave. "How will I know when I see my mine?" I said, almost as a parting shot.

"You'll know. I can see it already. Anyone can."

"Oh?" I said.

He dropped a card and pushed out his rubbery, moist bottom lip. Then he gazed at me with rheumy eyes. Painfully slowly, he lifted his bunched fists either side of his head, extending his forefingers upright, like they were two long ears. He made his fingers move minimally, and the skin under my collar flushed.

His hands dropped to the table and he went back to his cards. I let myself out.

I went home and made the cake. Emily Protheroe's wedding cake. It wore me out pouring all that love into the mix, baking in so much goodwill. I worked well into the night, and it exhausted me. But I made a fine job of it. I whispered into that cake. Only I know how much love went into it. Only me. In the morning I sent a lad with a message, and Emily and her mother came and collected the cake, and they were thrilled with it. They paid me well.

Because I made the cake.

twenty-two

In the afternoon Chas's van lurched to a halt outside the gate, and both he and Judith got out. Judith must have come straight from school because she was wearing her teaching clothes. She hardly seemed the same person in her pencil-skirt and with her hair piled in a bun. Chas carried a bloodied dead rabbit by the ears. He'd obviously spent the morning poaching. They came up the path, and he handed me his pretty peace offering.

"You might have skinned it for me," I said.

"Gratitude! Anyway you'll do it in one-tenth of the time I could."

It was true. I could skin a rabbit. I let them in and hung the rabbit in the back porch while the kettle boiled. When I returned they had a plan for me. They'd been putting their heads together about my future.

"Remember that odd chap you told me about?"

"What odd chap?"

"The one who came from Cambridge. The university bird. I was telling Chas what he wanted. And it turns out Chas knows the man."

I looked hard at Judith. Telling him what Bennett had wanted from us was tantamount to saying what we know and what we do. And I remember Mammy saying to me *the bed knows no secrets.*

"I don't actually know him," Chas said. "I know *of* him."

"Chas was at Cambridge," Judith said. "And he knows why Bennett was here."

"He wanted to make a few quid out of you," Chas put in. "Those Gardener and Murray books have really taken off, especially since the pair died. He wants to cash in."

Chas went on. He told me there was a fresh wave of interest. He told me that I didn't read the Sunday scandal sheets, but that *he* did, and that they would eat anything you gave them. In fact he said he knew he could make easy money just by getting a photographer and a journalist down and putting on a hippie show up at the farm. When I asked what sort of a show, he shrugged and said ten people dancing round a fire naked would do it. He knew it was all rubbish, he said. But it was money going free.

"You're mad," I said, "if you think I would do anything like that."

Judith tried to fend off trouble. "Fern! That's not the idea! We're not talking about dancing round a fire. We're talking about a book."

"A book?"

"Yes, a book. With pages, and words printed on the pages. You know what a book is, don't you?"

I admitted I did know what a book is. Judith talked at length. Together Chas and she had hatched an idea to solve some of my financial problems. Her idea was for me to write the book, and for her to help me, and for Chas to get it published. They didn't want anything from it, she said. Not a bean. Chas wasn't into money she said, and she'd have the pleasure of helping a friend in a spot. It wouldn't solve my immediate problems with the rent, she admitted, but it would help in the long run. And it would be so easy to write. Child's play, she said. Child's play.

"We've talked about this before," I said suspiciously. "And we concluded it was a bad thing."

"No," Chas dived in, "that's not the point. It's not as if you're actually going to give away any secrets."

"What secrets?" I said rather sharply. "What secrets do you think I have?"

"Give him a chance!" Judith said. "Listen to him!"

"The point is you don't give *anything* away. You just give them what they want. A few herbal remedies to make it sound authentic, and Bob's your uncle."

"You're suggesting I make it up?"

"In a manner of speaking. Look, Fern, if I *were* to dance around a fire, and I got paid for it by some bloke who then deliberately misrepresents it in his poxy newspaper, and his readers shell out for the paper knowing perfectly well that what those papers do is misrepresent everything, who is to blame? The wilfully gullible reader? Or the cynical newspaper? Or me, for dancing for money?"

I still thought it was a terrible idea, and I said so. I also reminded Judith that Mammy had strong views on such things.

Judith weighed in with, "You're missing the point. You wouldn't even have to fake it. You could offer incomplete recipes. Keep a portion back for Mammy, so to speak."

Then she must have read some hatred in my eye, because her manner suddenly hardened. "We're offering to help you here. I don't know why we're trying to persuade you. If you don't want our help, then you can stew in it." She got up and made to go.

Chas got up, too. "Well, kiddies, let's not have a fall-out."

But Judith was on her way. "Think on it, Fern. What else have you got going for you?"

I watched her march down the path, puffed with anger and pride. Her face was flushed, and her eyes were like hard glass buttons of spite. Chas followed behind her. The spring on the gate snapped back at Chas's legs. He stopped and looked back at the gate, as if he were contemplating some small revenge, as if it were a live thing that had wanted to hurt him.

"Judith!" I shouted. I ignored Chas and ran to the privet hedge at the border of the garden. "Judith, it's Friday! Friday!"

I know she heard me, but she made no answer as she climbed into the van. Chas got in and started the engine. Judith never even glanced at me through the window as they drove away.

I had three days in which to think about it and I had to clear my mind of all other things. I needed to think about what I was eating and what I was drinking and to prepare all the ingredients. I had to make sure I got enough rest, but I also had to make sure that my mind didn't go to sleep.

When Mammy was on her feet, and when we were gardening or walking or gathering or washing, she would creep up behind me and whisper near my ear. "Hark!" she would go. Or she would say "List!"

meaning I should listen. It wasn't that Mammy was telling me to listen to something in the fields or in the woods or in the streets: she was telling me to listen to myself.

"Listen to what a mean old girl you are," she would say, but with a chuckle. She wasn't saying that I was mean in particular; she meant herself, myself, everybody. Mammy said that in our everyday work, in our everyday thoughts we fall asleep, we lose awareness, we miss what is going on. And when we sleep on our feet like this, she said, we fall back on a grumbling and discontented voice in ourselves, on our lower instincts. And if only we could wake up and listen, then a dirty film of lazy thinking might be scrubbed away, and everything would look bright and polished, and we might be thankful.

And I missed that. Mammy speaking in my ear that way, at irregular intervals. Once or twice Judith and I had done it for each other, but it lacked the authority somehow. Mammy had a better instinct for knowing when you needed the imp of lazy thinking to be knocked off your shoulder.

I had a wind up alarm clock I used to set at varied times, to lift me; but if you set the clock, then you know the clock, don't you? Yet it was all I had. And if I was going to *Ask*, then I had to have some practice to make sure I didn't sleep or doze the whole way through.

If I only had Mammy to say "Hark!"

I had a shock when I arrived at ward twelve that day. I saw Venables, the Norfolk Eel, the vile estate manager, leaning over Mammy's bed and speaking in her ear. It turned my stomach. Meanwhile the curtains were drawn around the next bed, and nurses were wheeling out its recent occupant with a sheet over her face. I raced up the ward to confront Venables. "What's going on?"

He straightened his back. His face flushed, and he seemed startled. "Hello," he said.

"What are you doing?"

"A courtesy call. Simply to see how Mammy is progressing. I brought some flowers."

I saw at the foot of the bed a bouquet of spring mix still in their wrapping from the florist. I looked at Mammy. She seemed frightened and confused. "What have you been saying to her?"

"Calm down now. I haven't been saying anything. I've only just got here."

"Well you can just get out, can't you?"

Venables held his hands up in a gesture of placation. Then he turned to Mammy, and said, "I hope you get well quickly Mammy. Enjoy the flowers." With that he walked out of the ward.

One of the nurses had come by to see what the fuss was about. She picked up the flowers from the bed and suggested she put them in water. I told her no, that there were things that could be sprinkled on the flower heads, and that we didn't want them anywhere near Mammy. She looked at me very strangely, but fortunately she took them away.

"Mammy, I won't be in to see you for three days."

"Untie my feet, Fern," Mammy said. "Untie them."

That bastard had got her agitated. I lifted the sheets at the foot of the bed and made as if to loosen straps. "There. You're free. Mammy, did you hear me? I said I won't be in for three days."

"Tell that woman in the next bed to stop making faces at me."

I looked at the bed, emptied of its corpse not more than five minutes ago. There was a gap in the curtains, and I closed it. "There. That's stopped her game."

"She's been making faces at me all night."

"Well she can't now, can she?"

"Have you got everything you need, Fern?" Mammy said. "Because if not, you only have to ask."

"I know, Mammy, I know." I had an uncomfortable sensation that one of the other women on the ward was now making faces at *me*, and behind my back. I turned around. It was one of the painted old women across the ward, tilting her hand to her mouth, making a drinking motion and nodding at me suggestively.

So distracted was I by it all I failed to pay proper attention at my evening class. It wasn't that I thought MMM was wrong in her views—as I sometimes did—it was the hideous language she used to describe the ordinary.

Something about her voice chewed at the air like blunt episiotomy scissors. "The lie of the fetus describes how its long axis is placed in relation to the long axis of the uterus. Usually this lie is longitudinal, but it may be transverse or oblique. Normal presentation is vertex, and its opposite is breech."

If there was such a problem, Mammy would say, "Baby is upside down." Or, "Baby is lying across."

I stared very hard at these words on my notepad, and I couldn't see any extra value in them. Any at all. Vertex presentation? We say: headfirst. I counted up the syllables. That's three times as long to say the very same thing. Why had I come to college to learn words that added no more than a lot of extra noise to the sum of my knowledge? I had to stop myself thinking about it because it made me angry. All because of the ticket. The damned ticket. Mammy never had her ticket because she said *"headfirst."* Anybody who said "vertex pres-entation" to Bunch Cormell would get a split lip, and quite right, too. But I knew that if I was going to get the ticket, I was going to have to speak in this phoney three-times tongue.

I wondered in how many schools and colleges and universities and research centers and educational institutions up and down the coun-try this fraudulent language passed for learning. How many permits and diplomas, warrants and certificates, licenses and degrees it could earn you. How many *tickets* you could get just by pretending to be other, to speak *other* as if you had a hot potato in your mouth.

Then MMM promised to tell us about something called external version as a treatment when the baby is breech. I was staggered when all it meant was trying to massage the baby into the proper position. I'd seen Mammy do it (but she never liked to because it always hurt the mother, and it didn't always work). MMM told us that only a qualified doctor should attempt this, and I thought why? Why, when a midwife has touched more babies through a hard belly than doctors have felt their own arses? The only thing I've seen doctors massage is the clip on their bags when they want to prescribe sugared water to get you out of their way. It's because of the damned ticket.

"Miss Cullen! You don't seem with us again!"

Mrs. Marlene Mitchell had crept up behind me in her soft-soled shoes. I don't know how she did it, but it gave me the creeps. "I'm sorry, Mrs. Mitchell, I was thinking on what you'd said."

She put her mouth close to my ear and spoke in an undertone. "There's some anomaly with your registration documents. You must sort it out with the administration."

After class I went to the offices, but they were closed. I would have to come early the following week to find out the nature of the problem. Outside, Biddy saw me looking apprehensive.

"What's up then, Fern? You look like someone pinched a pound out of your back pocket." She had a packet of Black Cat Craven A and was withdrawing a cigarette. "Want a smoke?"

I rarely smoke, but that time I took a cigarette from her. We were near the building's front door, Biddy leaning against her bike, enjoying the evening air. After we had puffed away a bit the silence became uncomfortable. Wanting to make conversation, I said, "They're docking, aren't they? Tonight."

"Who are?" said Biddy.

"Astronauts. Up there."

"Are they?"

"Oh yes. Tonight. Never been done before. Very dangerous for them."

"Is it?"

Biddy looked perplexed. I'd heard on the radio that the crew of Gemini 8 were going to attempt to dock with an orbiting Agena rocket. Biddy's nostrils twitched once or twice while I explained to her the technical difficulties of the maneuver. She squinted at me strangely before taking a thoughtful drag on her cigarette. I was amazed she didn't seem to know anything about it. All that activity going on in space, and down here it seemed like most people didn't give a gnat's knackers. As Mammy would say.

MMM came out of the building, hem of her coat flapping. She looked down her nose at our cigarettes before skipping off to catch her bus.

"Bloody hell," Biddy went. "She'll tell us not to smoke around pregnant women next."

"All her big words!" I said.

"What that woman needs is—well I shouldn't say it—what she needs is a good seeing to."

"Seeing to?"

"Yes, a bloody good seeing to. A good shagging."

I tried not to look shocked, but Biddy saw that I was. She dropped her cigarette butt on the pavement and ground it out with her toe.

"Mind you, so do I!" she laughed. "We all do, don't we, m'duck?" Then she swung her heavy buttocks onto the stiff saddle of her bicycle and pedaled off into the night.

twenty-three

When I listened to my head things made no sense. Yet my heart told me a different tale. And even if part of me thought that *Asking* in this way could not possibly solve my problems, I felt a duty to Mammy to go through with it and thereafter let the pump run dry before moving on with my life.

It had been too long in me to ignore. The notion had been planted in my life on my seventh birthday and watered at the root on an almost daily basis. So why did I doubt? I wondered how many church-going Christian girls proceed doubting into their confirmation. Or do they surrender everything to the inducement of the pretty white dress and the snare of the lace gloves? I suppose they have the excuse of powerlessness, or of youthful compliance. But I had to either be free of Mammy or bound by her ways once and for all. I *had* to *Ask*.

The next two days comprised forty-eight hours of intense preparation, starting with the baths. I hauled water from the pump and heated it on the hob to fill the zinc tub. Dawn, noon and dusk of each preparation day. Of the nine ingredients required for the bath infusion I was a little short of sandalwood, but now I was committed I couldn't go out and get more, so I made it spin out with frankincense, which would have turned Mammy's nose up, but needs must. The care required to discard the water was a real chore. I couldn't drag the bath into the garden for fear of slopping some of the water, so it had to be taken out the same way as it was brought in, a bucket at a time, and poured into a hole in the ground. After each bath I burned the cloths or towels on which I dried myself.

I hadn't heard any more from Judith. I trusted she would come to shield me on the Friday, but I had no way of knowing if she would turn up. Now that I had begun the preparations I couldn't go out to visit her, and neither could I—for fear of contamination—send a message with anyone else.

Disaster almost struck on the Thursday morning, when I heard a rapping on the door. I was upstairs at the time and glanced out of the window. It was Arthur McCann, in his estate gear. I don't know what he wanted. I hid myself, lying on the floor as he knocked again. So persistent was he I thought he'd never go away. He tapped a third time on the window. Thankfully, he didn't try the door because he would have found it unlocked. I never had the habit of locking the door. But after he'd gone I went downstairs and turned the key in both front door and back, as again I couldn't risk contamination with any person at this stage.

During this time I drank only water and ate nothing but thin soup.

I was supercareful with the mushrooms and the catnip and the hellebore. I knew the dangers. Scrape the white warts off the glorious red mushroom? There's more to it than that. The month in which it is collected and dried means everything. Its habitat, likewise. Count the white spots, Mammy had said, and take care. Examine the collars on the stalks, and discard if swollen. See this one is not red but orange, watch out. Inspect the gills, and be cautious. Dry slowly, slowly. All those years I'd watched Mammy like a hawk, and I was glad I had. Fly. It can drive a person mad. I know it can.

That was Mammy's name for it: fly. I'd come to think of it as the ticket.

At dusk on Thursday I drew the final bath, but not before lighting a fire in the hearth. I'd swept out all the old ash and made sure that I burned no other wood than oak and certainly not coal. While it was blazing I boiled my pans for the bath. I steeped my sachet in the warm water: it contained equal parts basil, thyme, vervain, valerian, mint, rosemary, fennel, lavender and hyssop. After squeezing the sachet I sprinkled into the bath a handful of soap. Then I got in, and with the fire crackling around the oak logs I was able to let myself go into the flames.

I came to when I felt the water cooling around me. Then I got out, and I shaved my head plus all of my body hair and trimmed my fingernails and toenails. After that I had to empty the bathwater in the garden. I also made a small bonfire of all my hair and nail clippings and the towel I'd used to dry myself. I thought to burn Mammy's hair and nail clippings I'd brought back from the hospital, but some instinct made me leave them hidden in their jar on the shelf. Then I went to bed in the luxury of clean sheets.

I started to get pins and needles in my fingers and thumbs, a sensation that made sleep even more difficult, and yet I knew that above everything I would need a good night's sleep to be rested for the trials of the day. But every time I closed my eyes in the dark I had the most terrifying thoughts, and if I did manage to drift off to sleep, I would jolt awake with thoughts of William shouting in my ear. The jitters had me. With sleep eluding me I got up and checked and rechecked the dates, and I reaffirmed the positions of the moon. I knew I hadn't made a mistake, but I needed to occupy my mind to see off the terrors.

Finally, I did sleep, but I dreamed of a pair of ancient hands folding a black piece of paper until it seemed too impossibly small to fold any further, but the hands folded it again, and still again, and yet again, and each further impossible fold seemed horrifying to me, and then I woke into the gray light of predawn. I dressed hurriedly. I went downstairs and I made the infusion of tea and I gulped it down. The fire was still in from the night before, so I brought it back to life and banked it up with oak logs.

I stepped outside to go to the outhouse. I still had the pins and needles sensation in my fingers and thumbs, and my shaved head felt chilled in the morning air. As I hurried over to the outhouse first a robin hopped across my path, which was a good sign, then a toad, which was bad. The two together meant an unresolved situation, and I almost wanted to turn back. Even at that stage I could have put my fingers down my throat and retched. I would have been happier if I'd seen only my friend the robin. But I watched the toad hop onto the garden and squat somewhere in the rhubarb patch.

When I returned to the house I had to make a decision about the door, because I didn't know whether to expect Judith. I now thought she was about to let me down, though the implications for her had she done so would have been equally dire. I needed to keep the door locked, but if she were to arrive after it all started, then how would she get in? Finally, I left a sheet of newspaper outside, closed the door and turned the key, leaving it in the lock. I knew she'd figure it out. But for good measure I opened a side window a crack.

The tingling sensation in my fingers was beginning to spread to my hands and feet. I also felt my lips becoming numb. I calculated I had about ten minutes before I would have to sit in my chair and be content. I kept trying to lick my lips. I drank some water. I repositioned the chair so that it directly faced the door and front window, but I made sure that it fell under the shadow from the crossbeam and hanging herbs, so as to make it difficult for anyone looking in to see me. Remembering to fill a pint glass with water, I placed it on the floor by my chair. Finally, my muscles started to turn kind of slushy, so I sank back into the chair and let my arms fall to the side.

I could feel blisters of sweat the size of half-crowns appearing on my brow and running into my eyes, but my arms felt too heavy to lift to my face. My bowels churned. My tongue furred and seemed to swell inside my mouth. Reaching for the glass to take a sip of water seemed a superhuman effort and took every ounce of my strength, making the perspiration run faster. My heart thudded in my chest. I began to feel terribly frightened. Suppose I had made some kind of error after all?

I sat immobile for a while. I might have fainted clean away, I don't know. Then Judith came knocking.

She hammered on the door. Then I saw her face appear at the window, hand held angled above her eyes so she could peer into the gloom of my cottage. Perhaps I was too clever in concealing my chair, because she appeared not to see me. There was nothing I could do to attract her attention. My body felt like an anvil at the bottom of a pond. It was as much as I could do to keep open my eyelids. I made a vain attempt to move my hand, to make a motion, to signal her in some way, but I barely managed to twitch a finger.

She went away, and after a few moments I heard her shuffling about at the rear of the house. I heard her try the handle of the back door, but it remained locked from the time Arthur McCann had appeared. Then she came to the front of the house again, and peering in once more this time seemed to make out my lifeless shape in the chair.

"Fern!" she called, rapping hard on the window. "Come to the door!"

But of course I couldn't answer. My teeth tingled in my mouth when I tried to make a noise. After a while she went away, and the house fell silent.

Did I doze? I know that a log shifted in the fire and that brought me back to awareness. Some of the feeling had come back to my body, and though I had to make a supreme effort to do so, I managed at last to stand and shuffle about. I needed to drink some water but my judgment was skewed and as I reached for the glass my hand seemed to pass through it. I waved at the glass twice before becoming distracted by something outside.

I looked out of the window and saw three blackbirds perched on the washing line. They were chittering to each other, switching places on the line. Their eyes seemed mercurial and bright and their sleek feathers had a luster more blue than black and their orange beaks were more prominent than was normal. It occurred to me that these were what Mammy would call lookouts. I knew it was time for me to go outside, so I shuffled into my coat and made to leave.

But the tingling hadn't gone from my fingers, and, ridiculously, I couldn't find the strength required to turn the old iron key in the lock. I could grasp the key, but my fingers had no leverage. It simply wouldn't turn. So in the end it just seemed easier to rise above the kitchen sink and let myself out through the very window I'd left open earlier. Though when I did so the three birds on the line flew off instantly, so perhaps they were not lookouts at all. Perhaps they were just three birds on a line.

But outside it was the most splendid day in March! It was so bright that at first I had to shield my eyes. The sun was strong, but everything was bathed in cold, metallic light, shining like chrome but without diminishing the color spectrum. The water pump in the garden seemed huge, as did a single shimmering bead of water hanging from its lip

I lost a few moments, then I was walking along the street by the well. I paused to look at the crystal water trickling over the amber stones and into the clear well. Then I lost a few moments again and found myself standing against a five-bar gate before the track leading to the woods. Even from there I could smell the incipient spring blossom, cloying and thick. The earth, too, seemed to be opening up its scents. Grass and leaf mold and cow parsley and cuckoo spit on the tall weeds; brick dust where hard-core rubble had been dumped on the track to hold back the mud; lichen growing luminous green in the cracks weathered into the gray wood of the gate itself; living rust on the hinge. It was endless. I stood against the five-bar gate inhaling the compendium of odors, trying to separate and identify them. Far off amongst the trees I heard the cuckoo calling.

This sensual flooding must have seduced me into a loss of time and place because I confused several moments again and I came to my senses when the cuckoo's calling turned into a voice followed by a rattling sound, and I was back in my chair in the cottage. I must have returned there without realizing it. I looked at the fire. The logs had burned down a little. The rattling at the door caused me to look up, and I saw the key vibrating in the lock. Judith was at the door again, trying to push the key through from the outside. She'd found the newspaper and had slid it under the door to catch the key when it fell.

My walk had exhausted me, because I was paralyzed all over again. At last the key tumbled from the lock, but rather than fall clean it stopped for a moment in midair, then fell and stopped again. At last I heard the key hit the newspaper. Then the sheet of newspaper was pulled away with the key on it, and in a moment Judith had let herself in.

I was most surprised when Chas followed. "What has she done to her hair?" he blurted.

"It's nothing." Judith approached me, placed the palm of her hand on my forehead and looked into my eyes. Then smoothed at my blouse. "Blink twice if you feel all right."

I blinked twice.

"But she had such beautiful hair!" Chas protested, staring at me.

"I should have been here earlier," Judith said. She lifted the glass of water to my lips, and I drank. "I feel bad about it."

"Is she okay?" Chas wanted to know.

"I think so. Her lips look a bit dry, that's all."

Chas came and knelt in front of me, peering deep into my eyes. "Christ, her pupils are dilated. Just look at that!"

"She can hear everything you say," Judith said. "She's not like one of your potheads with a brain like mashed turnip. She's sharp enough."

"She don't look it."

I wanted to tell Chas to get out of my face. He was breathing on me. I was annoyed with Judith for bringing him here. All I could manage was a flicker.

"She blinked," he said.

"That's probably her way of saying piss off," said Judith.

Thank you, Judith. He looked doubtful, rubbed his jaw, then got up. "Is there anything to eat in here?"

"Don't touch anything. Brew some tea if you want to be useful."

Judith gave me another sip of water. While Chas was out filling the kettle she pressed her ear to my chest to listen to my heart. She seemed satisfied it wasn't beating too fast.

When he came back in I noticed he had a good poke about the place, though I don't know what he was looking for. More than once Judith told him to leave things alone. Even though I could only direct my gaze straight ahead, I could sense him behind me, eyeing every mousehole and nook. It made me uneasy.

Judith soaked a flannel and came over to mop my brow and my neck, and it wasn't until she did so that I realized how hot I was. She also wiped my chin—I think I must have been drooling. Then as they made tea I saw Judith mouth some words at him—obviously not meaning for me to hear. He grabbed her hair and kissed her full on the lips. She pretended to push him off. They were like playful kittens.

He went upstairs, and I could hear the floorboards creaking over my head as he moved around up there. Judith shouted for him to come back down. She told him to stop being so damned nosy, but eventually she followed him up there, and after a while it all fell quiet.

I've had enough of this, I thought. The rest had given me back my strength and I found I could rise from my chair and I went out again. At least I didn't have to leave by the window this time, since they'd left the door open. I'll vanish from the garden before they'll even miss me, I thought. Leave them to stew in it, I thought; I'd much rather be on my own.

And I came to my senses again still leaning against that five-bar gate, watching tiny red spider mites crawling in the lichen green splits in the chrome gray wood. And a voice that was my own but that sounded like Mammy in tone said *move girl, you should move if you're not going to get stuck here.* Because that was the problem. Getting stuck.

Mammy had said that was always the problem when *Asking*, getting stuck. You could gaze at a thing, like a stream of water or a mite crawling in a split in a gate-post, and it would carry off your soul and you were left, hollow, empty, not even present. And Mammy would say it's not just *Asking* that does this: it's life, and you can also get stuck and go to sleep in a corner of your life and then wake up seven or seventy years later and it was all gone. She said how you could blink during one of your school days and you blinked again and your own children were at school and you'd somehow got stuck and how we should never allow that to happen because we were too disposed to letting a life go by unheeded. And now, on this day, and under these lights, I knew exactly what she meant, and I said move girl, you've got to move.

And move I did, rediscovering my ability to set one foot in front of another, drifting through the marvelous splintering chromium light down the track running along the edge of the woods. But in that time

I noticed that something was happening to that chromium light: it was becoming tinged with violet and it was stretching. It had changed from soft, shining metal to another flimsier substance, like cobweb as seen on a misty morning, and it was falling off the trees and the bushes and the tall grasses as I passed through it and for a moment I had to laugh at my own foolishness because I realized this wasn't a substance or a color at all, it was merely the dawn, and it was passing, indeed had almost passed.

How foolish of me to have mistaken the dawn for a color. When it was actually a substance.

But with that realization came anxiety, because I also understood that I needed to find my territory, my position for the day, and quickly before anyone else should happen along. Then I saw the three blackbirds again on a branch up ahead and I felt a surge of joy because I was convinced they were looking out for me and I wondered if they were perhaps others from among the few. I stopped to look at them and leaned my hand against a tree to recover my breath. Even though I was not exerting myself, my breath came short in the excitement and anxiety of the moment. When I took my hand away from the trunk of the tree I saw that my fingers had been stained with the green dust that adhered to the bark.

I covered my hands in it until none of my lily white skin was exposed, then I proceeded to rub it into my face. It smoothed in like charcoal, but bright green, the color of the spring hedgerow, and there, at the corner sleeve of the woods I found my spot, in the tiniest break in a tangled hedgerow of blackthorn, dogwood and holly.

It was a lovely thick hedgerow, known as a midland bullock hedge and so-called because it was strong enough to contain a charging bull. And here was that tiny gap inviting me in, with a soft floor like a welcoming set or form, and I got in and the springy blackthorn and dogwood closed behind me with a whisper and I knew I might sit there all day in that thick hedge and not be seen. I prided myself that I'd found the perfect spot. Anyone happening by the path would have their eyeline cast ahead of him or her by the turn in the hedge and even if they looked dead on at me they might never see me. I was warm. I was comfortable. I was safe. More important, I was ready for what was coming. I closed my eyes and waited.

Though I must have got stuck once more. Because when I opened my eyes again I was back in the cottage. The sound of Judith and Chas descending the stairs had made me open my eyes. I panicked, because it meant that I'd imagined myself going out, that I hadn't been out at all, that I hadn't found my territory and that I hadn't settled in my perfect spot in the hedgerow.

But then Chas appeared first, looked at me, and said, "She's back."

"Thank goodness for that," Judith said. "Where have you been?"

Though I couldn't answer, because my tongue was still furred and paralyzed in my head, and my teeth seemed too big for my mouth. Yet I was relieved because their words showed that I had indeed been out and come back again. For a terrible moment I thought I'd somehow dreamed it.

Chas approached me and rolled back my eyelid. "You sure you know what's going on here, Jude?"

"She's fine."

"She looks green. What if she pukes?"

"Stop fidgeting. If you won't settle, you're going to have to go."

"You're right, I should go," Chas said. "I'm going back to the farm. Maybe take the dogs out or something. Will I see you later?"

"Possibly. Depends how this goes. Come on, I'll walk you to the gate."

They went out and left the door open behind them. They were a long time parting, and while they were distracted I let myself out again.

But no sooner was I outside than I was back in my soft den in the hedgerow, and I was startled awake by the sound of voices approaching. I recognized a voice amongst them. It was that of Bunch Cormell, walking the path with, all wrapped up, the very baby I had recently delivered for her. She was looking better than when I saw her last, and the whole family was out with her, perhaps on their way to Market Harborough or just the next village. They had a dog, too, that I feared as it bounded on ahead. But the dog, though it sniffed near the hedge, chose to ignore me. The farrier and his wife were talking about money problems while the children argued about the sharing out of Bluebird toffees. A spat broke out amongst the children, and the youngest boy, Malcolm, sulked and dragged his feet.

I watched them pass by me, so close I could almost have reached out a hand from the hedge and touched them. But I was deathly still, and they had no suspicion of my presence. Or wouldn't have had if young Malcolm hadn't loitered behind. He had a huge stick and chose that moment to toss it into the hedge where it landed close by. He stepped over the small ditch to retrieve his stick, and our eyes met.

He froze, as if he knew I could see into his seven-year-old heart, which at that moment I could; and all I could see there was terror.

"Malcolm, get and catch up with us and stop dawdlin'!" shouted the farrier.

But he couldn't move. He was pinned. And the only way I could release him was by closing my eyes. I waited. And I waited more. There was a sudden flutter, like a bird departing from a twig. And when I opened my eyes again he was gone, and the Cormells—all of them—were far off.

Whether he spoke about it to them or not I don't know. If he did, I trusted that they would think he was being fanciful because still sulking. Though I was angry with myself because the rule is that you should keep your eyes closed when anyone draws near. That's the rule, and that's why it's there.

But after they had gone everything became quiet, and I waited in silence for above an hour. During that time the sun rose higher in the sky and someone else came along—a local farmer walking by with an unsteady gait that threw his boots out wide—chuntering and snuffling to himself. This time I closed my eyes, and he passed by, and all became quiet again.

At the stroke of noon something happened. The stillness of the place became a soundlessness, and the sun locked into position in the sky, almost with a dull clonk like some kind of mechanism failing. It became like a painted sun on a canvas. It had hue and light, but it had no texture.

Then I heard them. Faintly at first. One or two, or three familiar calls of lapwings or peewits as Mammy called them. But they were so far away, almost in another world, or as deep as memory goes. Peeeee-wit! Perhaps more of a thought than a sound. Mammy would say listen, they are saying *Bewitched!* But then the calls were gone, and I heard another sound, approaching fast.

It was a feathering of the air. A rumor from the skies. A rustling, a shaking free, then suddenly, as if pouring from a tiny hole in the blue sky, was a gigantic flock of lapwings, hundreds and hundreds of them, diving in formation, twisting in the air like a long ribbon of black speckles and I could feel the fanning of their wings as they swooped over the hedge and my skin was popping, flushing and popping, and for a moment I thought: is this it? Is it the lapwing? And then I remembered that Judith had told me that first come the heralds, the harbingers, to mark the way.

They played the air currents. The tumult of lapwings winged through the blue sky, twisting and spinning the long, unwinding ribbon of themselves, spiraling like the tail of a kite, dipping and rising again, and it was so beautiful and overwhelming I wanted to cry. A few of the birds would get flung out of the ribbon trail only to settle in the field, just a few feet away from my place in the hedge, then they would fly up again, letting the air currents suck them back into the main formation.

On they went, testing the air streams, higher and higher, dipping and circling back toward me, trying for new formations until I realized they were looking for something. The formation changed, twisted, fattened and thinned. It was as if they were trying out new forms until suddenly I understood. It made me gasp.

My senses were crossing over. The tumult of the birds was a kind of whisper in my ear that somehow folded itself into twisted shapes in the air, an alphabet for me to descry. The lapwings, the thousand peewits, were trying to spell out words for me. They were skywriting, but in sound. At first it wasn't an alphabet I could recognize. It was like runes on ancient jewelry or the squiggles on stamps from exotic places, embossed on the air currents and hitting me like Morse code. Then at last the sounds fixed and set, and hung in the air, spelling out a brief message. I blinked up into the sunlit blue. Somehow in the tiny black speckles of the thousand lapwings was fixed a single word, simultaneously stitched into the sky and spoken to me in Mammy's faint voice, and it said: *Listen!*

And in the moment that I heard or read that single word the giant flock of lapwings wheeled and turned and were sucked back through the tiny hole in the sky through which they had first poured, and they were gone. Behind them was only an eerie stillness. And I was aware of the presence beside me.

I'd entertained no real doubts about what mine would be. It had spoken to me that evening at the Cormells'—and had not the far-rier's family been present this day? And had not William told me what mine would be? I never knew what Mammy's was, because she'd never told me. But mine was always going to be this.

The hare was poised next to me in the hedgerow, uncannily as though it had been there all along. It was a very large hare. Perhaps three feet tall to the tip of its ears. With me hunkered down in the hedge like that, it almost put us on a level. It sat erect, ears listening, resting on its powerful back legs, resting, but ready to spring away at the slightest start, quivering with a sense in which the next instant might change everything.

I swallowed, but almost afraid to in case the hare bolted. So far it hadn't even looked at me, but it turned slightly, and I felt a curious tickling inside my head.

Then the hare spoke.

The hare spoke not by moving its mouth, but by fixing its eye on me and whispering inside my brain, no more than an insinuation. The whispering corresponded to an increase in the pressure of the tickling inside my head.

I knew that I was coming unstuck in time because the tickling turned into the sensation of someone running hands across my shaved head, and I opened my eyes to see Judith leaning over me. I don't know when this was in the sequence of things, but Chas had now gone.

Judith, I realized, had a damp flannel cloth and was running it across my head and my neck. She folded the cloth and dabbed under my eye.

"Hope these are good tears, Fern," Judith said.

"These are just the tears," I said, or thought I said. I was surprised that the faculty of speech had come back to me. But when I went to speak again I couldn't manage anything. I could only lick my dry lips. Judith held the glass of water to my lips, and I was able to swallow a few mouthfuls.

I saw Judith glance at her wristwatch before looking at the door. Then she surveyed me thoughtfully, as if trying to make a decision. "I'm going to have to go out," she said. "I have an errand to run."

I tried to make a noise to detain her. I didn't want to be left.

"It's only for a short while. I'm going to lock the door, so you'll be safe."

Judith went out and locked the door behind her. I heard a brick clang as she deposited the key beneath it. I closed my eyes.

The hare told me how the world was made. It was a long story. The hare explained how the cracks between worlds had been fashioned the very first time a hare was chased across the fields by a dog, and it had no option but to escape into another world; and it explained that if it wasn't for the hares who kept these cracks open, no one would be able to cross over. The hare warned me that other animals and birds and men all claimed that their species had made and maintained the cracks, but that the truth was that it was the hares. It reminded me that hares could conceive a second time while already pregnant. This proved the point beyond all doubt, said the hare, because it had happened on the first time that the very first hare had occupied two worlds at once.

As the hare spoke I hadn't noticed it growing in size. Or perhaps I was diminishing. But after a while my clothes were hanging from me and I was little more than a baby girl, perhaps a yearling, perhaps two. I stepped out of my grown-up clothes. I enjoyed being naked. I could stand up and talk after a fashion. I looked at the hare's eye still fixed on me. Now the hare was almost twice my size.

The smell of its animal fur was overwhelming, but not unpleasant. I reached out to stroke the fur, but the hare shifted, inching away, tolerant, but unwilling to be touched. It continued with its tale.

The hare told me that we had moved into the time of Man, and that this was not a good thing, not even for men and women. It complained bitterly of the leverets killed in the blades of combine harvesters. It asked me if I had any idea how many combine harvesters there were in the country, and when I shook my head it specified an exact figure. The corn bleeds, it said pointedly, we bleed. I cried hot tears of guilt and I said I was very sorry, and the hare told me it wasn't my fault.

Then the hare began to tell me why hares chose not to burrow and of the making of the very first form and how hares got their powerful hind legs. At some point the hare's voice became Mammy's, and the hare was repeating all of the things Mammy had told me over the years.

It repeated things I hadn't entirely understood. That Mammy had been kept in that hospital for three long years. That sometimes they tied her arms and legs. The hare repeated all this in Mammy's voice. There were other young women in there, it said in Mammy's voice, for no other offense than for having children out of wedlock. Or for moral depravity, which she said meant being caught for doing what every woman wants to do and what men do with impunity. But Mammy's crime, and the reason she'd been put there, was because she'd threatened to tell.

The hare, in Mammy's voice, told me the list of names. The names of the fathers, and the names of the disowned, and the names of the cuckoos. It was a very long list, and I became confused, and perhaps I dozed or became stuck. Because when I lifted my head I was in hospital with Mammy and she was speaking to me now with urgency. "Too much for you to know, all this," Mammy said. "Oh the leverets, caught in the blades. And these are the names. You know why they put me in here, Fern? Because I threatened to tell. So let me tell *you*.

"Knowing this," Mammy said, "is the only thing that stands between me and them. They hate the fact that I know it. It galls them. But it keeps them afraid of me. It's my ticket, d'you see? But the time has come for me to pass it on to you. It's a burden, and one I've been keeping from you, but now it's a burden of knowledge you have take on. And here are the names."

And I listened, and I listened hard, and it was such a long list, and by the time she'd got to the end of the list Mammy had become the hare again. But then the hare stopped talking abruptly. I saw its huge ears stiffen. I asked why it stopped. Now Mammy's voice had gone and inside my head, the hare said, "Hearken!"

I listened hard. Far away, in another field, I heard the baying of two or more dogs.

Still inside my brain the hare said, "Now it begins."

I felt the prickle of its fear. "What begins?" I said. I felt frightened myself.

"Are you ready? I do so hope you are."

"Ready for what?"

"You must do it now. You have very little time."

"I don't understand!" I complained. My voice cracked. I was crying. "I don't know anything about this!"

"Are you ready to make the change?"

"What change?" I cried.

"Oh! You needed to be prepared. You'll be torn to pieces!"

My breath came short. Terror rippled through my skin, a cold wave on a colder sea. I panicked. I began hyperventilating.

"Breathe slowly!" the hare urged. "You will lose all your strength. Surely you know how to change!"

I heard the dogs again, a little nearer. Three of them, barking clear. The hare flexed its hind legs. It was getting ready to leave.

"No," I wailed. "No one has told me. Please don't leave me here."

"You have to remember."

"How can I remember what I never knew?" I sobbed.

"You're a chanter aren't you?" said the hare. "Everyone can at least say the rhyme."

And though I didn't know any rhyme I heard myself clearing my throat, half-singing, half-croaking the words:

> *I shall go into a hare*
> *With sorrow and sighing and mickle care*
> *I shall go in the devil's name*
> *An' while I come home again . . .*

"Good. Now I will give you something to help you." The hare moved closer. It licked the tears from my eyes. Then it opened its mouth and spat into my mouth. I smelled the grass and the corn on its saliva. Then it stepped back. "Time is running out. If you don't change, I will have to leave you. Now, remember."

I heard the dogs again, and I thought I heard a man's cry, too. I despaired. The warm saliva of the hare made me feel dizzy. I sat back on my haunches, very afraid. My stomach was in riot. In terror and desperation I looked into the black staring pupil of the hare's eye. In the shining polished mirror of its eye I could see myself as a baby girl, but distorted. My knees were drawn up to my chin. My feet seemed enormous. And my skin was bristling and quivering.

I gasped. But I had no time to speak. I head the yammering of the dogs as they broke into the field and raced up the track. The hare leaped from the hedge, and I with it, and we were sprinting across the field and I could keep up. I had speed and grace. But the dogs were big and strong. Two were old greyhounds and one was a whippet cross, and they, too, had speed. And they were gaining.

I heard the brick moved aside and the sound of the key inserted in the lock from the other side of the door, and I thought with some relief that Judith had returned from her errand. But it wasn't Judith who came in. It was Chas. I wanted to say: "Where is she? What are you doing here?" But though my tongue worked in my mouth, I still couldn't speak.

He sat down in the chair opposite me—Mammy's chair—and proceeded to roll himself a cigarette, which he spiked with pot. He lit up, sucked back the smoke and then after he'd exhaled it he said, "Judith got a bit caught up with things so she asked me to come and keep an eye on you. Make sure you were still alive, sort of thing. You are still alive, aren't you?"

I blinked.

"Good. Don't mind me. You trip out. I'll just relax. Keep an eye on you."

I didn't like him being there. I didn't like the smell of him. I didn't like the smell *on* him.

He sat back, smoking, regarding me steadily. At last he got up and came toward me. "You're drooling," he said. "Not very becoming, is it?" He used the ball of his thumb to gently wipe at the corner of my mouth. "There."

Then he did a very odd thing. He examined the small amount of spittle he'd collected from my mouth on his thumb, and he licked it. Kept his eyes on me and licked it thoroughly, like he was drinking it. Then he sat down in his chair again.

"Know what? I think I like you with your hair shaved like that. It's sort of foxy."

I closed my eyes so I wouldn't have to look at him leering at me, and I was back in the field. I opened my eyes again and my vision had fanned out to spectacular effect: perhaps to the 270 degrees one associates with prey animals and I could see, behind left, the dogs kicking up the earth as they sped toward us and, behind right, the cover of the wood. The dogs were yammering behind us now, drool stringing from their open jaws. My instinct was to go to the woods, but the hare ahead of me made a direct line across the fields and so I followed, only inches behind, matching it for strength and speed.

But the dogs were big, and with their greater stride they came upon us fast. Fear drenched my veins, and my muscles turned to useless slush, and for a moment I was ready to surrender: to just stop and be ripped apart. The lead dog came up on the right, snapping, inches from my hindquarters. Glistening saliva streamed from its jaws in a silver ribbon, sparkling in the sun. But then the hare turned at an astonishing ninety degrees, a perfect right-angle turn, and somehow I knew how to go with it.

The dogs couldn't match the turn. They went headlong three or four yards, trying to skid to a turn, crashing into each other until they could swing round and pick up the race again, and by that time we had already gained several yards. And I thought how strong! How agile and beautiful! And though I ran in terror, in dread and anguish, I knew that my nature had given me an advantage. I was nimbler. I was quicker. I could fool them.

But the size of their stride soon had them snapping at my legs again, and we made a second turn. This time the dogs yelped with frustration as they tangled once again. But now we were running toward the dog's owner. I could see he was a poacher, with a poacher's bag hanging over his shoulder, and I knew he carried a knife somewhere and that he wanted to rip my skin from my bones. I could smell him: that hot odor of a man, so unlike anything else that moves on the face of the earth. And then I saw his face, and I knew this man.

I opened my eyes and I was astonished to see Chas's face just an inch away from my own. He blinked. His breath fanned my cheek. Then he leaned in, and he kissed me, so softly, and so sweetly. I felt the kiss course through my body. I shuddered internally. At that moment the only feeling I had was in my mouth, in my tingling lips; lips that seemed to have swollen. I could taste the tobacco and the pot on his breath. Then he broke the kiss and sat back. He took a pull on his cigarette and breathed the smoke back into my mouth, and I don't know why but I wondered then if he had done that to me before.

"The great thing about you, Fern," he said, "is that you don't know what you've got."

And then he leaned over and kissed me a second time.

The man came lumbering toward us. I knew he was no danger. He would never catch us, the way a nimble dog might. But he could do us mischief by blocking our path on one side, and if he worked his dogs as a team, he might try to steer us to give them an advantage.

The dogs were yelping at our heels again. I could smell their breath now, and I could hear their jaws snapping at the air. The hare in front of me made a remarkable move. It surprised me by accelerating directly at the man. I knew only that I should follow. It caught the man off guard. Then when we were within two or three yards of him we made a turn followed by a rapid second turn to zigzag around him. We raced through a gap in the hedgerow and burst clear into the next field.

The man yelled, and the dogs squealed. The dogs muscled through the hedgerow after us, and I was beginning to feel tired though the hare showed no signs of weakening, and I knew it was because I was only pretending to be a hare. Out of one eye I saw the man vaulting a gate and running toward us as his dogs made up the distance.

Chas opened my blouse and my breasts fell forward and he froze and gazed at them for a moment, as if they were somehow dangerous. I felt a tiny bit of strength returning, but I was still desperately weak and hadn't got an ounce of energy with which to resist him. He leaned over and he licked my nipples. My heart hammered. My tongue stuck to the roof of my mouth. He sucked at my breasts and ran his tongue under the curve where my breasts met my rib cage; and then he planted kisses on my belly.

Then he pushed up my skirt and he tore down my knickers, and now I wanted to call out, to stop him, but I could barely move. It was as if huge weights were attached to my arms and legs. He parted my legs and hooked the backs of my knees across the arms of the chair, and I tried to signal frantically with my eyes to get him to stop, not to do this.

I wanted to shout to the hare that I couldn't keep up; wanted to say I'm not a hare, I'm a woman. The dogs were snapping, snapping at my heels, and I was running, running, and my heart was misfiring and my bones were ready to snap with the pain of exertion. The hare looked back, and I knew that it saw my distress and my failure to out-run the dogs. One of the dogs drew almost abreast of me and clamped its jaws around my heel and the pain stabbed through me and I saw only a blood-red sky and I was ready to die and be torn apart. But in that moment the hare in front of me slowed to a halt, quite deliber-ately, and let the other two dogs take it instead of me. The third dog left me and went for it.

Chas unbuckled his belt and lowered his trousers and his erection bobbed clear before he pushed inside me and I know a scream came from my mouth because it was almost the first sound I had made that day. It hurt. He humped at me without grace, the smell of his sweat streaming from him, his face red and ugly and contorted as he ejacu-lated inside me.

He shuddered to a halt and buried his head in my breasts. I leaned forward, and I took the soft part of his ear between my teeth and I bit hard and I didn't let go.

Chas smashed his fist into my eye trying to get away. He kicked wildly and hurt my foot. I bit down on his ear harder, and there was an explosion of his blood in my mouth.

I saw the dogs tear at the hare in a puff of blood that lined the sky. There was a moment of storm in the dry dust of the field. There was so much blood and fur in the air I could taste it. The dogs stripped the flesh of the hare between them. It had surrendered to them so that I could escape.

Exhausted, I ran for cover. I returned to the same spot in the hedgerow where I had waited all day. The grass was still beaten down like a hare's form. I licked the wound on my leg, and let myself go perfectly still. I even managed to still my breathing. I trusted to the camouflage of the hedge and hoped and prayed that the sacrifice of the hare would be enough to keep the dogs away.

twenty-four

I was bathing the wound on my ankle when Judith returned. Chas had gone. I had already managed to clean up the place. There was blood on the kitchen floor. I felt weak, tremulous, but I was relieved to be moving again.

"You've recovered, I see," Judith said when she came in.

"Yes."

"How do you feel?"

"Weak."

"What are you doing?"

"I scratched my ankle."

I still had my back to her as I dried my foot. When I turned she saw the swelling around my eye. "Fern! Whatever happened?"

"I was giddy, and I fell over."

Now she was all concern. "Sit down. You shouldn't even be on your feet. Look at you, you're shaking." She led me back to my chair.

I couldn't contain myself. "You should have been here, Judith!"

"I was only gone for half an hour!"

"You deserted me! You shouldn't have left me alone! I don't want to be alone!"

Judith dropped down to take a look at my injured foot. "That looks messy. What have you put on it? Here, give me that flannel."

She bathed my ankle gently, dabbing slowly at the laceration. Then she studied it closer. "This looks bad." She stopped dabbing. After a moment she looked up at me. "It went wrong, didn't it, Fern?"

"You shouldn't have left me."

"Tell me everything that happened. Please tell me."

I clamped my jaw tight. I compressed my lips.

*   *   *

It hadn't gone right but it hadn't gone completely wrong either. That is, events turned, as is promised to those who *Ask*, but not in any way I might have predicted. My first concern now that it was over was to go and see Mammy, and even though I was in no real shape to make the journey into Leicester, I did exactly that. It had been three days since I'd seen her, and she would have guessed what I'd done.

Even though I still felt groggy after the ravages of the day, I put on my leather jacket and went out. I couldn't face hitching a ride into town so I cut through the woods and waited at the bus stop for the evening service into Leicester. The wound on my foot ached. My eyesight was suffering from a flickering no doubt brought on by my experiences. The light wouldn't settle. There were patches of sky where it ran and spilled from the cloudless blue like quicksilver. The hedgerows, too, popped and quivered with life.

I heard a motorbike approaching so I hid in the hedge in case it was Arthur. As it happened, it wasn't. I thought the dogwood and the blackthorn were writhing and unfurling behind my back as I waited in the hedge. Some of me had been left behind. Or perhaps I'd brought the events of the day with me, and they roiled in my wake.

I was just in time to catch the end of the visiting period. The lights in ward twelve had been switched on. I attracted a few strange glances—I know I looked like a scarecrow or even some kind of demon with my shaved head and my bruised eye, but I couldn't disguise any of it. But when I reached the foot of Mammy's bed I cast around for help.

Mammy's bed was empty. It had been stripped, and the pillow was gone. Her personal possessions had been removed.

I heard footsteps coming up behind me. It was one of the nurses. "Where's Mammy?" I almost shouted. "What have you done with her?"

"You're her daughter, aren't you?" the nurse said. "Come with me."

I followed the nurse to the ward sister's office at the corner of the ward. The ward sister was in there, writing something on a wall chart. The nurse sat me down. "She's in the mortuary," the nurse said.

"Mortuary?" I said. "Why? When? When did this happen?"

"This afternoon."

The ward sister put down her pen. "I'll deal with this," she said. The nurse went out of the office. The sister took hold of my hand. "She was very old and very tired. She let go."

"I should have been here."

"Look," the sister said. "I know you weren't here. But in her confusion she thought you were. She told me as much. Though you'll be glad to know that her friend William was here when she passed away. She wasn't alone. He asked me to tell you that he would take care of everything."

I was shocked to discover that William had been with her in her final moments. I got up and walked out. I couldn't stand to listen to any more of it. I heard the sister calling after me, but I went out and I walked into the gathering twilight and I don't know if I got a lift or if I caught a bus or even if I walked all the way home.

Next evening I had a visit from the parish vicar, the Reverend Miller. When I opened the door the vicar was visibly shocked by my appearance. In fact he took a step back. "Fern!"

"I know I look a fright. What can I do for you?" I didn't want him to come in. I'd slept very badly, and I was still groggy from the depravitions of the previous day.

"I've come to talk about the arrangements."

"Arrangements?"

"William Brewer came to see me last night. I told him I'd come to see you." He blinked at me.

I let him in. He asked how I'd blacked my eye, and I told him I'd fallen over. From the things he said I could tell he thought I'd shaved my head in a fit of grief. Then he sat in the chair and leaned forward, pressing his knees with the palms of his hands, and blurted to me that he'd had a visit from Venables that morning and that Venables had said that it was the wish of Lord Stokes and the estate that Mammy not be buried in the churchyard.

I laughed. Of course I didn't give a damn whether Mammy was

buried in the churchyard, and neither would Mammy. I hadn't thought about it, but I expected the council crematorium to serve just as well. But then the vicar surprised me.

"Of course, I told him to go to hell."

"You what now?"

"I don't like the man, and I don't like the cut of his jib. And I told him that it was up to me to decide, not him and not Lord Stokes. I know Mammy had an aversion for the church, it's no secret. But God receives all into his heart and God loves—"

"The crow as he does the nightingale. Yes." I couldn't help myself.

"Exactly. So I have no objection. There's a place for Mammy, should you want it."

I admit I was astonished by this support from such an unlikely source. "I can't pay you. We've nothing."

"I've thought of that. We've a fund. I'll take care of it. Right now I'm more concerned about you."

"Me?"

"Yes. You're grieving, but you're not letting go. I don't like the thought of you here on your own."

And he actually offered to let me go and live with him and his wife at the vicarage, which he said had a choice of spare rooms. It was hard work persuading him that I was all right on my own. Incredibly hard work. But I couldn't see myself sipping from a mug of steaming cocoa as he stroked a guitar while his wife sang "Kum Ba Yah." Eventually I got him out of the house, thanking him for his generosity.

I was so perturbed by this unexpected alliance that after he'd gone I switched on the record player and played "Green Onions." I left the arm back so it would repeat and I turned it up really loud to block out the enraging chorus of "Kum Ba Yah" circulating in my head.

The day after that I had a letter from the manager of the Nationwide Building Society in Market Harborough. It informed me that my debt on the cottage had been paid off in full. Not only that, my rent for the next three months had been taken care of. I put on my coat and marched out of the gate up to Croker's Farm.

It was an exceptional morning toward the end of March.

When I got to the farm Luke was there, carrying some panes of glass. He couldn't take his eyes from my shorn head. I asked him where I could find Chas, and he pointed to the frame of a new greenhouse they were building. When Chas saw me coming he waved. He was also holding a pane of glass. He smiled stupidly and held the glass in front of his face, mashing his nose and lips up against the glass.

I could have smashed that glass with my fist.

He must have seen the expression on my face because as I approached he came from behind the glass. He lost his smile. His brow furrowed. "What's up, Fern?"

"Get away from me. It doesn't make it all right."

"Huh?"

"You can't ever make it right."

"Make what right?"

"If you think you can pay them off, and that's the end of it, you don't know me. You don't know me at all."

Chas put down the square of glass he was holding and scratched his head. He shouted after me, but I was already striding out of the yard. Luke said something as I passed, but I ignored him. Then Greta hurried over to me.

"Your hair, Fern! I almost didn't recognize you," Greta said. "Look, I need to see you. I need some help."

"See Chas," I spat back at her. "He's a great helper."

I heard her calling my name as I hurried down the lane, and the tarmac road undulated in front of me, like a set of lungs moving a rib cage up and down.

I was certain it had been Chas who had paid off my rent arrears to try to make up for what he'd done to me. It was how he worked. Same as with the record player he'd given me with "Green Onions," to buy me off after I'd helped him over the drugs. But then I began to wonder if I'd made a mistake in assuming it was Chas. What if I was wrong? What if it had been someone else? I tried hard to think of who might do such a thing. Of course I knew it was a gift from the hare, it had to be because of the *Asking*, but the hare would have to act through someone. It had to have an agent in this world.

I took a bus into Market Harborough and went to the offices of the Nationwide and questioned the manager about who had paid my rent. The manager turned out to be someone who had been to the same school as I had, though he was a good few years older. He sat at a polished walnut desk with his hands on the table, fingertips making a steeple pointed toward me. Hateful hateful hateful. Shifting his gaze from my shaved head to my bruised eye, he explained that the payment had been made anonymously; he even explained the word "anonymously" to me as if I didn't know its meaning.

I said it didn't seem right that folk could go around paying for things for people without revealing their identity. I asked him if it was legal, and he laughed in my face. He pointed out that I didn't have to accept the payment, that I could insist it be canceled and remain in arrears. But what I couldn't do was know who'd paid it.

I was so angry I tried to slam the door on the way out, but it was a heavy door on a sprung hinge, and it wouldn't close. In my efforts I knocked over a stack of leaflets. I only succeeded in looking foolish. The manager and his staff watched in silence as I left the premises.

From there I walked back to Keywell, determined to go up to the hideous pile—the vile Stokes Jacobean mansion—that owned my tiny cottage and a thousand acres of local land besides. My feet crunched the gravel of the long driveway as I passed the scruffy lake and the huge rhododendron bushes that were just beginning to bud. When I got to the house Lord Stokes and another man were mounted on horses in the quadrangle in front of the house, attended by grooms in cloth caps who toadied round adjusting stirrup lengths and tightening leather girths. Another chap, hands in his pockets, lounged against a brand-new Land Rover. He looked up at me from under a smart cloth cap and his fingers touched the paintwork of his new vehicle, almost protectively.

I walked straight up to one of the two grooms. The mounted men and the grooms went silent, and froze, and looked at me as if I were a ghost in chains. The horses turned and looked at me, too. Lord Stokes was a man with a collapsed face the hue of claret. His eyes were bloodshot and his droopy moustache was the color of a nicotine stain. His head withdrew into his neck, like a tortoise might, as he peered at me. Then his gray mare stamped and backed away.

"Stand!" his lordship snarled at the animal. "Stand!"

"Where do I find the estate manager?" I demanded of one of the grooms.

"You don't come 'ere," the groom said sharply with the vile, assumed superiority of those who wait on the rich. He pointed behind the house. "Get yourself to the offices, over yonder."

I turned and walked out of the quadrangle, but I heard Lord Stokes say, "Who the dashed hell is that?"

"Frightening the horses!" chortled the other rider. And they laughed.

I walked between some yew hedges and beyond a redbrick-walled kitchen garden, then along a gravel path to a set of outbuildings. A door stood open. Inside a gloomy office Venables, the estate manager, sat pushing a pen across a page.

He looked startled to see me. Perhaps he didn't recognize me at first. Then he relaxed and leaned back in his chair, pressing the tips of his fingers on the very edge of his desk. "What can I do for you?"

"Someone paid off my rent."

"Yes."

"I want to know who paid it."

He looked surprised. "You don't know?"

"No. Do you?"

"No idea. It won't do you any good, though."

"What do you mean by that?"

"We want you out. And we shall have you out, whether you have the rent or not."

"You'll have to pull the place down around my ears, then."

He leaned his elbows on the desk and locked his fingers together in front of his face, as if in prayer. He surveyed me gloomily. "That's easily arranged. Easily."

"I don't think you will," I said.

"Oh? Why's that?"

"Jane Louth."

His hands dropped to the table. "I'll pretend I didn't hear that."

"Linda Slipman. Julie Frost. Maggie Redman. But most of all Jane Louth."

His face darkened. I hadn't meant to use all that on him, but he'd pulled my tongue. It was done. He got up and came round his desk. Then he grabbed my face with his hand, squeezing my cheeks together hard, very hard. It hurt my mouth. I thought he would hit me, but I stood my ground and stared back at him. I knew I could make him fear my eye.

"Trying to threaten me, girlie?" He pushed my head back hard before releasing me.

I left his office quickly, and as I walked across the yard I saw Arthur McCann. I didn't stop, and he ran over to me, having to walk briskly to keep up.

"Fern, what did you do to your hair? Have you got a black eye?"

"I have to get out of here, Arthur."

"Are you all right, Fern? I heard about Mammy. I thought of stopping by your cottage again. Come and see you, like. Shit, are you all right?"

"I have to go."

I saw the confusion on his face as he stopped trying to keep pace with me. I felt bad, but I couldn't stop there and pass the time of day with him after what had happened in the office. I walked out of the property of the mansion the way I came, through those evil grounds where only the rhododendron bushes were beautiful.

And the rhododendrons were budding early that year. I wondered what that meant.

twenty-five

*N*ext day *I waited outside Judith's* house for her to come home from teaching at the school. Even while she was turning her key in the door, I told her what had happened with Chas. "What? What?" she said. She didn't believe me. She said it couldn't have been possible. "Fern, you're upset about Mammy. You're not making sense."

"Okay," I said. "Now I see where your loyalties lie I'll be off."

I made my way down the street with Judith calling after me.

On the evening of my class I left the village preparing to hitch a ride into Leicester when Chas's van drew up. I walked on, ignoring him, too. He drove a little way in front of me and swerved his van into the grass verge, blocking my path. Then he jumped out and confronted me. "I've been speaking to Judith. We need to talk."

I brushed him aside. "What on earth makes you think I'd want to talk with you?"

He grabbed my arm and held me roughly. "It's about what you said. What you told her." I looked at his hand where he restrained me. At last he released me. "But it isn't true," he said. "It just isn't true."

I walked on.

"Where are you going, Fern?"

"I'm going into Leicester. Leave me be."

"Let me give you a lift in the van. We could talk on the way."

I had to marvel at him. I stopped, waited for a few seconds, then turned back to face him. "You really are a piece of work, aren't you? You actually think I might climb in your van. You really do! It takes my breath away. It's really quite staggering what you think you can do."

"I believe you think something happened—"

"Think something happened! *Think?*"

"I believe you think something happened. But you've somehow got it wrong, Fern. I think you're so upset by what's happened lately that you've got it wrong in your head."

That was enough. I turned away and hiked toward Leicester, trying to hold back a taste of gall in my throat and a tingling fury that made me want to break something along the way. I'm sure I didn't look an attractive proposition to stop for, with my shorn hair and my black eye and my angry, tearful eyes. At the side of the road was a bench under an old elm, and I sat there for a few minutes having a blub.

I did eventually get a ride, and though I was a few minutes late for my class that evening, it suited me. I pulled a scarf over my head and slipped in quietly, taking a seat at the back next to Biddy. Biddy's greeting smile froze on her lips. "You all right, ducky? You look like Leicester's answer to Myra Hindley."

No sooner had she said it than I could see her regretting the remark. I had to think what she meant. Myra Hindley was about to go on trial for torturing children and burying their bodies on the moors. I'd heard a priest on the radio saying this was what happened in society when people took drugs and had sex and did anything they wanted without restraint.

MMM, pursing her lips and fluttering her eyelashes behind her spectacles, lectured the class on epidural anesthesia and barely noticed me. And wouldn't have at all if Biddy hadn't started in with her usual objections. First she fidgeted in her seat as MMM treated us to the new gospel of midwifery. She clattered her pencil to the floor. After that she made her lips pop. Then she pushed her seat back and rested her brow on the wooden desk, lightly tapping the desk with her forehead. Recovering, she sat up again and grabbed a fistful of her own hair.

At last it was too much. "Excuse me," Biddy shouted. "Excuse me."

"What now?" MMM said. By way of a digression she'd been talking about pushing.

"Excuse me, but I've never told ladies to push in the second stage. Never have, never will. It's only those who've got their eyes on the clock who would."

MMM flushed. It was something she did often. Perhaps she'd hit the time in her life that summons frequent hot flashes, but with her they were visible. I knew that one day she was going to lose her temper with Biddy and her interruptions. I wondered if this might not be it. "Biddy, midwives, like all nurses, carry a watch. It's regulation equipment. Why would you think we carry a watch if we're not supposed to use it? How would we know if the birthing were going on too long?"

"That's not what I'm saying," Biddy replied. "I'm talking about these hospitals where they just want the patient to get a move on, so the midwife and the doctors can go home and put their feet up. These sausage-factory hospitals. I'm talking about rushing, that's what I mean by the clock. Rushing."

"Have you finished?"

Biddy colored at that. "Not by a chalk," she said. "I'm making the point that to get a woman to push in the second stage won't help anyone. It may even be bad. At best it will only make 'em anxious that they're not doing it right, and they'll get all tense, and it'll set you back."

"Yes, Biddy. We all know you have strong views about *everything*." The two women had had earlier spats over the subjects of Caesarean births and breast versus bottle. "But we need to crack on."

But Biddy wasn't having that. "Well, are we all here to roll over and have our tummies tickled? Is that it? If you say something, do we all have to agree with you? I know some of the other members of the class agree with me one hundred percent about these things, but they don't say anything." Here Biddy switched her attention from MMM to the rest of the class. Her eyes were shining with anger as she looked round the room for the support she knew she wouldn't get. "Well is anyone going to agree with me? What about you, Dawn? Or Maria? Or you, Fern?"

I lowered my eyes.

"That's just it, isn't it?" said Biddy. "You want to keep your heads down and say nothing and collect your certificate. You don't want to do what we're here for, which is to educate ourselves, through argument if necessary. But this *line* you keep feeding us, this government line, as if there's only one way of doing things! I'm not a robot. And the women we work with aren't robots either."

"No one is saying they are," MMM said, trying to wrest back control of the class.

"No one is saying anything!" Biddy complained. "Is there not one woman in this room who agrees with me?"

No one spoke up. And yet on this issue probably all of us were in harmony with her.

Biddy looked astonished. Then she gathered up her papers and her pencil and walked out of the room. After a moment the lady called Dawn made a thin smile at MMM and went after Biddy. MMM, shaken, tried to recover.

"I'll not have it said that I won't allow discussion," she said in a warning tone. "I'll not have it said. Let's break off and discuss the matter, if it's a discussion that's wanted."

The trouble was nobody at that point much wanted to discuss anything. There was a cancerous silence, then the door opened and Dawn came back, but without Biddy. Though I knew she wouldn't come back. Biddy had just walked out of the whole messy business of helping women to have their babies. Like Mammy, she'd put herself on the outside. She'd torn up her ticket and stood down from her post at the portal of life.

"Dawn, we were discussing this wretched issue of pushing," MMM said fiercely. "If you had anything to add."

Dawn smiled thinly again. "Not really."

I heard Mammy's words whispering in my head, so I spoke up. "I wouldn't ask a mum to push in the second stage," I heard myself say.

Everyone turned to look at me. It was as if I'd removed my head scarf for everyone to see my shaved head. Not that I did so. It was as if I had.

"Good," MMM said. "That's good, Fern. If that's your strong opinion—and it's not mine—you are perfectly within your rights to stick with it. Why are you wearing your head scarf?"

I looked down at my desk. Someone in a previous lesson had

scratched something into the wood. It said: *Does she or doesn't she?* MMM didn't wait for an answer from me, but went back to talking about epidural anesthesia, and the entire class took many more notes than usual.

I went home that night thinking: Does she or doesn't she *what?*

twenty-six

*D*o you like an egg custard?" said the man at the door the following morning. He took off his hat and without invitation pushed past me to get inside the house. I was so taken aback I stood aside for him. "Only I do so like an egg custard, and the bakers had them fresh and I couldn't resist. It's the wonderful smell of them, isn't it? Cinnamon and the rest. You do like them, too, don't you?"

I said I didn't mind.

"I was rather hoping—and I hope you don't think it forward of me—that we might have a cup of tea with one of these. Is that rude of me to ask?"

I said I didn't think so, then I said, "Who are you?"

"Would it be all right if I sat?" he asked. "I get terrible rheumatic pains in my legs if I stay on my feet. Age. No, I was in the neighborhood and I thought to call to see how you are doing."

In addition to the bag of egg custards he carried a battered leather case. He set the custards on the table and the case down by a chair. Then he took his spectacles off and stroked a closed eye with a knuckle. I noticed how hairy were the backs of his hands. He wore a silver ring on his little finger.

After replacing his spectacles he smiled broadly. Then he took his coat off and laid it across the back of another chair before sitting down. He picked up his case, flicked open the metal clasps, rummaged through the contents, and closed it again. I'm certain he had shaved that morning because I could smell a sweet aftershave lotion on him, but he was so dark he was one of those men with a permanent blue shadow around his chin.

"What do you mean, you 'thought to call'?"

"Do have a custard," he said. "I'll feel so guilty if I eat them all myself." And then he giggled, like a girl.

I don't know why, but I found myself putting on the kettle. "Are you selling something?"

"Good Lord no!" he cried. "This is merely a social visit!"

I suddenly twigged who he was. This was Montague Butts, the colleague of Bennett, the Cambridge professor. I should have guessed it by his manner of speaking, which like his chum was all soft-soap. "Oh! You've come about the—"

"Indeed I have, Miss Cullen, indeed I have. I wanted to see how things were going."

The kettle boiled, and I made the tea. While I did so he fiddled in his case again and took out a manila folder and a notebook. From his breast pocket he extracted a heavy fountain pen, jet with swirls of amber. I handed him his tea and a small plate for his egg custard. He put them down on the floor and balanced the folder and notebook on his knee.

"How are things going? Things are going well enough," I said.

"And you're managing all right now you're on your own here in the cottage?"

"It's a struggle. But someone cleared a debt for me recently."

"How jolly kind of someone!" he said with a conspiratorial grin, and I wondered if it were Bennett and himself who had paid off the arrears. "Would you say you were coping?"

"Coping?"

"With the bereavement."

It didn't occur to me to ask him how he knew about Mammy's passing. "Everything is going to be difficult. I know that."

"Quite," he said, and he wrote some words in his notebook, grinding his teeth as he did so. "Why did you cut your hair, Miss Cullen?"

My hand darted to my head. "Oh, that."

"Yes, your hair." He looked across the top of his spectacles at me.

"A bit embarrassing," I said. "I caught head lice. Easiest way to get rid of them."

He was writing in his notebook again. "How did you catch 'em?"

"Local children."

"Really? What were you doing with local children?"

He was still looking down at his notebook, but though he was trying to disguise it, there was too much interest in my answer to his strange question. My skin prickled. I was suddenly on my guard again. "Just helping out with a local family. And of course if your heads get too close, well, they jump, don't they?"

"Indeed they do. Do you feel people are against you?"

"Against me? Well some of them are! What's that got to do with it?"

"Do you ever hear voices?"

I looked hard at him. "Do you mean for the book? Is this for the book?"

"The book? It could be."

"What are you writing down?"

"Oh I'm making an assessment, that's all. So do you hear voices?"

"I can hear yours well enough. What are you doing here?"

"Only a visit."

"Are you from Cambridge University?"

"No, I'm a redbrick man myself. Do you have lots of visitors from Cambridge University?"

I looked at the blue shadow on the man's chin and at the fat red maggot of his bottom lip, and I suddenly felt very cold and very afraid. "If you don't tell me why you are here, I'm going to get annoyed," I said.

"Do you often get angry, do you find?"

"Not especially."

"Got angry in the building society the other day though, didn't you?"

"Who sent you here?"

"Just someone worried about your well-being. A concerned friend. I don't know why you're getting upset."

"Which friend might that be?"

"Does it really matter?"

"You're a doctor?"

"You know, I really do wish you would tell me why you cut your hair."

Mammy, I thought. Mammy would know what to do in these circumstances. Why didn't I have her power, to deal with these priests and doctors, what Mammy used to call the juju men. I gazed evenly back at him, regulating my breathing as he sat with his glistening fountain pen poised over his notebook, and I knew that whatever he wrote in there it could go against me. His eyes had a mesmerizing strength, seeming to swim and to grow larger behind his spectacles.

"I'd like to stay and talk to you longer, but I've lots of work to attend to," I said.

"What work? You don't have any real work, do you now?"

"I have plenty."

"Like what?"

"I take in sewing. And laundry. All that on the lines in the garden. I have to get it back to people. Right now. So you'll have to go."

"Won't be dry yet, surely."

"Dry as a bone. Obviously, I get up earlier than you do." I stood up to show him it was time to leave. "You can help me fold it if you like."

He put his notebook back in his case. "No, I have my own errands to run. I'll be on my way."

At the door I handed him his bag of egg custards. "Do take these."

He accepted the bag and bade me good day. But on his way down the garden path he stopped and, very pointedly, reached out to touch one of the sheets hung out there. He rubbed it between a fat, putrid forefinger and thumb before proceeding down the path.

I knew it would be dry.

They were closing in.

Sometime after this doctor who wouldn't admit he was a doctor had gone I went out into the garden. There was an old stone sundial table there, with a rusted gnomon, where I often put bread crumbs out for the birds in winter. At one edge of the stone slab, where the shadow of the gnomon might fall, I placed a black pebble for each person I thought might have called in this doctor against me. There were six pebbles. At the other edge of the stone table, arrayed against the others like checkers on a squared board, I lined up white pebbles representing anyone who might have paid off my debt. That, too, added up to six. Three of the six people were represented on both sides, so I replaced all of these with brown pebbles.

I decided to go to the police house and find out what I could.

Bill Myers's police residence lay just outside the village. It was a curious house, with two porthole windows either side of the central door. Above the door was a large black-and-white enamel badge of the county coat of arms: the bull, the sheep and the fox courant. Bill Myers's wife, Peggy, whom I barely knew, came to the door. Her hair was fixed in plastic curlers, and the smell of setting lotion was overwhelming. She'd taken her dentures out so her mouth was rather pursed. She knew who I was immediately. With expressions of symphty she invited me inside, quickly refixing her dentures to tell me that Bill would be back for his dinner break in a few minutes.

I was left sitting in an untidy kitchen. The Myerses had four children, all of school age, and various items of their laundry were left drying around the place, hanging from a large clotheshorse and from an elastic line suspended between the walls.

Presently Bill arrived, and by that time Mrs. Myers had taken out her curlers and spruced herself up for his arrival. When he came in he skimmed his policeman's cap across the room to land in a chair, and they kissed as if they'd been parted for a fortnight instead of a few hours. Bill hugged his wife, then spotted me. "Hello, Fern, what brings you here? You know I was very sorry to hear about Mammy. Very sorry."

"Something's going on," I said.

"Do you want to go in the other room?" Peggy Myers said. She was already busy readying something for Bill to eat. I said no, I didn't mind her hearing; I don't know why. I told Bill about my visit from the unknown doctor. I let him know that I knew why the doctor had come.

"What makes you think someone will try to have you put away, Fern?" Bill said quietly.

But it was Peggy who answered for me, turning from the sink with a chopping knife in her hand. "Cos that's what they did to Mammy. It was back in the thirties, wasn't it Fern? Locked her up in the funny farm didn't they? When there was nothing wrong with her."

I nodded.

"Bill's mother told me about it, years ago," Peggy said. "She made enemies. They were scared of Mammy they were. Scared."

"This is 1966," Bill said. "They don't do things like that anymore."

"Ha!" went Peggy. "My eye!"

Bill scratched his head. "Hell," he said.

Bill and Peggy started a discussion about whether they really could still do that to people. I learned that all it took was a doctor's say-so, especially with me living alone. Then Bill furrowed his brow and turned to me. "You've got to tread carefully now Fern, cos there's been a complaint about you, you know."

"Complaint? But I haven't done anything!"

"Well you say that. But Lord Stokes says you went up to the manor house the other day causing trouble and—"

"Trouble!"

"—then the manager of the building society said you were in town throwing leaflets all round the premises—"

"That's not true!"

"And then the Cormells' lad told his teacher at school that he'd seen you sitting in the hedge with your face all smeared . . ."

My stomach turned over.

"And the teacher thought she ought to tell me, and well, this was so wild I went and spoke with the lad's father, and he said he saw you, too, though they're all fond of you the Cormells are, and the old man said you were causing no harm, just sitting in the hedge."

I tried to speak, but nothing would come out. My tongue stuck to the roof of my mouth, and my head was spinning. I looked at Bill. His mouth was moving, and I could hear him, but it was like listening from underwater.

"So what were you doing in the hedge, Fern?" Bill was saying.

I shook my head.

"I'm sure there's an explanation for some of these things. But I don't mind saying we're worried about you," Bill said.

"I want you to do something, Fern. I want you to look me in the eye and tell me you haven't been taking drugs at that Croker's Farm."

"I haven't," I said.

"You swear?"

"I swear I haven't been taking drugs at Croker's Farm."

"Because you start by taking drugs at Croker's Farm, then you end up cutting all your hair off and sitting in hedges and who-knows-what. That's exactly what happens with druggies. I've seen it."

"Don't push her," Peggy said.

"This is a small village, Fern. You've got to know how people are talking about you. They see everything."

We all went quiet. I might have knuckled away a tear. Then Peggy said, "Do you want a spot of summat to eat?"

I said I didn't. I told them I had things to do and I got up to leave. They both came to the door to see me out. "It's Mammy's funeral to-morrow afternoon, isn't it?" Peggy said. "We'll be there."

After my lecture from Bill I walked back to the cottage with a leaden heart. I don't know what my visit to the police house had accomplished, though I did at least come away with a picture of exactly how I was regarded in the community: as a mad little woman who shaved her head and prescribed herbal remedies, and who had tantrums in the building society.

It was so unfair.

twenty-seven

The motor of the vacuum cleaner whined from somewhere inside the house, rising and falling, and I thought I should knock louder the second time. The cleaner was switched off, and when Judith answered the door she showed no pleasure in seeing me. Her face was neutral. Her hair was tied at the back in twists, and she gave these an odd little shake.

"I want to talk," I said.

She let me in and closed the door behind me, then went back to the vacuum cleaner and switched it on. "Talk, then," she said above the din, running the thing along the carpet.

It was like watching someone plow a field. She ran the machine in a dead straight line from the top of the room to the bottom. Then she swung around and came back again, very slowly, very precisely, taking great care to overlap her previous track by about an inch. It was mesmerizing.

"You're not talking very much," she shouted above the drone of the motor. "I thought you said you'd come to talk."

"So I have," I said.

"What?"

"I said: so I have."

"What?"

I looked away. Judith continued to track up and down the carpet with bloodcurdling slowness. I glanced around at the obsessive tidiness of her house and at the matching furniture. It was all very modern, much like her. You could see she was proud of the appearance of her little terraced property, whereas I never gave mine a moment's thought.

After several more minutes and to my relief she switched off the vacuum cleaner. Then she unplugged it, carefully wound up the cable and stowed the machine in a cupboard. Then she turned a tiny plastic key in the cupboard door. Only after all this did she invite me to sit down and when I went to lower myself on to the sofa she protested, directing me instead to sit on a hard chair at the table, where she joined me, blinking at me like a cat might blink at a spider, the blue of her iris compromised by the leak of green. And then I told her all about it, but this time with nothing left out.

Whereas previously I'd only told her about Chas's assault, this time I gave her the complete story about the *Asking*. About what happened. About being seen in the hedge. About being bitten by the dog. About Chas and what he did. And through it all—through my retelling of the entire story—I swear that Judith did not once blink her wide-open eyes.

"You should have been with me, Judith."

"I know. I left you unprotected."

"So you believe me?"

"I believe that you believe it."

"That means no. You're in love with him. You can't believe he would do such a thing, and you won't hear a word said against him."

Judith folded her arms and looked at the wall.

"All right," I said. "That's not what I've come about."

When I told her about the visit from the doctor she actually went white. After a moment she got up, crossed to the cupboard, unlocked it, took out the vacuum cleaner, unraveled the cable, plugged it in and switched it on. She began carefully tracking up and down the carpet again. I'd had enough. I got up and tugged at her elbow. "But what should I do for goodness sake? What should I do?"

"Sit down," she shouted over the din. "I'm thinking."

After some more minutes of pushing the vacuum cleaner up and down the room she switched the thing off, unplugged it, carefully wound the cable and restored it to the cupboard. After she'd turned the key in the cupboard door, she said, "We need to go and see William."

*   *   *

The sun was descending behind William's cottage by the time we arrived, a red disc tangled in the sooty branches of a tree. I'd only been there on that one previous occasion. A small, smoky bonfire was burning in the garden, and William was out working on his beehives. I don't know if I imagined it, but I thought I could hear the bees humming in their white boxes. The smoke subdued them, causing them to gorge on honey should fire prove a threat. It was almost as if I could hear them talking. William turned round and looked at us through his protective headgear, as if tipped off to our presence. Then he resumed his work. He wasn't going to be hurried away from his bees.

Judith pushed open the door, and we went inside. The grandfather clock ticked. The room was scented with herbs hanging from the rafters. William's insufferable deck of cards was on the oak table by the window. Judith and I sat in a difficult silence, waiting for William to join us.

At last, after perhaps twenty minutes, he came in. He'd taken off his headgear and was scratching the back of his hand.

"Been stung?" Judith asked him.

"Can't keep bees without getting stung," he said, crossing toward the kitchen. Then he stopped abruptly and looked hard at me. "Hear that?"

I blinked back at him. He went through to wash his hands then came to join us, taking a seat at the oak table. "Normally I'm immune," he said to Judith. "Don't feel it anymore, you know? But if I feel it, it's 'cos they want to tell me something." Then he turned to me. "What is it they want to tell me?"

You irritating old bastard, I thought. I looked at his hands, and at the dirt under his fingernails, and I felt like walking out of there.

"Anyway you've saved me a journey. I was coming to tell the both of you that you've got to be ready tonight. We'll come for you at one o'clock. "You'll have to sit up and wait for us."

"What for?"

"You'll see. Just be ready with your coat, and waiting."

Bewildered I looked at Judith. But she said, "Never mind that. Tell William what you told me." I then heard myself repeating the story I had told to Judith earlier. Only I added to it. I told him about the lapwings in the field, and about the things the hare told me in Mammy's voice, and about its sacrifice, and things about Chas and the day the police raided his farm. After a while he closed his eyes, but he wasn't sleeping. He opened them now and again to let me know he was still with it. And when I'd finished the telling of it, it was dark outside, and Judith must have switched the low lamps on inside, though I hadn't noticed her get up.

William's brow wrinkled. "Warned you, didn't I?"

"Yes, you did."

"This came about because you're not mentally strong enough to do these things. You're half-cocked. What did you hope to achieve?"

"I wanted help. I asked. And I got it."

"Someone paid off your rent? You think that's it? You're half-cocked. You don't believe it anyway."

"I believe in some things. More now I've seen."

William turned to Judith and flicked his head backward, but minimally. It was a little gesture of dismissal and disgust. As if to say: What would you expect from this girl? "What do you think it's for?"

"The *Asking?* Only what Mammy told me."

"And what was that?"

"She said you can only knock on the door. You can ask for help, but that's all. She said you could bend events to your will, but you can't break what has to be."

He smacked his lips as if someone had coated them with mustard. "Yes, that's Mammy's bilge all right. The point is you got what you wanted, didn't you?"

"The rent? You mean that the rent was paid off?"

"I'm not just talking about the rent." I was confused. I looked at Judith, but she colored and looked away. It dawned on me what he was talking about.

"Oh yes," William said. "That's what I told you before you went ahead and did it. You weren't clear, were you? Didn't clear your head beforehand, did you? Now if there is ever to be a next time, perhaps you'll think on it."

I thought about what he was saying about Chas and my feelings for him. I didn't like where this was going. There was a horrible circular logic to his words. "But William," I protested, "was I in the hedge or in my home? I mean how is it that the Cormells could see me in the hedgerow? How is that possible?"

"You didn't disguise yourself well enough, that's all. You should have taken more care."

"But I wasn't really there, was I? In the hedgerow, I mean. I wasn't actually *there*."

"What's she raving about?" he said to Judith.

Judith shrugged.

"What I mean is, I was in my own cottage. Dreaming it. Or at least my body was."

"Judith, get that doctor," William said.

Judith laughed. She actually cackled at my discomfort. It was the first time I'd seen her break a smile since I'd first reported Chas's assault to her. And it wasn't funny.

"You mean I was actually there in the field? And I was dreaming that my body was in the cottage? Is that what happened?"

"Nurse!" William shouted, and Judith cackled again.

"I admit I was so far gone," I said, "that I wouldn't know whether I was in one place dreaming about the other or vice versa."

The smile went off William's face. "Are you trying to be funny, girlie?"

I know I blushed. "What I mean is, if I was in the hedgerow and not the cottage at all, then perhaps I imagined the thing with Chas. I mean it's possible, isn't it? In which case I've made a terrible mistake in accusing him."

"Did Mammy teach you nothing in her time with you?"

I felt confused, wrong-footed. "About what?"

He looked at Judith. "You tell her."

Judith folded her arms tightly. "I'm not telling her. It's not my job to tell her."

The old boy cocked his head on one side and stared hard at me again, poking his tongue inside his cheek. I was sure he was enjoying this even though he pretended to look displeased. He said nothing. The silence was unbearable, so I broke it again. "Let me ask you this: I made all the preparations very carefully, and I sat down in a chair in my cottage. Did I then get up and go out or did I hallucinate it?"

"You got up and went out."

"Yes, but what I want to know is: if I'd have chained my leg to the floor, would I have been able to go out and sit in the hedge?"

William said, "You'd have been in the hedge with your leg chained to the floor. Obviously."

"Obviously," Judith added.

"I don't know why," I said sourly, "but it's not obvious to me."

"That's because you live in a world where things either are or they are not. And you shouldn't have stepped into this world where things both are and are not. Mammy's at fault. She should have looked at you and told you not to. You weren't fit for it. Not everyone can be."

I looked from one to the other of them, and I had a sudden suspicion. "Why are you being so hard on me? Is it because Mammy passed on her list of names to me and not to you, Judith? Is that it?"

Though they didn't answer, it shut them up, which was answer enough. William gathered his cards and started shuffling in with his arthritic hands. "Who do you think sent this doctor?" he said.

"Any of six."

William seemed to know some of my suspicions without me having to tell him. "Rule out Judith. She's one of us, whatever you say. Rule out the vicar. He's a chump, but he doesn't want to harm you. Four most likely?"

I named four people. William turned up the four knaves from his deck and spread them on the table. Turning up a fool, he put that down, and he gave me a look. I knew the fool was supposed to be me, but I wasn't going to give him the pleasure by saying as much. Then he turned it facedown and told me to put my finger on it. I resisted. He grabbed my hand with his bony fingers and dropped it on the card. "You a fool or a knave?" he said.

"Neither."

"Turn it."

I turned over my card, and it had become a knave. I looked at the four knaves and one of them had become a queen of hearts. Then he told me to turn it again and keep my finger on it this time, while he put his finger on the other end of the card. "Fool or knave?" he said.

"Neither," I said again, and he slipped the card suddenly so that it passed under one of the knaves. I stabbed my finger on it, but when he told me to turn it, this time it had become a queen of hearts, and the knave was back in its old place.

"So, you became a hare?" he said. "Did you?"

"Yes," I said, and he slipped the card, lightning fast, under the next knave, but this time I was sure I didn't let it off my fingertip, but when I turned it, it had become an ace of clubs.

"Fool become a lady; lady become a hare," said William. "Are you ready?"

This time I was determined to keep my finger on the card. William was fast. He whisked it under the next knave. I turned it, and now it was a two of spades. You had to admire the trick.

"What did the hare do when it was cornered?" he said.

"Ran straight at the poacher," I said.

"There's your answer," William said.

"My answer? What answer?" I felt bewildered, and not just by William's gnomic remarks about the hare but by his wizardry with the cards. "How did you do it?" I asked him.

He started laughing. "How did I do it?" He turned to Judith, who also started laughing. "How did Mammy pick her? Eh? She's like a five-year-old! How did I do it? It's card tricks, girlie! Card tricks!"

And then the pair of them were cackling and hooting and hugging their ribs. I looked from one to the other, this wizened man and this misfit young woman, and not for the first time I wondered what kind of people on earth Mammy had left me with.

twenty-eight

I had no problem in sitting up until the small hours, since my mind was running on the thought of the funeral the following day. In one sense I was relieved that William had completely taken over the arrangements, but in other ways I felt sidelined. I had no experience in these things, but I felt it was somehow my responsibility to Mammy.

I'd left William's cottage in rather bad humor, what with the pair of them cackling at me. What's more, the distance between Judith and me was growing. I was feeling even more angry and isolated. Before I left, William had told me to leave a single candle burning in my window for them, though he wouldn't be drawn about what was going on. I made up a fire in the hearth, and I sat and waited.

At exactly one in the morning William and Judith arrived. Judith was tight-lipped and wouldn't make eye contact. William refused to say where we were going. He told me to put on my coat. I climbed into Arthur's leather jacket with the death's-head on the back. William glanced at it, and said, "For God's sake." Judith looked slightly pained.

I followed them in silence along the field path and into the woods. The moon was struggling into its last quarter, but was muffled by clouds, and its light was weak. The grass underfoot was wet, and the night air served up a bone-invading damp. I was shivering and clasping my coat and scarf at my throat as I followed a well-known track deep into the woods. The bluebells were in shoot, not flowering yet but already exhaling a sweet perfume. White moths were also out everywhere, flitting from the new ferns and the trees, disturbed by this passing cortege, flitting and resettling.

We came to a small clearing guarded by oak and ash trees and shielded by holly bushes. Several other figures, perhaps a dozen in total, had already assembled there, though at first I couldn't recognize any of them in the darkness, and I doubt if broad daylight would have helped. William went amongst them, dispensing gruff greetings. Though they had battery-powered torches, someone had set flickering candles burning in jam jars at the foot of an oak.

To my astonishment I saw that a deep grave had been dug near the candles. A thrill of horror flashed through me as I thought they were going to kill me and bury me in the woods. Then I saw a military-style medical stretcher drawn up near the grave, and I realized they already had their corpse. The body was draped in a sheet of muslin cloth.

"Mammy!" I breathed. "Oh Mammy!"

William immediately came across to me. He gently cupped his leathery old hands around my face. His soft eyes peered into mine. "You understand?" he said. "You understand?"

I couldn't speak. I nodded, and he stepped back from me and went to join the others by the yawning grave. Large clumps of green bluebell shoots had been carefully lifted with their root soil intact and set aside in neat slabs. More white moths flitted around, excited by the candlelight and the odors of the disturbed ground. I approached the grave. I wanted to look into the black earth, into the soil pit where we all go. If I could have done I would have lighted Mammy's journey.

It was too dark to see even to the bottom. Someone had dug with a wonderfully sharp spade, so precise and sheer were the sides of the fresh pit. There was a beautiful efficiency in the cutting of the earth. The spade had sliced through a tangle of white, cottonlike plant fiber and tree root. The black soil at the lip of the grave gleamed with moisture. The smells rising from the hole were yeasty and strangely sweet. I looked up from the grave and saw, on the other side of the hole, Judith. She tried a sympathetic smile.

"Stand aside," a stranger's voice said, and I realized he meant me. The men had lifted Mammy from the stretcher and were waiting to get on with things. Then the voice said, "Stone the crows. What the hell are you wearing?" William looked at the man and shook his snowy white head in disgust.

The men had four ropes looped under Mammy's body. The ropes were new, bleached white and elaborately knotted at intervals. They tossed the ropes across the grave and the other mourners stepped forward and took them up. Judith motioned to me so that I might go and share her rope end. I recognized another woman whom I couldn't place at the time. She was sharing her rope end with yet another woman who was sliding her dentures out along her bottom lip. Others were strangers to me. I counted heads. There were thirteen mourners, myself included.

Mammy was hoisted into position and carefully lowered into the black hole. The shuffling feet around the grave kicked up the scent of leaf mold and released dozens of white moths that flew up or settled on the muslin sheet covering the body. When the body touched the floor of the grave we all let go of the ropes, letting them fall into the hole.

William cleared his throat, and said simply, "Mammy Cullen has come back to you."

I didn't know if we were supposed to repeat the words, as in a church catechism, but no one added anything. All that happened was that everyone stepped back, as if William's words had been a cue. If so, it was lost on me. Perhaps I expected more, but there was nothing. One man with his spade filled in the grave as everyone watched in silence. When it was filled, he and William took up the clumps of shooting bluebells and carefully transplanted them back into the disturbed earth, and as they did so the white moths streamed from the plants in a small cloud, each like a tiny point of light, so many that I was astonished.

"The moths!" I couldn't help myself.

William stopped in his work of replanting the bluebells and looked glumly back at me. Then he continued. When the job was done it seemed that only very careful inspection of the earth would reveal any sign of the grave. William got up from his knees, his joints cracking, and wiped the dirt from his hands. It was over.

William approached me, still brushing soil from his hands. I think his leg had gone numb from the kneeling, because he weaved toward me like a drunk. "Don't you know when Mammy is talking to you?"

"What?" I said.

"I'm wasting my breath, aren't I? You know nothing about it."

"Leave her alone," Judith said. "She's grieving." Judith took my hand. Her own was warm. "I'll walk home with you and sit up. You won't want to sleep the rest of the night."

I looked round to see what William and the others were planning to do. They had already gone, slipped through the trees. There was neither sound nor sight of any of the other mourners who, moments earlier, had been gathered around the grave. They had vanished like spirits. The candles were gone, too. The shooting bluebells looked as if they had never been disturbed. Even the moths had settled. The only sound was of the huge oak at the head of Mammy's grave, creaking slightly in the breeze.

The sound of that tree creaking has never left me.

Judith did walk me back to the cottage, but when we got there I persuaded her that I wanted to be on my own. There were things I wanted to do, and there was already too much distance between us. She kissed me lightly on the cheek and left.

Once inside I switched on the lamp and I took out a notebook. I put that "Green Onions" record on the record player and left it playing quietly, with the arm off so that it might repeat over and over. Then I sat at the table and I wrote. I wrote everything. Everything that Mammy had told me about everyone I knew, and about those I didn't know. At first I just wrote notes, filling up several pages with names. Then I started again and wrote in full sentences and proper paragraphs.

I started with the names of those higher up and worked my way down. And I had such a lot to say. Such a lot.

I wrote on into the night, with "Green Onions" for company. The moon going into her last quarter shone clear and cold through the window. I heard, above the muted music, the owls screeching outside as I wrote. I heard the dog fox barking and the badger coughing in the lane. I filled three notebooks with my tight, small scribbling. I wouldn't have thought it possible to write for so long without a break. I paused only to massage my aching hand or to answer a call of nature. I wrote when it all went still, and I continued writing through the first birdsong and past the trailing off of the dawn chorus.

My pen whispered to the page. It poured out like heartache. And though I was writing, writing in a kind of fury, in a fever, with my pen stroking at the leaves of the notebook, it felt to me like a running, a kind of sudden freedom, a haring through the fields in which my paws left imprints and trails of signs in the grass and earth underfoot, from which the meaning spoke itself.

Ultimately after my writing marathon I fell asleep in my armchair and was awoken by the sound of someone knocking on my door. It was Greta. I struggled to my feet.

She was smiling again, damn her eyes. "Gosh, Fern, you look like you've only just woken up."

"I have."

"But it's the middle of the day!"

"Really. I suppose you'd better come in." I remembered my notebooks on the table. I swept them up and placed them on the hidden shelf behind the tea caddy, next to the secret jar of Mammy's hair and nail clippings.

"What have you been doing?" Greta beamed at me. I grunted, and she said, "Wisewoman things?"

I'm not sure what she meant by that but I wasn't going to encourage her. I was still half-coiled in my midmorning sleep. I also had the afternoon's "funeral" to think about. I asked her what had brought her to me.

"This is not going to be easy to say," she told me.

I suspected instantly that Chas had sent her to do his pleading. She would let me know what a decent man he was, how he was above that kind of behavior. She would appeal to me that I'd made some sort of a mistake. "Spit it out," I said.

"Right. Okay. I'm going to say it with no beating about the bush. I'm going to tell you, straight off the bat—"

"Greta!"

208 | Graham Joyce

"Okay. I'm pregnant. I want you to get rid of it."

Suddenly I woke up. I'd got her wrong. Maybe I was slipping in my ability to see through people. But here she was, smiling at me as if across a cake full of lighted candles at her birthday party and telling me she wanted an abortion. "You didn't have period pains the other day, did you? How far gone are you? Don't lie." I said this automatically.

"Ten to twelve weeks," she said. I thought, stop smiling will you!

"It's Chas's?" I thought, this complicates my feelings. But she shook her head. "No?"

"Luke."

"You're certain? I thought you said Chas was . . . also your boyfriend."

"I did. Well, I said he was also my lover. But it's not Chas's."

"How can you be sure?"

"A woman can be sure, Fern."

Her smile was starting to look goofy, and deeply irritating. I suspected she had some airy-fairy mystical notion of when she conceived. Women always say this, and it's rot. About these things Mammy would always say you can't trust yourself, and you can't trust your heart because your heart will only tell you what your heart wants you to be told. I knew that the only way a woman can be sure in such circumstances would be a blood test, and I told her so. The smile, at least, dropped from her face, and I wanted to shout Hurrah!

"In some ways you're very clever, Fern," she said sharply, "but in other ways you're like a little girl. It couldn't be Chas's child because he has problems in that department."

"What?" I said, genuinely shocked.

"He can't get it up. Can't get a hard-on. How plain do you want me to put it?"

I felt dizzy. This couldn't be possible. I had to get out of my chair, turn my back on Greta for a moment. I tried to conceal my bewilderment by putting to her a number of questions about Luke. Did he know? What was his opinion on the matter? Though I barely listened to the answers Greta offered.

Luke knew, she said, and wanted to keep the child. But Luke already had two children at the commune by different women, and another two offspring in other parts of the country. He was wonderful yet irresponsible, she said; decent but feckless.

It was a woman's right to choose, she said. I agreed with that sure enough. It always has been and it always will be. Then she said she hated to get rid of this baby but needed to because she had had enough of the commune life. She said she was sick of the drugs, tired of the aimless living, hurt by the emotional debris of the promiscuity and angered by the way these hippie guys trailed their "chicks" and their babies around the commune free from the most basic of duties and emotional obligations. It's not enough just to grow your hair long, she told me. She wanted another kind of life, not one of conformity, no, not going back to winding the machine, she said, but on to a life where she could build what she called a "new ethos." No longer one of the outsiders, it would be "in and against"; it would be radical and challenging; it would be a new bohemian alternative that would bring out the best in people.

It was quite a speech. She sounded like Joan of Arc. And she never smiled while she said all this. And though in one way I loved hearing it, I couldn't keep my mind off what she'd told me about Chas.

"Where are you?" she said. "You seem miles away. Are you going to help me or not? I know you can."

It didn't occur to me to ask how she knew I might be able to help her. It was dangerous information. Many of the women in the village and around knew what Mammy did, and many would guess I could do it, too. Few of them would tell the men. It was a half secret, if there can be such a thing. But I set to work right away.

Greta watched me as I mixed the herbal abortifacients. I said, "Mammy never liked doing this, and I don't either. I don't want you to think I do it lightly."

"I don't. I've sworn to myself I'll never be so careless again."

I'm sure I sniffed at that, but I think she meant what she said. When I'd gathered together the ingredients I instructed her how to use it and to come to see me if she got terribly ill. "The last one we gave this to died," I told her.

She looked at me. Well you would, wouldn't you?

"You'll be all right," I told her. "Anyway, it's either that or the Leamington dwarf with his knitting needles."

"Are you angry with me about something, Fern?"

"No, not you. It's just that I think I'm going mad. And there are people in the world who would like to see me go mad. You'd better leave now. I don't want you telling Luke nor Chas nor anyone else what I've given you there. You can tell Judith, that's all."

"Credit me with some sense! And have you heard about Judith?"

"What about her?"

"She might be suspended from the school."

"Whatever for?"

"Being seen with undesirables, no doubt."

I didn't know whether by that remark Greta meant me or the folk at Croker's Farm. My mind raced. "Now if you don't mind, I've got to get myself ready for Mammy's funeral this afternoon."

"That's another thing," Greta said. "Can Chas and I come?"

twenty-nine

*I*t was very odd, watching the burial of a coffin you know to be empty. That and listening to the rites and obsequies, though the Reverend Miller presided over this emptiness beautifully. I felt bad that he'd gone to all this trouble, paying for a plot and ordering a simple headstone just to bury a box of bricks.

William was there, and Judith, who of course managed to make herself look sexier and juicier than ever in her mourning clothes and coal black, broad-brimmed hat and black nylons. There were others whose faces I recognized from the previous evening, though they never gave any signal. I was still amazed by it all. It was not as if I didn't know that Mammy wouldn't have wanted to be buried in a churchyard; that she felt no affinity with the local church; that she thought her proper resting place would be somewhere in what remained of the old forest. It was the degree of the organization that surprised me, the machinery of the deception, the dedication to the alternative by the few.

And of course there were many others there who didn't know either. Bill Myers in his police uniform and holding his cap under his arm, and Peggy looking sombre. The Cormells, with Bunch red-faced and openly weeping. Emily Protheroe who would soon be eating her wedding cake, and her mother. One or two other families were represented, too, though not nearly so many as the number of families Mammy had helped over the years. Not nearly so many. But of those who were there, I let everyone know that Venables and the estate hadn't wanted Mammy buried in the churchyard. That even in 1966 this was how these people behaved. I wanted everyone to know how spiteful these people were.

But there was Greta, smiling beatifically and Chas, too, shirtless, having made no concession to the funeral dress code, wearing a leather waistcoat under a corduroy jacket. Though Bill shuffled un-comfortably whenever Chas drew near to him, I was glad they were there to swell the numbers and show their respects. But it was when the Reverend Miller said, "*My days are swifter than a weaver's shut-tle*" that something started to happen to me.

I started to come undone.

Then later when he read from the psalm: *"As for man, his days are as grass: as a flower of the field, so he flourisheth. For the wind pas-seth over it, and it is gone."* I know it's so ridiculous because it wasn't as if Mammy was there at all and I hadn't shed a single tear during the night at her real burial, but it began to flow, and I felt myself swaying and unable to reconcile the thought of Mammy in the ground and astronauts in space and Judith with her arm linked in Chas's, and I know if Bill Myers hadn't stepped over and caught me by the elbow, I might have fallen in with the box of bricks; and then Peggy held me by my other arm.

The people came up to me after it was over. Bunch Cormell, still weeping, hugged me dearly. Bill and Peggy kissed me. Others shook my hand. Greta kissed me. Chas came up gingerly, and said, "I'll al-ways think of her whenever I'm on the loo." Then Judith tried to hug me, but I said yes, you're faster than a weaver's shuttle, what? she said, yes, I said, how could you be so careless? Careless? she said you're the one who hasn't taken enough care, and with that I grabbed her hair and I swung at her and my fingernails flailed at the skin on her neck and she lashed back at me and then there was Bill and Peggy and Chas between us.

"Feelings are running high!" the vicar shouted with stunning ob-viousness. He lifted his arms in the air. "Feelings are running high!" And then I was led away from Judith and the graveside and finally I let go and cried so very hard I thought every drop of moisture in me was shed and I had become so brittle I might crack and break.

But I did stop crying, and eventually they all drifted away and, having rejected their invitations, I was left alone. I thanked the vicar. He was very kind and allowed me to use the vestry to straighten my-self up a little before I went on, because I had important things to do.

Still in my black mourning clothes, I walked up to the mansion. The ugly Jacobean pile. Along the leafy gravel driveway, past the festering duckweed pond, slipping between the match-flare rhododendrons, like a shade. This time I didn't go to Venables's offices behind the house. I deliberately went to the front door, where I was confronted by a flunky, one of Lord Stokes's stooped and crusty retainers. The man hadn't a hair on his head. He looked like he wore his master's castoffs. I swear I saw a dead fly fall from him as he shuffled forward.

"Do you have an appointment?" he asked, kindly enough.

"Tell him I'm Mammy Cullen's daughter, and I have some information he needs."

"I know who you are," the wizened flunky said, "but his lordship won't see you. If you have business, you must take it to the estate manager."

Just then Arthur McCann was passing. "Fern, here you are again." It was a kind of question. Then he said, "I'll deal with it, Geoffrey," and at this the front door was closed in my face. Arthur led me away. "They wouldn't let me off work to come along this afternoon," he said. "Or I would have."

"I know that. It's all right, Arthur."

"You know your name is mud up here, Fern. Mud."

"I know that, too. I've got to see Lord Stokes. I found something in the cottage he needs to know about. Something Mammy left behind. Information about people. I need his advice on what I should do with it."

"What kind of information?"

"I can't tell you, Arthur. But it's really serious."

Arthur blinked his white eyelashes. "Wait here but stay out of sight. I'll see if I can get you five minutes." With that he darted through to the walled garden behind the house.

A few moments later he returned. "He'll see you right now. It had better be good, Fern."

"Oh it is," I assured him.

Arthur led me to a glass door admitting to a wonderful library at the rear of the house. He opened the door and ushered me in, closing it after me while he remained outside.

Lord Stokes sat on an elegant couch, one leg drawn up on the upholstery and an elbow hooked over the back of the couch. Even though it was a warm day, a log fire roared in the hearth. A newspaper was on the couch, open at the racing pages. His lordship regarded me steadily with bloodshot eyes, sucking the ragged ends of his nicotine-and-white moustache. His pink jowls quivered slightly.

"*Mffffffff,*" he said.

I didn't know if this was a command or an expression of contempt. I knew I should wait until asked to sit down, but no such invitation seemed forthcoming. The minor aristocracy are amongst the rudest of all people.

"*Mffffffff,*" he said again.

"I don't know what *mffffffff* means," I said.

His face darkened. His white eyebrows moved in opposed directions. "Wha' d'ye wan'?"

"I've come to ask your advice."

" 'Vice? Wa' 'vice?"

"You knew Mammy Cullen, I think. Lived in your cottage by the wood?" He nodded. "I'm her daughter by adoption. When she died I had a clean-out. I found some old writing of her ideas." I brandished my notebooks.

"Wha's got to do wi' me?"

"It has sensitive information. About people in the entire district."

Without offering to get up he raised a liver-spotted hand. "Give a look hya."

I crossed the room and offered him one of the notebooks. His nostrils twitched, and he patted the sofa, evidently looking for his spectacles. As he did so I noticed a small silver ring on his little finger, just like that worn by the doctor who had tricked his way into my house. Eventually he found them on an occasional table drawn up by the sofa. It took him an age to clip the wire around his ears. Then he fell back in his sofa, reading the page at which I had opened the notebook.

I watched him closely. His lips moved slightly as he read. The light from the fire shone yellow in his rheumy eyes. He made tiny incomprehensible sounds as his reading progressed. "*Mm . . . eh . . . ffff . . . mmm.*"

At last he let the notebook sink to the sofa. Then he looked at me across the top of his spectacles. "Gibberish," he said.

"But what about the names?" I insisted, but quietly.

"Names?"

He picked up the notebook and scrutinised it again. He shook his head slightly. Then he read some of it aloud in a voice that might have stripped the oils from the ancestral portrait over the fireplace. "*The best way to make a cake is as follows. Lord knows how many folk get this wrong. Has the recipe never been written down before I wonder? A few tips on preparation first. Love must go into the baking of any cake. Child or grown-up, infant or adult, who doesn't know this? Mammy Cullen knows this above all things. Also, mind your mood. Rid yourself of all mean thoughts before baking this cake. Of this, more later. Another tip is to look at the position of the moon before commencing . . . dah dah dah . . .*what is this rot about names, girl? What's it got to do wi' the price of potatoes?"

"You have to look harder."

"Dammit girl!"

"You have to read the first word of each sentence. The first word only."

He looked at it again, reading silently this time. Twice. Dim, very dim, but he got it. Oh yes. Put that on the three-thirty at Ascot, I thought. Then he was staring hard at the page, no longer reading any of it. The silence was unbearable. I shifted my weight onto my other foot. A beautiful antique clock on the mantelpiece whirred into life and struck the hour with delicate, almost faint chimes.

"Did I do right in bringing it to you?"

"Mffff."

"Only I didn't know what should be done with it."

"Mffff. Other chaps mentioned? Eh?"

"Lots. The doctor. The chairman of the Conservative Party. The head of the Chamber of Commerce. The—"

"Nuff o' that. Got the drift. Mmm."

"It's not on every page. You have to know where to look."

"Indeed."

I bit my lip. "So is it all right?"

"All right?"

"You see there's this man from Cambridge University. A Mr. Bennett. And he didn't notice it. And even someone as clever as yourself didn't notice it. So that must mean it's all right to go ahead and publish it."

"Publish? Publish?"

"The man from Cambridge. He's interested in all this herbal medicine. Hedgerow cures for ailments. Folk medicine. Which is what the notebooks are about. He wants to publish them."

Lord Stokes turned his attention on me as if truly seeing me now for the very first time. And for a change he spoke clearly and emphatically. "Are you completely blithering insane? Well? Are you?"

I was completely cried out from the afternoon. But I manufactured a crestfallen look. I made my lip tremble. I forced fat tears to appear in the corners of my eyes. I even impressed myself. "But you yourself didn't notice, and the man from Cambridge said if we published it he would pay me enough to cover my rent for your cottage—and—and —and—" My sobs were just about stopping me from getting it out.

His face turned puce with anger and puzzlement. It made his white eyelashes and moustache appear to flare, and his forehead was cracked with lines like a dried old riverbed. "Cottage? My cottage? Never mind the bloody cottage! You can't damned well publish this wretched thing, you silly little sop!"

"But Mr. Venables wants to evict me!" I whimpered.

"Geoffrey!" his lordship roared. "Geoffrey!" After an age the flunky from the front door appeared. "Get me Venables, Geoffrey, and *quick abite it.*"

The idea of this old cadaver Geoffrey being quick about anything almost made me giggle. I restrained myself and dabbed my eyes with a tiny handkerchief. Lord Stokes glared at me evilly. When Venables appeared, Stokes said, "D'you know this girl?"

"Yes. She occupies one of your cottages by the—"

"She's to be left alone. Rent-free. All that. Until I say different."

"But we already—"

"Never mind that. My cottage, my decision. That's that. Off you go."

Venables turned and went without looking back at me.

Stokes waved the notebook at me. "This the only copy?"

"I'll check around the cottage to make sure."

"You do that. And be sure to let me know. Good girl. Now then, be off with you and if you see that bastard from Cambridge sniffing round, you know what to tell him, don't you?"

"Yes, your lordship."

"On your way, then."

I slipped out of the library the same way I came in. I heard another roar from the library. Arthur was hanging around outside, smoking a cigarette, waiting for me. He stamped out his cigarette and came to usher me away, taking me by the arm. "What are you up to, Fern?"

"Nothing."

"Nothing? Sparks are flying round here. I've just seen Venables raging." Arthur walked along the gravel drive with me, between the rhododondrons. I thought he was going to shout at me, but then he said, "Look, can I drop by sometime?"

I told him I'd like that. I felt a little afraid after what I'd done, and I knew I needed friends now. We left it vague. He promised to come by one evening.

thirty

I *had a good ear, Mammy had* always told me. "You've got a good ear, which is why you've got a good voice. You're a chanter sure enough."

She used the old word "chanter," where she said that she was merely a singer. She knew so many songs but she admitted she couldn't sing half so well as I. "You'll never want, really want, if you're a chanter," Mammy said. "You can chant for your supper. You can chant a man to want to sit beside you. You can chant people to do your bidding, if you're careful enough."

"Can you show me?" I'd asked her.

"Not on your nelly! Like all these things, it can go off wrong. Anyway, I've told you before as I'm no chanter. I'll teach you the songs, and you find for yourself how to use 'em."

Oh Mammy, I thought, I will miss your songs, and the trembling voice in which you used to pass them on! Then I thought about that song of the hare on the day of *Asking*, and I couldn't remember Mammy giving me that one. I wondered whether she had in fact given it to me; or whether I'd simply picked it up elsewhere, with my good ear. Sometimes, at a stretch, you could hear what other people were thinking. Other times you didn't need to be in earshot to hear what people were saying.

Sometimes in order to listen I could make my ears grow tall. I thought I could hear all of those who paused along the way, or in the marketplace or in the High Street. I could hear gossip unspool from their lips and tongues into the shell of another's ear. Gossip set up a vibration around the district, quite beyond words, like the waves that fed my battery radio; a disturbance in the ether; an air current. But one I felt even from behind the walls of my little cottage. I could hear it from beyond its range. The gossip, fanning out.

I could also hear the chirrup of the tiny wren in the hedge, which meant visitors. Venables came early.

I'd got all my washing out. The sheets hung wet and heavy on the line, and the spring sunshine filtered down on my cottage garden. I sat on the front step, peeling potatoes in a bowl of water. I heard the gate hinge warning me of his approach, but I didn't look up. Only when he stood over me, blocking the sun behind him, did I do so.

"Not clever," he said. "Not clever at all."

I picked up a large potato from the bowl. It had sprouted an eye, so I cut it out before peeling it.

"Whatever you think you can achieve by doing this, you're wrong."

I squinted up at him from my seat on the step. "I asked his lordship for some advice, and I got it."

"He's not as stupid as you think."

"How stupid do I think he is?"

"You wrote that notebook yourself. All of it."

"Did I? Did I write your name in it all those times, too?" I took my kitchen knife, and I began to whet it on the granite step near my haunches. I went back to the potato, and I got its jacket off in one long coiling string of peel. I held it up for him to see.

He had half a smile—no a quarter, no, not even that—fixed to his face. "You've succeeded in making things worse for yourself."

"Worse? Come after my cottage, will you? Send me the doctor, will you?"

He stooped down, so that his soft eyes were level with mine. Then he leaned in and spoke quietly, confidentially, the movements of his lips barely stirring the air near my cheek. "You think you're clever. But you made one stupid mistake. Old Mammy Cullen didn't write it. She couldn't even write her own name. She was an ignorant, illiterate old woman."

My hand closed over the handle of my potato knife, but he saw it. He clasped his own over my knife hand. With his other hand he grabbed me by the ear and knocked my head against the angle of the wall behind me. "Listen," he said. "Do you hear that?" He knocked my head against the wall a second time. "That's the sound of your own head hitting the wall of a padded cell. Listen to it again. You're already there, in that padded cell. This conversation isn't happening. You're already there. You're just remembering this."

"Jane Louth," I said, twisting away from him.

But he was gone, slipped away between the white shrouds of my drying sheets.

Oh it was a day for visitors. Bill Myers came in the afternoon, parking his panda car in full view outside of my cottage and taking off his peaked hat as he walked up the path. He'd had a bad haircut and it made his ears look pink and glowing. Though I shouldn't criticize people's hair.

He tapped gently on the open door. I was pouring off last year's elderberry wine into individual bottles. "Got a lot of washing on the line, Fern."

"Oh yes." I stopped my bottling and wiped my hands on my pinafore apron. He refused the offer of a cup of tea and placed his soft policeman's hat on the table.

"What you been up to, Fern?"

"Up to, Bill?"

"Yes, up to. Went to the big house, didn't you?"

"I don't deny that."

"You threatened Lord Stokes with certain information—"

"That's not true; I—"

"Stop it." He was sharp in cutting me off. His face hardened. "Now just stop it, Fern, this is very serious. The word being used is 'blackmail.' Do you know what that is?"

I nodded.

"You can't go round making threats to people. It's a serious criminal offense."

"But they can break the law, Bill. They can do what they want. They can get girls in the family way and pay them off to get an illegal abortion and wash their hands of it, then they jump up and down and say the law, the law, and what are you going to do about that, are you—"

"Fern."

"—going to put them in prison for buying abortions? No you won't, you'll just let that go or you'll prosecute the ones who do the abortions not the ones who buy them, and if you do, you're just as bad as them or even worse, because you jump up and down for them. Is that what the police are for, to jump and down for those who are powerful?"

"Stop it, Fern."

"Well?"

"Now listen. I've always had a soft spot for you, but it's come to an end. I know what you did that time at Croker's farm, too, but I let that go, didn't I? Well, I ain't letting it go no more. I can't. I'll tell you one thing about Lord Muck at the hall: he may look stupid and may even be stupid. But he's got power. And if he says I'm to charge you, I shall charge you, and your feet won't touch the ground."

"Is he saying you're to charge me?"

"He hasn't made up his mind."

"He daren't risk it, that means."

Bill got to his feet and made a big show of fixing his cap on his head, just so. "You're out o' your depth, Fern. I can't help you no more. You ought to ask yourself whether this village is the place you want to be, now that Mammy's gone."

"What are you saying?"

"I'm just saying."

"You're not a policeman, Bill. You're a ticket collector."

He shook his head with incomprehension at my remark. Then he showed himself out, making bold strides down the garden path. I watched him from behind my drying sheets. Watched him switch on his motor, check his mirror and steer his panda car out into the road.

It was a day for men. My third visitor was a sour-looking William. He was dressed in a collar and tie and a dark suit with a gold fob chain hanging from his waistcoat. His black boots were polished to a high shine.

"What are you looking so glum about?" he said, finding me in the garden.

"I might say the same of you."

"I always look glum. Glum's my stock-in-trade. What's your excuse?"

He said he'd had to come into Keywell on business, though what kind of business he didn't reveal. I groped at my laundry on the line. It was dry. "Make yourself useful. Help me fold these sheets."

He cracked a smile at that and took hold of the corners of the sheet I held out to him. "Now that sounds like Mammy."

"What have you come for, William?"

"I want to see what this nonsense is about between you and Judith."

"I'm angry with her because she took sides with someone against me. She's gone over to the soap-dodgers."

"Judith's under threat of being put on List Ninety-nine. Do you know what that is? A list held by the Department of Education and Science naming teachers with criminal records or those suspected of gross moral turpitude."

"Turpy what?"

"Turpitude. Child molesters and the like. Drug users. That sort. Someone at the school says she's been seen talking to or 'consorting' with known drug users. Who saw her, and why they thought it important enough to tell the Department of Education and Science I don't know. But she could be suspended from her job."

"What's that got to do with me?"

"You're another person she's been told not to be seen with."

I let the sheet fall from my fingers. It trailed in the mud. "What?"

"That's right. So you'll be doing her a favor by keeping away from her. Though I know Judith. If she wants to do a thing, or see a body, she'll do it. She at least knows who her friends are."

"She's no friend of mine."

William wiped a finger under his nose. "The reason Judith didn't believe you is because Chas can't get a stand, at least not with her. She keeps no secrets from me. None at all. Like I said, she's knows who her friends are. Can you say the same?"

I looked at the washing, crisp and white, bleached and dried by the sun. Then I ran at it, dragging it all from the line, grabbing as many sheets as I could and trampling them into the wet earth by the water pump. I shrieked and kicked at the white linen. I screamed and got down on my knees and rubbed the beautiful clean sheets into the dirt until they were filthied and muddied. Then I squealed and tried to tear them with my hands. Finally, I fell sobbing onto the pile of muddy sheets.

William stood over me, pushing out his bottom lip, but looking across the gate. He was embarrassed. "Come on, Fern. Get up."

"Am I going insane, William? Am I?"

"Come on. Stand up."

"I hate all this washing," I sobbed. "Hate it."

"I know you do. Get up. Let's go inside. We've got to make a bit of smoke."

"Smoke? Whatever for?"

"To quiet the bees," he said.

I felt so wretched. I couldn't stop the sobbing, and I had to ask him "William, were you and Mammy once lovers?"

"Maybe we were. We all had our youth. Then we had a fall-out. And I know what you're thinking, and no, I'm not your bloody father."

I got to my feet. "You're Judith's father?"

"As far as any man can be sure, I'm sure I might be." William gathered up the big, spoiled pile of laundry in a bundle and carried it into the cottage. "You'll have to do all this again," he said.

thirty-one

*A*fter my next midwifery class MMM called me aside and hit me with crushing news. The administration had searched my references and couldn't find any record of a basic qualification in nursing. These credentials were a prerequisite of the course. MMM had my original application form and showed me a box, clearly ticked, saying I was a qualified nurse. An adjacent box asking for my reference number had been left blank.

I admitted I must have ticked the box in error. I wasn't accustomed to filling in forms, I explained.

MMM looked bewildered. She took off her glasses and glowered at me with half-closed eyes. Then she sucked the earpiece of her glasses. It was impossible, she said, impossible. And so disappointing, she said, what with me being her most promising student. This last remark was news to me, of course, but of no help. I asked if I could still come to her lectures, but she avowed that there would be no point. No basic qualifications would mean no diploma at the end of it.

It was a long journey home. Perhaps it was all expressed in my face, because no one wanted to give me a ride. Though it was a beautiful spring evening with blackbirds darting in the dusky hedgerows, I couldn't feel any of it. When I got to my cottage I found Arthur sitting on my step and smoking a cigarette. I was heartened to see him. I so needed to be distracted from my worries.

"How long have you been waiting there?"

"A while. Want to take a stroll to the Lion?"

I'd never been to the Red Lion, though I'd passed by it many times and wondered what it was like, so I heard myself saying yes. It was very quiet inside. Two grizzled old boys sat in opposing corners of the lounge bar drinking pints of mild and passionately ignoring each other. A couple sat at a table holding hands and whispering. On one wall there was a huge stuffed pike in a glass case. The landlord seemed to know Arthur well enough. I didn't know what I wanted to drink. The landlord tilted his head forward and said lots of his lady customers liked a Babycham. So that's what I had. Arthur bought himself a pint of bitter and a Babycham for me.

We sat down at a table. Arthur set his bitter down on a beer mat and I put my Babycham on a beer mat, too. When Arthur sipped his beer I sipped my Babycham. It was fizzy and very sweet, and maybe it put an idea in my head about Arthur, but it made me snigger for the first time since Mammy had died.

"What?"

"Nothing," I said.

"What?"

I shook my head. Actually I was thinking about what he had in his pants that day, and whether it had ever gone down.

"Do you like your Babycham?"

"I quite like it. I wouldn't go mad for it though."

"You don't have to go mad for it."

"No, well I wouldn't."

I took another sip to show Arthur I didn't mind it. Then I looked round the pub. One of the old boys stared at me across the foamy top of his pint of mild. I ran a hand through my shorn hair.

Arthur told me his good news. He'd been selected to carry one of the three "Bottles" or barrels of ale in the Hallaton Easter parade. Hal-laton was home to an annual and ancient festival known as "Hare Pie Scramble and Bottle Kicking." The position of Bottle carrier was highly prized by the local lads. Arthur swelled with pride as he told me.

"That's so nice Arthur!"

"Yeh. It is, ain't it?"

"Wonderful."

We looked around the pub again, at the other drinkers. Then Arthur cleared his throat. "They're out to get you, Fern."

"Are they?" I said lightly.

"Someone ought to stick up for you. To protect you."

"Would you do that then, Arthur? Stick up for me?"

"I would, Fern." He took a sip of his bitter. The creamy head smeared his upper lip. "I would if I could think how to."

"That's nice." There was a silence, and it was broken by laughter coming from the room on the other side of the bar. "I didn't know there was another room."

"The Smoke Room. Beer a penny cheaper in that room. I get in there with my biker pals some nights."

"I'll bet that's a laugh."

"It is." He missed my irony, but went on, "See that back room? You can be in there without being seen and catch everything that's said in here. One time I heard Venables talking to Jane Louth. Right? He'd knocked her up, and she said she'd been to see Mammy. And he says, *'That's no good, you've got to take these.'* I was going to tell you all this the night I came round your cottage. But it got lost." The recollection of that evening made him squint into his beer.

"But what was it? What did he give her?"

"No idea. I could hear but not see. Anyway, I'd heard him say it works for sure."

I looked into the bubbles of my Babycham. I could think of a few things it might have been. But mostly I thought, *poor Mammy*. Because now I was sure she hadn't made a mistake, but she'd gone to her grave thinking she had.

"Another Babycham?" said Arthur.

"No. One of them's enough for anybody."

After we'd finished our drinks Arthur walked me back to the cottage. We stood at the gate for a while. We agreed it was a beautiful evening. I looked up at the stars, and Arthur asked me what I was looking for.

"Satellites. Sputniks and the like."

Arthur told me that the first commercial satellite had just been launched into space. I didn't know what that meant. "Nongovernment, Fern. Business. Private."

I was appalled. "You mean *anyone* can put one up there?"

"If they're rich enough. Yes."

"But that's terrible!"

Arthur shrugged. I was going to tell him about the dead dogs and monkeys in space but it seemed so unromantic, and I thought he was going to try to kiss me. But he didn't. I was a little disappointed when we said good night.

The next morning another letter arrived. I thought I understood it, but I wasn't sure how to respond, so I took it along to someone who would know for sure. At Croker's Farm Chas, Luke and two other hippies were still building their monster-sized greenhouse. Chas was puttying around some glass when I approached him. The gray putty was all over his hands. I took a deep breath. "I'm still not sure if I was wrong," I said, "but if I was, then I'm sorry. Very sorry. But I'm still not sure that I was." Then I turned on my heels and walked away.

"That's an apology?" I heard him call after me, but I ignored it and went inside the house. I asked another woman where Greta was and was directed to a bedroom upstairs.

Greta lay on a mattress on the floor, her head propped up with pillows. She was reading a book, and though she was pale, she didn't appear too bad. The room reeked of incense. She looked up at me, and with only the faintest flicker of her old infuriating smile, she said, "Hi."

I sat on the floor and held her hand. "How are you?"

"Not bad. Feel sick all the time."

"It'll pass. Drink lots of water. These joss sticks aren't good. It's all the wrong smells. I'm going to put them out. I've bought a tea made from lemon and vervain—"

"Herb of Grace," Greta said.

"That's what my Mammy used to call it. And here, look. I'm going to stick a sprig above your bed." There was a postcard tacked to the wall, and I used the pin to stick the vervain over it. "That will stop you having the nightmares."

"How did you know I had nightmares about it?"

"How can you ask me that question?"

Greta started crying. "Come on, Greta, you made a decision. Now be strong in it." These were Mammy's words. Mammy always said if there was no suffering in it, then it never needed a decision in the first place. I told Greta I would go and make her some tea from the vervain and lemon.

When I returned with the tea she'd stopped crying and was looking a little brighter. She seemed grateful for the tea anyhow. "Tell me how you've been," she said. "Take my mind off things."

"My trouble for your trouble," I said, and I showed her the letter.

She read it and frowned, her eyebrows knitting. "It's from the local Health Authority. They're going to make an assessment, it says here. My God! Can they do this?"

"That's why I brought it to you, Greta. You having studied the law and all."

"Well I suppose they can," she said. "I suppose this is how it's done."

"What will they do on the day?"

"They'll tie you in a sack, then they'll throw you in the river," Greta said. "So to speak."

"So to speak," I said.

Greta smiled back at me, but rather thinly.

thirty-two

I *went to Mammy's grave in the* night—not the fake grave, the real one in the woods. I sat with my back against the broad oak, and I talked with Mammy. The moon was strong and clear and if I half closed my eyes, I could easily see her, sitting with her back to a neighboring oak, talking to me in the silvery light, taking in the moon.

Now perhaps I was going a little bit mad at that time, and I'm not sure if I saw it or I simply remembered it. Or perhaps in remembering it I somehow saw it all over again. What's the difference between memory and imagination if there is no one who can tell you whether a thing happened? Mammy was talking to me about my singing, how I was a chanter and I shouldn't hide my gift. "See them little babies?" she says. "What's the first thing they do when they're out?"

"They wail," I says.

"That's right," she says, "they wail, because they're hurting at the world, blinking and smarting at the sudden violence of the light. But after a while they stop, because the hurt falls away, and they see only the beauty, but they don't know what it is. And when you're a-chanting, that's what you're doing."

"What, hurting?"

"Yes. You're wailing. But you're on the way to mending it. To making the hurt fall away. All singing is about a hurting, ain't it? Oh, there's funny songs here and there, but there's a hurt even in them if you listen. And though the song can't put it right, it makes the hurt fall away for a moment, and let's you see what's behind it. And a fine chanter like you, well, that's what you give people."

I said I understood. I thought perhaps I did.

But Mammy would never stay serious too long. She got to her

feet, and she kicked off her shoes. "Come on, Fern, count me in. One little last dance afore we go in. One little last dance."

I got to my feet, too, and with the moonlight drenching the woods and pouring between the trees I clapped my hands to count time and I gave her a lively "Marrowbones," that being her favorite tune forever. And she hitched up her skirts around her knees and she danced, with such a look of happiness and wicked joy etched on her features that I could barely hold the tune for laughing.

"Look at these old bones!" Mammy called as she kicked up her legs amid the bluebells. "Look at this old bag of bones a-dancing under the moon! And we don't care what they'll think of us!"

And I clapped my hands for her, and I just couldn't keep the song going for laughter. The moon was on her. She seemed to call it to her, and it soaked her as she capered and danced. It drizzled from her. It was her mantle. I could never love her more than at that moment.

And then in the next moment I was alone, under the tree where she was buried, and Mammy was gone, and I didn't know if I'd just recalled her shade to the world or only remembered something that happened, and I knew that dwelling on such an idea could tip you over the edge.

That very night someone desecrated Mammy's churchyard grave. They had cracked the headstone and painted vile words on the stone, and they had scattered all the flowers that had been placed there. I was informed of this by a local woman I barely knew. She was full of sympathy. She couldn't understand how anyone could be so hateful. Mammy had helped a lot of people, she said. Did I think it was those long-haired yobs at Croker's? I said no, they weren't bad people at Croker's, and I knew it wouldn't be them. She asked me if I wanted her to get some people to tidy up the grave. I thanked her and said I'd see to it myself.

I had other things to think about. Greta had suggested that I find some people who would speak up for me at the assessment, so I went to Bill Myers and showed him the letter. He and Peggy Myers sat me down and we discussed it, but not before they'd both expressed their outrage at the spoiling of Mammy's grave. Bill was livid, and he said if he found the culprits, he would give them a pasting, and Peggy said she would, too. They both said they thought I had enough to put up with without this. They wanted to know if I'd been to the churchyard to sort it out, and I admitted I hadn't.

But sympathy only extended so far. When it came to discussing the letter and the pending assessment, Bill said he couldn't speak up for me. "I'm caught between a rock and a hard place, Fern. A policeman's friends often find out that his allegiance to the law usually comes before friendship. That's why we're outsiders, Fern, we bobbies. We have to stand apart."

She doesn't want to hear all that, Peggy said, she wants to know if you'll speak up for her. I can't, Bill said, because it might even come to it that's she's charged, and I have to stay out of it. That's sitting on the fence, his wife said. It may well be, Bill said, but that's the position I'm in. You owe your life to Mammy Cullen, Peggy said, when you were newborn. What's that got to do with Fern? Bill wanted to know. She brought you back from the dead, Peggy insisted.

Peggy looked at me and told me how Bill had been written off by the doctor but someone had sent for Mammy in secret, and she came and spat a herb oil—I knew what it was—into Bill's throat and Mammy with her own lips had sucked the oil and the plug of phlegm from Bill's throat and doused him in cold water and put mustard oil between his shoulders and he came back from the dead and here he was, the great lump of him.

Bill looked thoughtful at that. I sensed a row breaking out between the two of them, and that's not what I wanted. I thanked them and got up to go. As I went out I thought Bill looked sad.

Peggy followed me out into the hall. I said to her, "They want to put me away, just like they did with Mammy."

"There's a difference," Peggy said. "When Mammy was put away, my mam told me, it was true she was a little bit crazy for a while. She'd lost her husband, then she lost her son. She went around for a while trying to conceive as if she didn't mind who the father was. But then once they have you inside that bloody place, well. Did you know they sterilized her when she was in there?"

I was shocked. "I didn't know that."

Peggy nodded. "Look, Bill might not be able to speak up for you," she said as she let me out, "but I know someone who can."

I looked her in the eye to try to decipher her meaning, but she gently closed the door on me.

As I made my way back to my cottage another lady stopped me and expressed her horror at what had happened at the churchyard. She said she didn't know what the world was coming to if even the dead couldn't be left in peace. The desecration had upset everyone.

That evening I was visited by William, Peggy Myers and a woman I'd never seen before, an old lady suffering from dowager's hump and the disadvantage of very thick spectacle glass. I didn't even know that William and Peggy were acquainted. William had his hands plunged in the jacket pockets of his dark, official-looking suit with the fob chain. He behaved as if he'd never met me before in his life, said nothing and looked as if he cared even less. I asked them all in.

When they were seated, Peggy Myers was cordial enough, though William looked bored, surveying the cottage with an air of mild disapproval. I thought it better not to let on that I knew him. It was the lady with the dowager's hump, rubbing her arthritic fingers together, who came to the point. "We've come about the pie, m'dear."

"The pie?"

"Yes, the pie."

"Well in previous years it was Mammy shall we say," and here she stopped and plucked at something invisible on the tip of her tongue, "Yes Mammy who helped with the pie. Though she declined more recently over the last few years because it is such a lot of work, making the pie. So over the last few years we had Carlton's bakery sort it out, though nobody thought too highly of it. So we're going back to making it ourselves this year."

"Yourselves?"

"We three being on the committee, shall we say. Me being chairman. And we thought to ask you."

"To ask me?"

"To help with it, m'dear. Not all on your own. But to bring us a bit of Mammy in the mix. Shameful, that business at the churchyard. Shameful."

I was stunned. My eyes filled with tears.

"There," Peggy said. "Told you she'd say yes. This year's pie will be the best yet."

"Is the girl up to the job?" William growled. "I want to be convinced she won't make a hash of it."

"Of course she can do it!" Peggy growled back.

William clenched his teeth, folded his arms and looked away.

"Well?" said the committee chairman, still nursing her arthritic knuckles.

"Well?" was my feeble response.

"Can you?"

"Yes. I can."

"That's it then, m'dear." With that the committee got up, Peggy and the old lady seeming pleased with themselves, William looking like someone overruled. And as they left William turned and looked at me. Without a word. Without a flicker on his lovely sour old face.

After they had gone I sat back in my chair and thought about what had just happened. I'd been offered the job of joining the pie-making.

Hare pie.

That hare pie. Over in Hallaton they had been making the hare pie for the festival for so long no one can remember when it first started. The church kept trying to stop it. The church hated it.

Mammy told me that well over a hundred years ago they did stop it. But then it started again. Some say it didn't even get started until a hundred years ago, but others say there was a parson in the eighteenth century: he tried to stop the pie, and the parishioners smashed his windows and daubed the words "No Pie No Parson" on the rectory wall. He put the pie back quick enough.

I don't know. I think it's one of those things that has no beginning and will have no end. There will always be a hare pie, and there never was a hare pie. But it wasn't true what the old lady said, about Mammy tiring of making the pie. They stopped her. Or another parson, or vicar, stopped her. It was after they'd had her inside for those years. They never let her back in the kitchen again. Poor Mammy. And how she loved to bake. "How they hate you if you're a little bit different," she would say. "They hate you so." To which she would add, "And it ain't necessary."

But then here they'd come, asking me. The three of them, and I wanted to say, what? Ask the hare for hare pie? But you don't say anything. You are asked, and you put on your apron and bake. That's what you do.

Though what I know, because Mammy told me, is there hasn't been a hare in that pie in how many years. "It's beef and ham, it is. Beef and ham. What sort of a hare pie is that?" Mammy was appalled. Because on hare pie day it's the one day of the year when you can eat a hare without being cursed. That's the point of it. That's why we have permission. I would never eat a hare on any day but Easter Monday. You are cursed with cowardice any other day. Everyone knows that. But somehow and for reasons beyond my sight this year it had fallen to me, and I would give them a hare pie. I would.

And the first thing I did was to go into the woods to tell Mammy.

Arthur found out soon enough, and on the Wednesday he came calling. What with him carrying one of the barrels of ale for the Bottle Kicking we both now had a role to play in the festival. He was cock-a-hoop, and I was busy busy busy.

"Have you been to tidy Mammy's grave?" he asked me, knitting his eyebrows.

"Not yet," I said.

"It's all the talk. I'd like to get hold of the person who did that."

I had plenty of other things to think about. I had to make ready a giant pie by Easter Monday. I also was scheduled for my "assessment" the next day, which was the day before Good Friday. All I could think was: if they are going to lock me away, how am I going to make the pie? I wondered if anyone had considered this.

I spent the evening before the assessment cleaning up. Greta had told me to make the place look spick-'n'-span. She told me to lift some of the stranger-looking bunches of herbs down off the rafters, and to gather up a few of the more sticky bottles and jars off the shelves. It felt like an insult to Mammy, but I did as Greta suggested and stored everything in the lean-to. I even took down the jar of Mammy's nail and hair clippings from the hidden shelf, but I couldn't bring myself to throw it away. I returned the jar to its hiding place.

I dusted and polished every nook. I scrubbed the floor, and I wiped down the paintwork. I washed the chair covers and the tablecloth, and I laid it all out as pretty as I could. I worked hard.

Even though I'd worn myself out with cleaning I didn't sleep well that night. I kept thinking about Mammy, how she was delirious and slipping in time and telling me about when she was locked up in that awful place. I thought about them sterilizing her without her consent.

In the morning I put a jar of spring flowers on the white tablecloth, and in the mix I included some bright yellow sunny coltsfoot for peace. I was still arranging the flowers when an officious-looking woman in a smart business suit appeared at the open door. The woman wore half-moon spectacles and carried a folder. Her hair was scraped back and tied behind.

My heart skipped when I realized who it was. "Greta! The suit!"

Greta sat herself down. "Place looks nice." Laying her folder and a pen on the table, she said, "It's all in the act, Fern, you know that."

"No I don't know. Where did you get the suit?"

"Stowed away. Haven't had it out in nearly two years." She looked at me across the top of her spectacles, and if I hadn't known her, I would have felt intimidated. "Shall we rehearse a few things?"

At ten o'clock sharp Dr. Bloom, the local GP who'd ushered Mammy into hospital before she died, arrived with the other doctor—the one who'd insinuated his way into my house with egg custards. A tall and rather gaunt woman followed them. Her face was red and chapped as if exposed too often to the wind on the fells, and her hair was pewter gray, cut into an unfashionable bob. She said her name was Jean Cavendish, and she introduced herself as a "social worker."

I'd occasionally heard the term "social worker" without really knowing what one was. I was about to ask her what a social worker does exactly, when I heard Greta saying that she thought everyone would be more comfortable sitting at the table for the proceedings and that there was a chair for everyone.

The egg-custard doctor looked at the chairs as if they were slimy. "And who might you be?" he asked.

"I'm Greta Dean. I'm here to counsel and advise Fern in the process of this assessment."

"I didn't know anything about this," said the egg-custard doctor, looking round at the others.

Greta sat down and pulled out a chair beside her for Jean the social worker. Jean accepted a seat, and so did Bloom. At last the egg-custard doctor took a seat, eyeing Greta with suspicion. "It's simple enough. Fern has hired me to ensure that all the legal issues are correct."

"Hired? I'd be very surprised if she could afford a solicitor!"

"That's Fern's business, surely." And then Greta beamed him one of those smiles that had always infuriated me. I was so glad to see it used on the man in this way that my spirits lifted. "Could I ask you to introduce yourself?"

"This is all a little bit formal, isn't it? We—"

"Fern refers to you as the egg-custard doctor after you came upon her with egg custards. I really can't in all conscience refer to you as the egg-custard doctor."

This got a repressed giggle from Jean the social worker, and a sniff from Bloom. Jean said, "I think it would be a good thing if we all introduced ourselves properly."

So we went round the table. The egg-custard doctor said his name was Glaister and that he was employed by the County Health Authority to "help in these matters." I'll bet you are, is what I thought. I went last after Greta. "I'm Fern, and I'm not bats."

Greta blinked at me. She'd warned me not to make any reference to that, but I'd forgotten. Then Glaister tried to take control of the meeting. Without anything being said, he decided he was chairman of the proceedings. "Shall we crack on then? Firstly, Fern, I want to tell you that this is an informal and friendly meeting set up to establish a few things, that's all, and that we will ask you a few questions and you can be relaxed about your answers."

Greta interjected immediately. "Though it's important that you understand, Fern, that while this may be an informal meeting, its express purpose is for Messrs. Bloom and Glaister, and Miss Cavendish, to make an assessment of your mental health. They may, at the end of this meeting, recommend that you would benefit from hospital treatment. If they do so, they have full legal power to make that happen. Do you understand that?"

"Yes," I said.

"In that case," Greta said, "you need to understand that while this meeting is informal, you don't have to regard it as completely friendly."

"Are you qualified in the law?" Glaister said.

"Fully," said Greta.

"Do you have the credentials?"

"I'll show you mine if you'll show me yours." And Greta smiled that toothsome smile.

"Stop it, George," Jean said to Glaister. She'd obviously known the man for years. "Let's get on with it."

And then the questioning began.

And while it went on I thought of Mammy, and of the years we had been together, and of her many kindnesses and her occasional bad temper. I wondered now if she'd adopted me because they'd scorched her ovaries. I knew—because she'd told me—that Mammy had brought me back from a hospital where there was another patient who couldn't keep her baby. Now I realized what sort of a hospital it was. My natural mother must have been a patient there. Possibly my father, too. There was no point in speculating. I truly didn't care. Mammy was my real mother through and through. Blood may be thicker than water, but I know that kindness is thicker than blood.

I remember once when I'd gone with Mammy to a difficult birth. The mother was hardly in her first flush of life and seemed like a mature woman to me. I'd just had my first period and Mammy joined up the dots for me and said look at this one, this is where it all leads. Anyway, we went to the woman and found her in such agony that Mammy had to use all her skills and all her craft, and we were together in her house the whole day and most of the night. The woman screamed and wailed. And afterward when the fat bonny little thing was safe and gurgling in her arms, she said, never again, never again.

Ha, you all say that, Mammy told her. But the woman insisted. She wasn't going to let her bloke near her. It wasn't going to happen. She'd keep her fellow away from her with an ax before that happened again, and could Mammy give her anything else for the pain? There she started crying all over again, and where for many women it would be a joy and a relief, for this woman, as is also the case for many, it was a sorrow and a hurt, because there was no love in her house.

Mammy gave her one of her special concoctions and after a while the woman settled a little. The woman wished bitterly that her own mother was there, her having died some years before. Well, Mammy was the only mother of the moment, so while the woman cradled her new baby in her arms, Mammy got up on the bed and cradled the mother, and hushed her and soothed her and poured love into her ear. "You know," she said, "there's something in us that makes us forget the pain, and there: we go and do it all over again. But the pain will all fall away, I promise you."

I remember it seemed a shock to me at the time, to see Mammy mothering this grown woman. Now that I know a lot more, not at all. And then Mammy spoke softly to the woman and stroked her hair, but all the time it was into my eyes she looked as she spoke. "And after all the pain and the suffering has fallen away, that's when."

"Could you answer the question, Fern?" asked Jean.

"Fern?" Greta prompted.

I was so distracted I had to ask them to repeat the question.

"Do you hear voices?"

"I hear Mammy's voice. She helps me in times of difficulty."

Greta winced visibly. She'd coached me not to say such things and again in the distraction of the moment I'd forgotten.

"Do you believe in magical acts?" Bloom asked.

"You're going to have to define what you mean by magic," Greta said.

I said, "I can't imagine anyone living without the hope or expectation of some magic in their lives."

"Have you ever performed an abortion for anyone?" Glaister asked.

"What's that got to do with it?" Greta said. "It's got nothing to do with any of this."

"No, I don't see your drift, George," Jean Cavendish said.

"Can we ascertain, Dr. Glaister," Greta said, looking over the top of her spectacles at him, "how you came to be involved in this particular case?"

"I beg your pardon?"

"I can see how Dr. Bloom and Miss Cavendish are involved here, since this is their professional catchment area, but I'm not sure how you came to be interested in Fern."

"I was called in. Professionally."

"By whom?"

"That's not for me to say nor for anyone else to know."

I noticed the silver ring on the little finger of Glaister's pudgy hand. It was the same as the one worn by Lord Stokes. "They're Freemasons," I said. "Lord Stokes, Dr. Glaister here, Mr. Venables, and lots of others."

Bloom looked at the ceiling and blew out his cheeks. "For God's sake!" went Glaister. Jean Cavendish looked hard at me.

Mammy had told me that the men who had had her put away before and during the war had been Freemasons. She'd said you could never prove it. She'd said it was a secret band of men—often in positions of authority—who worked to help each other, and if you crossed one of them, they formed against you and did each other's work. "Thick as thieves," she said. I remember asking her if it were true that there were secret societies, to which she said what are we? And though I'd never thought of we few as quite like that, since we carried no insignia nor did we make oaths or secret handshakes and the like, I supposed that was what we were. Though you should never try to name them, she told me. And when I asked why not she'd said that they would make out you were far-fetched and mad, and they would conspire to have you put away.

I knew everyone who was a Freemason because Mammy had listed them for me, and I'd coded them in my notebook. Every businessman, local politician, police officer—no, Bill Myers wasn't a Mason as far as I knew—civic dignitary, and every local authority employee (and it didn't escape me that maybe that's how my credentials at the College of Midwifery had suddenly come to be checked) who was known to us was listed. They were our opposite numbers, our shadow forms, a kind of mockery of ourselves Mammy used to say.

Dr. Bloom said, "Fern, do you think people are conspiring to get at you?"

"I would say that in this case," Greta put in quickly, "there are definitely people who are out to manipulate Fern."

"What's that supposed to mean?" said Glaister sharply.

"Yes," said Jean Cavendish. "We are acting in Fern's best interests after all."

"What I mean is that even if a person is paranoid, there may still be others conspiring against them."

"So you agree that your client is paranoid?" Glaister said.

"Aren't we all a little paranoid?" Greta tried. "I mean your reaction to my previous remark was somewhat paranoid, wasn't it?"

"This is getting ridiculous," said Bloom. "I'm pretty convinced I've heard enough anyway now, what with all this wild talk of Freemasons."

Jean Cavendish had her hand under her chin. She appeared glum. She swiveled her head and looked at Bloom. "Well I'm not all that certain."

Greta seemed relieved. Bloom and Glaister had made up their minds a long time before this mock-trial had ever been mooted, and we all knew it. Cavendish was my only hope.

They talked endlessly. The questions were interminable. They asked about my childhood and about my relationship with Mammy when I was a girl. Glaister tried to bring up abortions again, but Jean Cavendish ruled him out of order. I couldn't concentrate. I just couldn't remain focused. Even though I knew it was crucial to stay with the discussion, I kept drifting off.

Then I did hear voices, but outside the door. There was a knock, and Greta went to answer. When she came back she announced that she'd asked a few people to offer a character witness. I wasn't surprised by this, since Greta and I had discussed it beforehand, but I didn't know who would stand up for me on the day. Glaister didn't like it at all, but Jean Cavendish said she didn't see how it could hurt. Greta went outside and brought in Peggy Myers.

Peggy introduced herself as the area policeman's wife and gave as good an account of me as anyone could. I blushed to hear some of this goodwill spoken in front of me. She also mentioned that my standing in the community was high enough to be asked to bake the hare pie. Peggy also made a speech about the desecration in the graveyard and looked like she wanted to pin the charge on someone in that very room.

After Peggy left Greta brought in a second character witness. She'd decided to play it like a court of law for exaggerated effect. But no one was more amazed than I was when this second woman appeared. It was MMM.

She bustled in and sat upright and somehow made the others feel she was doing them an enormous favor by being there. But she turned this to my advantage by describing how she'd given up her precious time to speak for me. She told them I was one of her most promising students and that for my age I knew an enormous amount about midwifery, even if some of my ideas were a little old-fashioned. I'd got my head screwed on, she insisted, in all the right places.

Things became a little sticky when she revealed the mix-up over the application form. Glaister pressed her on whether she thought I'd deliberately misled people in filling in the form. MMM said that the form was complicated, and in her experience there was no relationship between bureaucratic skills and bedside craft. She said that she would always be prepared to recommend me providing I saw through the proper period of training.

I was moved almost to tears by this unexpected tribute, and MMM nodded briefly at me before leaving. I looked to Greta, since it had been entirely her idea to recruit her from the college. After MMM had gone out, Jean Cavendish gave me the first sign of encouragement. She did this by compressing her lips and raising her eyebrows at me, as if prepared for the first time that day to concede that I wasn't after all a complete imbecile.

I wanted to slap her.

I was even more astonished when Judith appeared as my third character witness. Greta and I had discounted her because of her possible suspension from school. If Judith were seen to be supporting me, then her position might be further imperiled, especially if the assessment went against me. I had no right to expect her there after the inexcusable manner in which I'd treated her. But here she was, and so shamed was I by her presence, I had to look away.

Though I was disturbed by what did happen when she made her entry. Precisely because all eyes except mine were trained on Judith as she came into the room, no one else saw it. It was Bloom. He colored instantly. Judith, appearing in her most conservative schoolteacher clothes, sat and as she spoke up for me pinned Bloom with a commanding gaze. Indeed she never took her eyes from him for a moment. Whereas Peggy and MMM had addressed all three of my interrogators, Judith looked only at Bloom for the entire time she spoke. It wasn't what you would call a glare or a glower. It was more at ease than that. But throughout he stared back at her like the startled hind before it bolts for cover.

"I'm a local schoolteacher and I'm here to give a character reference for this young woman, Fern Cullen," Judith said. "She's a perfectly ordinary and respectable young woman. She's been upset lately because she's still grieving over the death of the woman who was a mother to her all her life. Grief can make anyone withdraw. Anyone.

"Her mother, Mammy, was an exceptional woman who performed

a lot of services for women in the district. She helped many desperate women—and I mean desperate—in ways that often had to go unthanked, and she herself was never served well by some cowardly men who hid behind the cloak of authority when the chips were down.

"But hopefully these are different times. Mammy was a strong woman, and I daresay Fern misses her badly. Well, people wear their grief differently, don't they? Some show it. Others don't, then find that it comes out later at odd moments. Others bide their time, and for them it becomes a kind of anger.

"Fern is no different from anyone else. I don't know what this is about. I've heard talk about her state of mind, but talk is cheap. Reputations can be ruined by talk. You all do important work. But if you make the wrong decision here today, you could be seen as vindictive. Mammy's reputation was similarly ruined, and she had to fight all her life to win it back. The wrong words out of place could easily ruin a reputation, for anyone.

"Fern has a community of friends here to help her through the difficult times of her bereavement. My own mother, Doll, was a friend to Mammy, though when my father chose between them they stopped speaking forever. Otherwise, I would have been a better friend to Fern over the years. Well make no mistake, we will change that, and we will help her now. We will. That's all I have to say."

Judith stood, pushing back her chair. It scraped the floor hideously as she did so. She went out, leaving a stunned silence behind her. Bloom gently scratched the inner shell of his ear. Cavendish, with her chin on her hand, looked from one to the other of the two men.

Glaister pushed his spectacles up the bridge of his nose. "Well I didn't understand a single word of that."

"I'm satisfied with what I've heard today," Bloom said. "I think the girl is better off in the community."

"What?" went Glaister. Cavendish swiveled her head toward Bloom.

"Policeman's wife, senior midwife, respected schoolteacher. It's obvious she's well thought of."

"That's quite a somersault, Dr. Bloom," Cavendish said.

"Well thought of?" said Glaister. He looked poleaxed. "So was Lucrezia Borgia."

"Fern's not a poisoner," Greta snapped.

"No?" Glaister said. "Not what I've heard."

"Well, what is this anyway?" said Bloom. "The star chamber? I'm satisfied."

"I'm not," Glaister said.

"I think I am," Cavendish said, closing the file in front of her. "Indeed, I think I am."

Greta looked at me across the top of her spectacles, and she beamed that ridiculous smile of blue sky heaven. I allowed myself a nervous smile back at her, but all the while I was thinking about Judith and Bloom. And I thought: Judith, you've also had your own sadness. Poor Judith. Wonderful Judith.

thirty-three

I heard nothing after they went away. Ever. They never wrote to me, nor did they communicate their conclusions in any way. Though these three worthies had decided not to exercise their informal power to declare me insane and have me whisked away to the same horror house of Mammy's torment, neither did they declare me sane. I suspect I had fallen into the category of unproven.

Thankfully, I had other things to occupy my mind, namely a huge pie to bake ready for Monday morning. I would spend Good Friday gathering together all the ingredients; Saturday chopping and preparing; Sunday for baking. I was getting help with the pastry making— that being a very fine and underestimated skill—from two other ladies, who were to come with the giant tin tray and roll out the pastry. Our domestic ovens not being up to the size of the thing, they were then to take away the pie to the bakery, ready for Easter Monday.

Meanwhile I had two matters to attend to. Firstly, I went to the churchyard. Someone from the church had fixed the stone and dealt with the worst of the mess. I tidied it up a bit more and wiped off the unpleasant words that had been painted there, knowing it would scrub up easily enough. I set new flowers in a vase, and after I'd finished I thought it looked quite smart if anyone was bothered.

I had further business at Croker's. I washed my face, and I smoothed my hair. It was beginning to grow out again, a little tufty, but I could almost like it. I even put on the tiniest touch of eye makeup and lipstick. Just a little.

When I got to Croker's the sun was warm, and there was a modest breeze streaming from the west. The hedgerows were writhing and tangling beautifully, and the ditches were a melee of forget-me-not and primroses and purple vetch. It all gave me a confident step. Chas and Luke were sitting by their greenhouse development, constructing and smoking cigarettes. The greenhouse was built and ready and smarting with new glass. There was also another man I hadn't seen before. He wore sunglasses, which was ridiculous because although the sun was out, it really wasn't all that bright. Perhaps he wasn't either. He looked at me with his mouth hanging open.

Chas looked up, and said, softly, "Hey." Luke waved his lazy hand at me.

"What will you grow here?" I asked.

"Herbs," said Luke. "There's a lot of interest in 'erbs these days." And for some reason they all laughed.

I colored and asked Chas if I could have a word with him. He got up, dusted off the seat of his jeans with putty-soiled fingers and beckoned me away from the other two men. As we made to walk away I heard the man with the sunglasses say, "Foxy." Then I saw Luke put his finger to his lips in a kind of warning.

When we were out of earshot, Chas said to me, "Hear you're making a pie. Can out-of-towners come to this thing on Monday?"

"People come from all over. Pie for everyone. I've come to apologize. Properly this time."

"Oh?"

"I think I made a mistake."

"I think you did."

"Maybe it was something I wanted to happen, and you wanted to happen, but neither of us would let happen. Maybe it was something that hatched out between us, but in another place." Somewhere in my head I heard Mammy say *The difference imp.* I think I said it aloud.

"The what?"

"Mammy always used to say that feelings between people made things happen in another place, and we couldn't control it. When something should happen but couldn't." I felt myself blushing. "*That 'difference imp.'* That's what Mammy said. Anyway."

Chas smiled. "Have you been eating those red mushrooms?"

"Don't mock."

"Sorry."

"No, I'm the one who is sorry. I maligned you, and I'm apologizing. I've come to repay you."

"You don't have to do that."

"Yes I do. I'm giving you permission to catch two hares. You see this pie? It's a hare pie, but they make it with beef, which is no good to anyone. And Easter is the only time we can eat hare. And I give the permission. It's very special. The hare won't mind at this special time."

Chas scratched his head. "And you get to give the permission?"

"Yes."

"Why?"

"Mammy gave me the permission."

"Why you?"

"That's for me to know. Will you do it?"

"Haven't you got to hang a hare for three days?"

"Not essential."

"And this is your way of apologizing? Having me run round for a couple of hares?"

"Yes. You're a good poacher, and I need them by Sunday midday at the very latest."

"You're a strange one, Fern."

"Strange can be good, though."

He let some air escape between his teeth. "Beautiful," he said in an underbreath. I don't know if I was meant to hear it. He turned away from me and walked back toward Luke. Then he whistled his dogs. Two old greyhounds and a whippet cross came bounding from the house, yapping, jaws open, eyes glinting with avidity.

"What's happening, friend?" said the new hippie, the one with dark glasses.

"I'm going hunting. Going to check my traps. You coming, Luke?"

"No, I'll stay here and relax hard," Luke said, in the middle of rolling himself another reefer.

Chas was already on his way.

"Dig that," said the man with dark glasses, his mouth still hanging open. "I mean totally."

I spent the Saturday chopping vegetables, and I flung open all the doors and windows of the cottage and had my record player blasting "Green Onions" for anyone who wanted to hear it. I chopped mainly potatoes and onions, yes green onions, it had to be green onions—and I made stock. It was a lot of work. Chop chop chop. Several pounds of each. I kept a very sharp knife and I whetted it on the stone step of my threshold. I chopped herbs, too. And there were other things to chop, very fine and secret things I would have powdered if I could. I undid bunches hanging from the rafters. I took down old jars from the shelf, and I chopped as fine as I could.

In the afternoon a butcher, pink-faced and sprightly, came in a white van delivering the beef to mix with the hare. He brought it wrapped in bloodstained brown paper tied up with string. He asked me where I wanted it, in that way they do. I got him to put it all in the sink.

Then I set about chopping the beef into small cubes. That was a long job. While I was doing that the flour and the lard arrived. The grocer was chipper, stacking it on the table as I continued to cube beef. "You've got your work cut out for you," he said. They'd also thought to send seasoning. Goodness, I told him, I can run to seasoning! We shared a laugh over that.

And with the vats all simmering on the stove in the evening I sat and chopped and powdered insofar as I could. I was disturbed shortly after dark by Judith, who was on her way to see Chas at Croker's. I let her in and resumed my work, there being no need to hide it from her.

"What's that you're doing?" she said innocently enough. Then she looked at the clippings jar, and said, "Oh."

"You disapprove?"

"No. Carry on."

"I saw Chas," I said.

"I know. He hasn't time for me. Too busy haring. For you."

"Do you know what?" I said, putting down my chopping knife and my pestle. "Here's one that is said to put lead in a bloke's pencil. Mammy told me this, and I'll bet you've never heard of it."

"Go on."

And when I told her she was amazed, and admitted she'd never heard of it. "You could try it," I said.

"I might give it a run," she said.

I didn't know how to mention the assessment without raising the question of Bloom. Judith seemed sad. I asked her why.

"This thing with Chas," she said. "I like him a lot, but I'm not sure I want to be a hippie. Plus I want to keep my teaching job. What about you? Been chucked off your midwives' course, haven't you?"

I got up to attend to a steaming pan. "Yes. Come and help me strain these potatoes."

She couldn't stay long. "Thank you, Judith," I said. "Thank you."

She ran a hand through my hair, searching me with eyes that leaked color the way a curative plant seeped resin. Then she was gone. Afterward I went back to chopping and powdering into the night. "Mammy, you were wrong about Judith."

I remembered Mammy sitting in her chair and administering her snuff. She would take it right back into her sinuses and blink and pause before answering a challenge like that. "Sometimes I am wrong," Mammy would say. "Sometimes I am."

Early Sunday morning Chas came with his two hares for me. Killed with the dew still on them. No, I didn't feel sad for them. It was their sacrifice. I took them by the ears from Chas and weighed them in each hand. Not bad, I thought. They wouldn't make a complete pie, not even half a pie, but they would mix in well with the chopped beef, and this year the Hallaton Hare Pie Scramble would be fought over a true hare pie. I told Chas not to say too much about it, since some folk might have a distaste for eating hare. I mean amongst other things there were rumors you could become homosexual after eating hare. I don't know where in the world this sort of nonsense comes from, but it keeps coming.

"Led me a dance, they did," Chas said.

"I don't care. They're going in the pot."

"What else is going in that pie?"

"Taters. Onions. Beef. That's about all. Now if you'll clear off, I've lots to do."

"Don't I get a cup of tea as a thank-you?"

"No. I don't want you under my feet."

He rubbed his face with his hand and showed no sign of shifting. "I was talking to Greta, you know. We agreed that, in a strange way, whoever it was that messed up Mammy's grave did you a favor. I mean it turned the village people around, didn't it?"

"Where's my knife? Have you seen my knife?"

"I mean it couldn't have worked out better if you'd done it yourself, could it?"

"Here it is. Shall I show you how to skin these hares?" I said.

"No, Fern. I'll leave it to you. I reckon you're the best skinner of the two of us."

Our eyes met, and that difference imp leaped again. "That's right," I told him. "I am." And when he saw me starting to deal with the hares he left.

First you chop off the feet at the first joint; then remove the head at the first joint below the skull and slit the skin of the stomach from a point between the forelegs to the hind legs. You can pull out the paunch after that. Then you slit the skin from the opening in the stomach around the back to the opposite side. If you catch hold on the back and pull the skin first from the hind legs, then from the forelegs, off it comes like a jacket. Mammy used to make gloves out of rabbit fur once upon a time, but nowadays there's no profit in it.

She made me a pair once.

I chopped the hares up and boiled them, and I disguised the meat amongst the beef. By the time the two pastry ladies arrived at my house I had all my pie mix bubbling away in two great vats and I'd played "Green Onions" so many times, I didn't care if someone came in and broke the damn record.

The pastry ladies weren't known to me. Taciturn, white-haired women, they came with bright smiles and shining eyes. I fancied they'd been baking the hare pie pastry for a thousand years. They set out their store without even so much as a critical glance around the cottage, so intent on making their pastry were they. They even— gently—took over my kitchen and steered me around it without making me feel displaced or under their feet.

They brought with them their own mixing bowls and utensils and an enormous baking tin for the pie itself, and they stored them in the larder to keep things cool until ready. It was a marvel to watch them mix the lard and the flour, building the dough and flaking it between their fingers, working silently and in mesmerizing rhythm. Working in a kind of shining light they part-baked a sectional bottom for the pie using my oven, and these sections they cut and laid into the giant tin tray.

Then they stood back and looked at me with those gleaming eyes. "Your turn now," one of them said.

I suddenly became nervous. They watched me intently as I ladled in the pie mix, spreading it evenly to the four corners of the baking tray. I was about to ladle more when one of the ladies stopped me simply by raising the palm of her hand. Then they added the thick, top layer of dough. When they were satisfied, they covered the pie over with a cloth.

They insisted on cleaning up my kitchen behind them, and before they had finished that task two men came to carry the pie away to the bakers. It was to be baked that night. With my kitchen clean, the ladies took off their aprons, put on their coats and carried away their cooking equipment. After they had gone I realized that not more than eight or nine words had passed between us during the entire time they were there.

I almost began to doubt of their existence at all.

thirty-four

*T*he *drinking was already well* under way by the time I got to the Fox Inn on Monday at lunchtime. They had set up an ale tent on the grass beyond the duck pond, and the fine weather had brought the revelers out in force. The sun was busy, too, though there was a chill in the air when the wind picked up. Nevertheless the Master of the Stowe would have pronounced it a perfect day for the annual Hare Pie Scramble and Bottle Kicking.

I passed through the ale tent looking for Arthur. He told me he would be drinking at the Fox Inn from midday. He'd no doubt want to get stoked up for the Bottle Kicking and in any event the parade left from there before it moved down to the church of St. Michael's. I couldn't see him, but I saw Venables enjoying a pint of bitter with a couple of his cronies. Their heads turned my way. Venables made some remark, and they all cackled.

I went instead to see if I could find Arthur inside the pub, and there he was, supping foamy ale with Bill Myers and other men in a bar crowded with footballers and pipers from the marching band. Bill was known to like to mix it in the Bottle Kicking. Often in the scrum a few old scores were settled, and though Bill was always fair with me, he was known as a bruiser and a hardcase. Unlike Arthur, Bill came from a neighboring village, so he kicked for Medbourne. Traditionally only Hallaton men were allowed to kick for the Hallaton team, whereas the Medbourne team comprised blades from several of the smaller surrounding villages.

They were already well oiled. Both Arthur and Bill cheered when they saw me, and they waved me over to their table. They wore striped football jerseys and dirty industrial boots; their eyes were moist and their faces red. Bill yelled to a friend at the bar to get me a drink. I said no, I'd just come to see the procession of the pie, but Bill insisted, and Arthur told him I drank Babycham, so I had one of those.

The men were in raucous mood, good-natured but clearly spoiling for something. I noticed that a pint of beer might only be raised to the lips three or four times before it was emptied, as if for these men it was a hard-and-fast quaffing rule. They joked, they teased, they broke into song easily. One man I'd never seen before stroked my hair and asked me for a kiss.

"Get off her or you'll answer to me," Arthur shouted, and the company laughed as if his was the funniest remark in the history of funny remarks.

Arthur winked at me, and said, "How's yer pie?"

"My pie is all right. How's your Bottle?"

"My Bottle is here," he said, and he reached down and picked up the small ale-filled wooden barrel he was commissioned to carry during the procession. On sighting the barrel held aloft, all the men cheered and broke into song. Arthur looked at me and blushed. He was so proud to be carrying the Bottle that year. He'd won the right—when one of the older men retired from the honor—by scoring a goal for Hallaton the previous year. And there was something about his pride and humility mixed that made me want to put my hand on his arm. Instead, I sipped my fizzy Babycham.

When they finished singing Bill embarrassed me by getting to his feet. "Gentlemen, we have a songbird amongst us! A lovely songbird she is. Let's have her give us a song!"

Now it was my turn to blush. I waved my hands in protest and shook my head vigorously but then there were nine or ten men on their feet, and chanting, *"She'll give us a song, she'll give us a song, she'll not take long, but she'll give us a song!"*

I looked for the door. Arthur knew what I was thinking, and said, "Better give 'em what they want."

"No way out, lovely girl," Bill put in. "No way out."

I got to my feet, and the chanting men fell back into their seats. One burly figure made it worse by lifting me by my waist as if I were as light as a pin and standing me on a table. Bill was right, there was no way out. I knew my voice was good, but I felt crushed with embarrassment. The rest of the pub fell quiet for me.

I cleared my throat, and it just happened at that moment that one of Venables's cronies came into the taproom and, seeing me up there on the table, put his hand to his mouth and blew an ugly lip-fart. Instantly, every man around me leaped to his feet roaring displeasure, waving fists at the man and lashing their arms in the air. Suddenly they seemed like a colony of wild things at the waterhole in a brief, defensive frenzy. Venables's crony colored and ducked smartly out of the room. Just as quickly the men slumped back in their seats and fell silent, fixing their eyes on me, and I was momentarily afraid of the hair-trigger nature of the switch from masculine cheer to imminent violence.

But with order restored, Bill said, "On you go, Fern."

By this time the pipers and drummers of the marching band had gone silent for me, too. Better make it a jolly one I thought, even though I was trembling. I knew there was only one thing to do with such embarrassment and self-consciousness, and that's to deflect it elsewhere. So I fixed my gaze on Arthur, and I sang. I gave 'em that old one, "The Brisk Young Butcher," and they loved it all right.

> *When he arrived at Leicester town he came upon an inn*
> *He called out for an ostler and boldly he walked in*
> *He called for liquors of the best he being a roving blade*
> *And quickly fixed his eyes upon the lovely chambermaid.*

Nine verses, and Arthur never took his eyes away from mine, nor did I take mine from him. They whistled and stamped and called for another song, so I gave them "The Coal-Black-Smith," which is a right dirty song when you think of it, and they whistled and cheered and stamped at that, too, but I got down off the table and told them that would have to do.

The beers were going down like ninepins and I got my arm twisted to have a second Babycham. Bill's way of teasing Arthur about my gazing at him through the song was to jiggle his eyebrows and to lean over and grasp Arthur's cheek between his leathery thumb and fore-finger. Arthur didn't seem to mind, at least not until the third time it was done.

But then I must have drifted off, and Bill noticed me looking sad. "Cheer up, Fern, might never 'appen."

"Oh it's that Venables. He was in the ale tent mocking me as usual."

Bill looked thoughtful. I also noticed two burly figures in red-hooped rugby football shirts who seemed to take an interest at the mention of Venables's name. Then Bill shrugged. "Medbourne's a bit short of numbers this year. Ain't that right, lads?"

"Could do wi' one or two more," someone agreed.

Bill got up. "Let's get out and recruit from the ale tent." A few of his drinking pals drained their glasses and staggered out after him. I asked Arthur if we should follow, too, but one of the men in the red-striped shirts put out a gentle hand and touched my arm. "No m'duck, you and Arthur stay here with us a bit."

"That's right," said Arthur. "Stay with us Hallaton men a bit."

One of the men *would* buy me another Babycham and wouldn't take no for an answer. Though rough-looking, they were nice fellows, and they pretended to be interested in my singing and in how I knew the songs; but I couldn't get past the feeling that they were detaining me for a reason.

At one-thirty it was time for the procession. All the pipers and drummers from the marching band drained their glasses and went to muster for the parade, and the rest of the footballers went, too, leav-ing the bar eerily quiet. I couldn't stay there, so I went out to watch the procession, but first I passed through the crowded ale tent. I no-ticed Bill Myers and some of his drinking pals standing with Ven-ables. Bill had his arm around Venables's shoulders, and they were sharing a joke, obviously enjoying each other's company. I felt hurt that Bill could be so fickle. Venables, laughing uproariously, was red in the face.

"One more before we go," Bill shouted.

"No, I'm slaughtered!" I heard Venables protest.

But one of Bill's chums was already pulling in the beers from the ale-tent bar. I saw him deliberately spill a bit from one glass and top it up with a huge splash of vodka from a quart bottle. Then he secreted the bottle in his pocket and passed the doctored beer to Venables. The men raised their glasses and started up some sort of a drinking chant, where they all downed their beers in one. Venables included.

I left them to their boys' games and went out to the street in front of the Fox Inn. The procession was lined up and ready to go, and there, at the front, was the Warrener in his green cape and holding a staff. Behind him, glory of glories, were two young women from the village carrying the great pie between them. My pie! My hare pie.

Following the pie were the bearers of the three "Bottles," including Arthur; and behind them a motley crew of local dignitaries, assorted footballers, and committee members including Peggy Myers, the sweet hunchback lady, and William. He kept checking his fob chain and looking irritated with everything. William saw me and he let pass the nearest thing to a grin I imagined he could manage. I'd seen that half-stopped grin only once before, when he'd suggested we "make some smoke": the sympathy-garnering churchyard atrocity had been his idea.

At a command from the bandmaster the marching band stiffened to attention, sticks poised a fraction above the drumskin, pipes ready at the lip. The three Bottle Bearers each held their barrels aloft with one hand, and the Warrener prodded the air with his staff. The band struck up loud, and the procession moved off, and every hair on my body stood thrilled and erect.

I watched the procession move down the hill toward St. Michael's church. More footballers came spilling out of the ale tent to catch the tailcoat of the procession, amongst them Bill Myers and Venables. Bill and one of his pals were supporting or coaxing Venables to join in the parade. Each had an arm locked round Venables's arms, as if they were holding him upright. He was clearly very, very drunk. I heard him protesting in a good-natured and humorous manner that he wasn't dressed for the football, but Bill and company were jocular and wouldn't hear of it. No one else was taking much notice that Venables was a late recruit into the game.

I followed the procession all the way down to St. Michael's, where it halted in front of the wrought-iron gates at the east end of the old church. There was the vicar of St. Michael's, waiting to perform his duties. I'd heard he didn't like doing this. He'd made his feelings known about what he called primitive rituals several times. But like many vicars before him, he knew the warnings handed out in the eighteenth century, and like that parson before him, he was compelled to dirty his hands with pie gravy.

For it was his duty to carve up the hare pie and offer it to the people in the scramble. By now there were hundreds of villagers from all around the region, their ranks swelled by tourists and sightseers, pressing forward as the vicar sliced up the pie. The pie was then snatched from his hand and flung, as was the tradition, at the crowd.

There was a roar of delight as the crowd surged forward. The vicar was jostled as pieces of pie were torn from him and flung at the pressing throng, pastry, gravy, meat, potatoes and all the rest slapping in folk's faces and exploding in their hair. And those who held up their hands caught the pie as it flew and they stuffed it, shrieking, in their mouths. The people at the front of the crowd jostled the vicar again, almost having him off his feet, imploring, pushing out their hands for pie. With barely concealed ill temper, the harried vicar doled it out. The people ate it. They turned back for more, pushing and shoving to get at it. They flung it farther out into the crowd. And as I saw the fragments of pie dispersing and soaring through the air, I whispered, *"Fly to them, Mammy! Fly to the people!"*

It was done.

After the Hare Pie Scramble came the Bottle Kicking. Part of the procession, leaving the scene of the scramble behind them, wound up the grassy hill of Hare Pie Bank, where all the players assembled. The chairman of the Bottle Kicking match threw one of the "Bottles" into the air. This he repeated twice. When the Bottle hit the grass for the third time, the men fell upon it in a furious scrum. This was a game like few others. The touchlines were represented by streams at each end of the great field, about three-quarters of a mile apart. Between the streams lay hills, hedges, water-filled ditches, country lanes and barbed-wire fences. There were no rules. First-aid stewards from the St. John Ambulance Brigade, themselves an annual fixture, stood by to attend to the inevitable wounds, fractures, and other injuries.

I watched as the mob of straining, groaning, jostling men locked into combat, failing to make an inch of progress on either side of the muddy field. There were two kinds of players—the mad bloods who launched into the center of the fray risking every limb, and the skirmish players who stayed on the periphery. From a safe distance I saw fists fly, then a slight lurch—not more than a single yard—downhill. Then the lurch was corrected back to the start position.

Chas, Luke and the man with sunglasses were there. They seemed to have joined the skirmish, but only on the very safe extreme periphery of it. In fact they looked stoned out of their heads. They each made a nervous short foray toward the skirmish, flapping an arm at an imaginary "Bottle" or enemy before laughing like hyenas and withdrawing for a rest and another smoke. Still, they seemed to enjoy it.

I also saw Venables, still drunk and still protesting, carried into the very grunting epicenter of the struggle by Bill and one of the men wearing the red-hooped shirts. Briefly, I saw Arthur's face. He was seriously gasping for air. Then the scrum swallowed all of them. I turned away and went back down into the village. There is only so much of this you can watch.

It was only some time later that I found out that Venables had been injured in the melee. I have no idea how it happened. In the central scrum of fifty or more bodies no one else would have seen either. These things happen by accident. I would imagine that Bill Myers, in securing a grip on the Bottle might have found his fingers slipping and his elbow crashing back and breaking Venables's nose. I expect Arthur, in trying to make progress through the scrum, might have inadvertently brought his knee under Venables's jaw, and that was what dislocated it. I guess one or both of the burly men in red-hooped shirts, whom I later found out to be Jane Louth's brothers, might in trying to get advantage have accidentally pushed Venables arm so far up his back that it broke a bone. Who knows how he had his teeth pushed in? You can't keep speculating, and the older men, stalwart critics of the game, observed that it was never wise to wade into the annual Bottle Kicking while the worse for wear with drink.

Everyone knew you went into the Hallaton Bottle Kicking at your own risk. And what's more, they remarked to one another as seasoned observers, it was never meant to be a game for girls.

thirty-five

Somebody won the game, but in truth no one cares too much to remember the score. It's always the event that matters. Who were the victors, who had scored the rare goals and what had happened in which muddy field was a subject of endless debate in the pubs of Hallaton and the neighboring villages that very night. Arthur told me that Medbourne had won two–nil though he seemed perfectly happy in defeat. In fact all of the men, Arthur, Bill, the Louth brothers and every single male who took part in the skirmish looked happy. As if they'd worked something out of them. Or maybe had something put in.

I was talked into drinking with them that evening, and I said I would as long as I didn't have to drink that horrible Babycham stuff. I asked Judith to come along for female company but she'd arranged to see Greta, who'd promised to help her in the dark matter of List Ninety-nine and her teaching career. Proper village advocate Greta was becoming. Even so, I somehow couldn't see Chas and his band of gypsies downing bitters and cracking funnies with the likes of Bill Myers. Anyway, it ended with us supping at both the Fox Inn and the Bewicke Arms in Hallaton that night. Hallaton men drank happily with members of the Medbourne team, out of whom just a few hours earlier they were kicking lumps. Arthur had earned a fresh, juicy black eye, just as mine was fading. Bill had three vicious claw marks down the side of his face. They all made light of it.

"Shame about that Venables bloke," Arthur said beerily when we were ensconced in a nook of the Bewicke Arms.

"Yes, shame," said Bill. "Nice bloke he is and all."

"Yes," said one of the Louth brothers. "Shame about that Venables bloke."

"Still," Bill said, holding aloft a foaming pint of bitter. "Cheers to all the players."

"Cheers!"

"Cheers!"

Well I raised my glass to that. I was drinking half-pints of bitter. I don't know what Mammy would have thought of me sitting in pubs, downing beer with the men. But I decided I liked it.

I decided I liked Arthur, too. And the more I supped from my glass, the more I found my liking grew. I took a fancy to his blackened eye. I wanted to put my lips to the violet-and-yellow swollen skin and kiss it away.

"Are you two going to spend the evening eyeing each other up?" Bill said at one point. "Because you're putting me off my ale." I blushed, so he saved me by changing the subject. "What will you do now you can't complete your midwife course?" he asked me.

I explained that MMM had told me of a grant I could apply for, to get a proper qualification in nursing. And then after that I could go on to become a qualified midwife. That seemed to be the thing to do.

"All aboveboard, sort of thing," he said.

"Yes."

"And what about the cottage? Will you keep that on?"

"I'll fight to keep it. And I'll try to find a way to pay you back for the rent."

Bill froze for a second. Then he said we needed more beer. He gathered up the glasses and rushed to the bar. But he was too late, because I'd already seen that it was his turn to blush.

At chucking-out time Arthur offered to walk me home. Though it was a little chilly out, it was a lovely clear evening, so we walked across the fields instead of going by the lanes. I felt warm enough, wrapped in my death's-head leather jacket that Arthur seemed to have forgotten belonged to him. We walked alongside the church and up past the motte-and-bailey earthworks. We sat on the hill of the earthworks, and it was while I was looking for a satellite in the night sky that Arthur kissed me. The kiss went on. When it stopped

I looked back across the lighted village and I heard my blood pumping in my veins.

"Are you all right?" Arthur asked me.

"I'm very all right."

We walked on and he held my hand and I don't believe he noticed I was trembling. When we reached the cottage he kissed me again at the gate, then he made to go.

"No, Arthur, I want you to come in."

"Ahey?"

"I said I want you to come in."

"Yeh, I heard you."

"Well?"

When we got inside he took off his jacket. "I've got funny memories of being here the last time," he said.

"Undress me."

He swallowed hard, but we went upstairs and he did undress me. He was all fingers and thumbs. Then he got naked, and I didn't know whether to feel disappointed or relieved that he didn't have the broom handle he was showing the last time. We got into my small bed. He looked agitated.

"It's the Bottle Kicking, Fern. I've been running around so much all day, I don't think I've got anything left."

I let my head fall back on my pillow, and I laughed out loud.

"What?"

"I'm not laughing at you. Honestly. It's all right. Really. There will be other times. Just hold me and kiss me."

He fell asleep pretty soon after that. I did, too.

I woke up in the slate gray light of predawn. He slept on, but his cock was hard again, and I felt it creeping against my thigh. I didn't know what to do so I got out of bed. I peeled back the sheets so I could look him. I sat naked on a chair, just gazing at this sleeping man, with his full erection.

Then I covered him over, and unsure of what he might want when he awoke I got dressed. I left him a note and went for a walk. It was a shimmering morning, with the sun cracking over the hill to the east.

I walked the rolls, just as I might have done with Mammy. And on the crest of one undulation of the land I saw a multitude of hares, boxing and playing in silhouette. I got as close as I could. Then they sensed me, but instead of darting they froze. Motionless, they could have been a ring of stones on the hill.

Then they dispersed, and were gone. I walked to the top of the hill, and I looked down. Mammy's words came back to me again. She said you have to look beyond what hurts you. She said you must listen to the sounds behind the sounds. She said that eventually all the pain falls away, and what's left behind is only beauty.

Acknowledgments

Special thanks to Anna Franklin, author of *Hearth Witch*, and to Dr. Dave Tull, both of whom readily answered all of my dumb questions. Heartloads of thanks to Sue, always, and to Simon Spanton, Tracy Behar, Luigi Bonomi, Chris Lotts, Vince Gerardis, Wendy Walker, Ilona Jasiewicz, Nicola Sinclair, Brigitte Eaton (at jungawunga.com for superb web support), Phil Wheatley, Bill Sheehan, Pete and Anne Williams, Helen Willson and Daniel and Julie Hanson. Thanks also for wonderful support from colleagues and writing students at Nottingham Trent University.